In less than a heartbeat Angel was in her arms. Even as their lips met, Rett pulled Angel down to straddle her lap. She had not forgotten the way Angel tasted or the smell of her hair. Sensation evoked and reinforced memory as Angel returned her kiss.

Shoulders . . . the hollow at her throat. Rett bent Angel back in her arms to relearn the texture of the soft skin with her teeth and tongue. She slipped the straps of the tank top out of the way. Beautiful olive skin pulsed with the beat of Angel's heart. Angel yanked the tank top down with an earthy groan of desire. Rett filled her mouth with Angel's breasts and trembled with an ache between her legs that could take a lifetime to ease.

"Not here . . . oh . . ."

Rett's fingers slipped past the hem of Angel's shorts, remembering the way to welcoming heat and wetness. She put her other arm around Angel's waist to pull her closer.

Angel groaned out her name as Rett's fingers slipped inside her, then she burst into tears. Rett murmured, "Hold on to me, it's okay."

"I didn't want to love you again." Her hips moved convulsively. "Don't stop." Angel put both arms around Rett's neck and hid her tears in Rett's hair. "Don't stop."

WRITING AS KARIN KALLMAKER:

One Degree of Separation
Maybe Next Time
Substitute for Love
Frosting on the Cake
Unforgettable
Watermark
Making Up for Lost Time
Embrace in Motion
Wild Things
Painted Moon
Car Pool
Paperback Romance
Touchwood
In Every Port
All the Wrong Places
Sugar

WRITING AS LAURA ADAMS:

Christabel

The Tunnel of Light Trilogy:
Sleight of Hand
Seeds of Fire

Daughters of Pallas:
Night Vision
The Dawning

Unforgettable

Karin Kallmaker

Bella
BOOKS
2004

For Maria

How wonderful we never had to go through this P.S. There are no horseflies in romance novels.

Ten Makes a Celebration, Loud, Loud, Loud!

About the Author

Karin Kallmaker admits that her first crush on a woman was the local librarian. Just remembering the pencil through the loose, attractive bun makes her warm. Maybe it was the librarian's influence, but for whatever reason, at the age of 16, Karin fell into the arms of her first and only sweetheart.

There's a certain symmetry to the fact that ten years later, after seeing the film Desert Hearts, her sweetheart descended on the Berkeley Public Library to find some of "those" books. "Rule, Jane" led to "Lesbianism—Fiction" and then on to book after self-affirming book by and about lesbians. These books were the encouragement Karin needed to forget the so-called "mainstream" and spin her first romance for lesbians. That manuscript became her first novel, In Every Port.

The happily-ever-after couple, mated since 1977, now lives in the San Francisco Bay Area, and became Mom and Moogie to Kelson in 1995 and Eleanor in 1997.

All of Karin's work can now be found at Bella Books. Details and background about her novels, and her other pen name, Laura Adams, can be found at her own website.

1

"...has indicated that the cabin has reached cruising altitude. For your safety and comfort..."

"This is all about you being cozy and comfortable. You could get up off your ass once in a while!"

Rett shook her head against the stiff airplane seat and tried to find a way back to sleep that didn't include reliving that humiliating fight with Trish. She was so tired and wanted so much to sleep all the way from La Guardia to LAX. She hadn't slept well all week, not with every word Trish had said pinging around in her head.

"Can I get you something to snack on while lunch is being prepared?" The nasal-voiced steward was back again. Rett was unused to the solicitousness of first class. She'd been hoping the more comfortable seating would turn out to be worth every mileage point she'd cashed in for the upgrade, but that would only be the case if she got some sleep. Still, it was nice to be waited on hand and foot.

"Some water," Rett mumbled. She was behind in her daily intake and sleep seemed unlikely. She drank the bottle down in a few gulps and closed her eyes.

So tired . . .

". . . on the right, you can see the thousands of lakes that cover Minnesota, as well as Lake Superior . . ."

"*You're so superior. So you can sing. Whoopity-fucking-doo. We're taking in less money this year than we did last year and you're running out of time for that Ms. Nice Girl act. You want to be famous, you gotta act that way.* "

Thoroughly disoriented, Rett opened one eye and saw the steward delivering a freshly tossed Caesar salad to the man next to her.

"You're awake," the steward said cheerily. "Would you like the filet or Chicken Newburg?"

Rett cleared her throat. Her voice still came out a froggy squeak. "Chicken." She put her hand to her throat. "And more water."

Swallowing produced the merest nuance of pain that made her singer's reflexes wince. She'd overused her voice all week, enjoying the band she'd been appearing with, as well as the appreciative, swing- and jazz-loving audience. She sang as long as anyone would listen, not wanting to go back to the hotel to replay The Fight one more time.

She didn't want to break up with Trish, but maybe it was inevitable. Trish was right — she'd be forty in just three weeks, and she was running out of time for all sorts of things. God, it had been a gruesome fight. She'd seen Trish dismantle other people, but Trish's barbs had never been directed so relentlessly at her.

She was so tired . . .

". . . the great visibility means both sides of the plane can see the Continental Divide all the way to the horizon . . ."

"*You want to expand your horizons? Stupid little thing, people like us are stuck in Woton, Minnesota. You were nothing when you were born, and you'll never be more than nothing.*"

Rett woke up clutching the arms of her seat. She'd gone from Trish to her mother, good God. She knew she was tired, but what on earth was happening to her that she was coming so mentally unglued as to dream about her mother after all these years?

Afraid to go back to sleep, she picked at the hot fudge sundae the steward urged on her. She found herself blinking back tears and cursed herself for letting the tears get that far — damn it, her throat was tensing up and the resulting ache and diminished volume would last at least twelve hours. Her throat was already sore enough to require some time over the vaporizer. Trish would say vapor therapy was just an excuse not to go out to some party or some premiere or another pointless opportunity to make "do lunch" promises to people she'd never see again. No one ever remembered Rett Jamison.

Stop that, she admonished herself. *You've got enough grief to think about without dumping more self-pity on the heap.*

She rested her forehead against the cool window. She was so tired . . .

"Stop it, please," she had pleaded. "Nothing you say is going to make me beg some producer for a callback."

Trish snarled, "Beg? Is that my job?" She kicked at a bath towel on the floor. "I work my butt off and now you act like you're above a phone call? As if you're anybody! As if you could ever get anywhere without my help!"

Trish had never been this angry with her before, but Rett didn't want to give in. "You always told me to concentrate on my craft and you'd take care of all the messy details. You get fifteen percent for it." Rett didn't want to bring up money but there it was.

"I deserve more. That audition was damned hard to set up and you won't even make a follow-up call."

"Naomi set it up, not you. And Naomi hasn't suggested that any kind of follow-up call is necessary."

Trish trembled with anger. "Don't bring that bitch up. Next you'll be telling me you made more when she was your manager and not just your agent."

It's true — oh, how Rett wanted to say it. It took

4

the little self-control she had left to keep the words off her tongue. Shakily, she began, "I'm leaving for New York in two hours —"

"Which is why you should march your ass over to that phone and call that producer. I schmoozed at four parties to find out who was producing that movie."

"I think it'll backfire." Mere discomfort at self-promotion was not what was making her stubborn. She trusted Naomi, who had been her agent for a long time, to let her know when calling a producer might be necessary. Getting this singing part in a Disney animated movie was the chance of a lifetime and she didn't want to screw it up.

"What the fuck do you know about it? You don't know anything about the business of keeping Rett Jamison, Inc. in the black. You don't trust my judgment. You're so fucking Midwestern sometimes. Christ, you are so pathetic. Look at you — buttoned to the neck and a tighter ass than Nancy Reagan. I don't know why I even bother."

"Don't do this, Trish. I have to get on the plane —" Rett stirred in her seat, wanting to end the relentless playback of their fight.

"I might not be here when you get back," Trish had snapped. "I have other places I can be. Just remember that money is tight while you're in New York."

". . . cool New York morning to a pleasant sixty-seven at the terminal in Los Angeles. We'll be starting our descent in just a few minutes. The tailwind that

5

helped with the wonderful visibility during our flight
is also getting us to the gate forty-five minutes
early . . ."

Suddenly, Rett could hear Louis Armstrong crooning "What a Wonderful World." The words floated in
her sleep-befuddled brain and she wanted to stay
inside the song where the skies were blue and Trish
was not yelling at her. She'd dreamed she was singing
a duet with Chet Baker, or had it been Tony Bennett?
No, no, it had been Ella Fitzgerald or even Rosemary
Clooney. She was reliving the past week, when she'd
crooned their songs and the crowd had begged for
more. She should feel like a million bucks, like a star.

She felt like a popped balloon.

A pert voice drowned out what was left of her
dream duets. "We are beginning our descent into Los
Angeles. The captain has turned on the Fasten Seat
Belts sign . . ."

"Can I get you anything else before we land?" The
nasal-voiced steward for first class was hovering again.

"Water," Rett said automatically. He was back in a
flash with another bottle of spring water and Rett tried
to shake off her fatigue while she sipped. She felt a
little better for the rest, but her days of glee- fully
running on less than three hours' sleep were long over.
She lacked the emotional reserves to cope with the ugly
situation between her and Trish. She sighed.

"Rough trip?" The man next to her was putting
away his computer. When they'd first boarded she'd
been afraid he would want to talk the whole way, but
as soon as there had been a "computers okay" announcement, he'd headed for cyber-broker land.

"Just tired. I don't bounce back the way I used to.
Once upon a time I could sing until three A.M. and be

ready at nine for studio work. And I could do that for weeks on end."

"I hear that." He stowed the computer in the overhead bin, then eased back into his seat. "There was a time when I'd get off this plane and go right to two meetings, a cocktail party and a lengthy business dinner. Now all I want is a soak in the spa and bed."

"That sounds fabulous," Rett agreed, then realized her fervent agreement had sounded like a come-on. She looked sideways at him. "I have a Jacuzzi tub at home and that's where I'm headed."

He looked relieved. "Same here." There was a brief, awkward silence, then he said, "Did you know you hum in your sleep?"

Rett blushed. "No, I didn't." It was not a personal tidbit she had ever expected to learn from a man. "No one has ever mentioned that."

"I think it was a Cole Porter song."

"I sing a lot of Cole Porter," Rett admitted. "He's a favorite."

"Of mine, too. Do you perform around L.A. somewhere? I have a friend who likes that kind of music — jazz, that sort of thing."

"I'm appearing at the Newport Jazz Festival in late July. With David Benoit and others."

"I'll have to get passes." He whipped out a Palm Pilot and jotted frantically with a minuscule stylus. "Rett Jamison, right?" He grinned. "I saw it on your luggage. We'll look for you. After your set I'll tell him I heard you sing in your sleep — that'll raise his eyebrows."

Rett's gaydar beeped. "Just don't tell my girlfriend that — she's not the understanding type." Actually, Trish was the understanding type, but Rett wanted to make sure he knew she had received his message and replied in kind.

His bass voice was now tinged with a slight Southern accent. Atlanta, she thought. "I doubt you'll remember me by then, but if you do see me in the crowd, wave. I'll be as cool as the other side of the pillah."

"I'll remember," Rett said. "I never forget a face. I never forget just about anything, for that matter." A photographic memory — near-perfect recall — was a blessing for a performer and allowed her a wide repertoire. It also kept every single word Trish said fresh and unrelentingly painful in her mind.

The steward took away her empty water bottle and a few minutes later the plane touched down smoothly. A glance out the window confirmed that the captain had been right. May in L.A. meant mild breezes, blue sky and warm sunshine. Today looked like no exception. It was still a little nippy in New York, especially at night.

Her cell phone chirped as she walked out of the terminal in search of a shuttle. The digital readout said it was Naomi Grey, her agent. "I just got off the plane," she said without a hello. "At least let me catch my breath."

"I need to see you right away." Naomi sounded only mildly apologetic. "I'm about five minutes from the airport — I'll give you a lift home."

"I'll let you have your way with me if it means not having to take a shuttle. You know my stop would be last and it would take three hours to go twenty miles." Rett felt a wave of relief. "I'll even talk business. Well, I'll listen business. I'm pretty worn out."

"I know, sweetie. But it can't wait."

She stood at the curb and wondered what Naomi had to convey that was so urgent. A new gig, maybe? No, Naomi would not have waited to relay something mundane. She'd have left a message. Unless it was really, really good news. For a moment Rett's heart pounded. Maybe she had gotten a callback from Disney. She'd be an actress's singing voice in an animated feature. If she got that callback the entire fight with Trish would be moot.

She quelled her enthusiasm. By definition, a performer's life was one long series of rejections interrupted by moments of glory. She was lucky enough to have the rejections down to a minimum. She had found her steady niche and that was more than most performers could say. Besides, she just wasn't lucky enough to solve her problems with Trish that way. It would only be a temporary fix at best.

Naomi's Audi veered across several lanes to brake at the curb. Rett tossed her suitcase and carry-on into the trunk and lowered herself into the passenger seat. Naomi had always liked low-slung cars.

Rett waited to ask questions until Naomi was safely onto Century Boulevard. She deeply distrusted airport shuttle drivers and was convinced driving around an airport was more dangerous than flying. "So what's the news that couldn't wait?"

"I'll buy you a drink and then tell you."

Naomi was ill at ease; Rett could see that now. No Disney deal, then. "I don't need to be anesthetized for bad news."

"I do," Naomi said shortly.

"We can have a drink at my place."

"We need some privacy."

9

Rett mulled that over. A bar was hardly more private than her place. But it was likely that Trish was home, which meant that what Naomi really wanted was privacy from Trish. Great, just great. Trish and Naomi had always had problems and she'd always played the peacemaker. She couldn't do that right now, not since her relationship with Trish was barely breathing.

Trouble between the two women was not new. From the beginning, it hadn't been smooth. Four years ago Rett had changed her relationship with Naomi from agent-manager to just agent so that the love of her life could be her manager. Trish had managed several starlets and another singer early in their careers — all were doing well now. Trish could give Rett a hundred percent of her attention. They were in love. It had seemed logical to Rett at the time, but now she asked herself why the other talent Trish had managed all moved on to other managers after a few years. It was a disloyal thought and one Rett didn't want to pursue at the moment. There was too much on her Trish plate as it was.

Naomi had accepted the decision with resigned grace, but the tension — tension Rett had believed was just both women's competitive natures — remained.

They were settled in a booth at a hotel cocktail lounge when Rett admitted, "I don't think I have the energy today to smooth over some problem between you and Trish." She didn't want to tell Naomi about the fight and that Trish had threatened to leave.

Naomi sipped her vodka tonic and grimaced. "You won't have to. You know I don't like her. I've never made any bones about that. I know she thinks I bad-mouth her to you but she has no idea — neither do you — of how many times I've choked on what I wanted to say. This morning I found out something that cinched things for me. It's her or me, and I don't expect you to pick me. She's your lover and I accept that."

Rett found herself blinking in confusion. Naomi wanted to stop representing her? The idea had never crossed Rett's mind. Naomi had been her agent for ten, no twelve, Christ — a lot of years. Naomi was the kind of agent who got to pick and choose her clients. Shit — they were both threatening to leave her. It wasn't the first time Trish had done that, but it was definitely a first for Naomi. And Naomi didn't make idle threats.

Loyalty to Trish should have kept her from asking. She should ask Trish's side first. But she couldn't help herself. "What happened?"

"I found out three days ago you got a callback from Disney."

Rett swallowed her excitement. Naomi's face was too gloomy for this development to last. "And?"

"Trish didn't tell you about it, did she? I told them to check with Trish for your calendar. Today the casting rep at Disney phones — a courtesy to me since we've known each other since diapers — and says the callback is off."

Naomi's long-time friendship with the casting person at Disney was one of the reasons she'd gotten the initial screening. Dreading the answer and already suspecting what it was, Rett asked, "What happened?"

"You're too difficult to work with."

Rett stared at Naomi for a full minute with the sound of blood rushing in her ears. Difficult to work with? *Me?* When her brain stopped buzzing in disbelief she realized what must have happened. Her incredulity mutated to rage. She said hoarsely, "I think I'll take that drink now." When Naomi returned from the bar with a vodka tonic for her, Rett was beyond anger. Her voice shook. "What exactly happened?" She downed about a quarter of the drink and listened to Naomi confirm her suspicions.

Naomi's expression was wooden, though Rett couldn't tell if it was anger or resignation. "Although Disney recognizes that you have the rare vocal quality their composer is looking for, you are not so valuable to them that they can send a limo for you and provide sumptuous surroundings for your five or six guests. I called in a valuable marker to get you that audition and callback and she fucking wasted it — for both of us."

Rett was now so angry she could spit. The precious callback that Trish had wanted her to beg a producer for had landed in their laps — and it wasn't enough for Trish. She'd decided that Rett Jamison needed to play the diva in order to become one.

It was one thing for Trish to look out for her and another to be unreasonable. She'd never been able to make Trish see the difference. It was like the water thing. Most people didn't understand why she required room-temperature water before a performance, but the last time someone had inadvertently brought iced water Trish had gone off the deep end at the poor waiter. She had wanted to tell Trish to stop — just ask for the right thing and let it go, but she'd been frozen. Frozen because lately when Trish got angry like that she tended to be cruel to everyone, and the last thing Rett needed before a performance was Trish's verbal slice-and-dice turned on her. When

Trish turned cruel Rett just didn't know what to do. She'd been dodging Trish's temper for the last couple of months. The Fight was just the culmination.

She had to face their problems now. The past week she'd been trying to think of how to patch it up because starting over was too daunting. But how could she patch it up — an opportunity like this would likely not come again. And if word got around that Rett Jamison was a pain in the ass, well, she might never know that was why she was losing gigs.

How could Trish have fucked up so badly?

She took a deep breath, aware that Naomi was watching her. Anger is a force, she told herself. Anger can finally get you off your butt and ready to do whatever it takes to change things.

High-handedness with Disney was the last thing she could afford. How often in the last year had she cringed when Trish flippantly informed her that some other agent or promoter was a jerk and they couldn't waste their time on jerks unless they paid above usual to make up for the slime factor? When they asked for more money, sometimes the jobs went away. How often had Trish followed those pronouncements with reminders that Rett wasn't making any more this year than she had last year, yet their expenses had gone up? How long had Rett had the sinking awareness that her career was cooling off when she could least afford to fade away? Forty was a steel wall for many singers.

When she'd left for New York, she'd felt like a failure. The bank balance was as low as her self-esteem. She would have to economize during the trip, Trish had informed her. The coming summer was looking slow, unless the Disney deal went through.

The funk that came with walking the extra blocks to less expensive restaurants and delis and going without room service when she was particularly tired had made it harder and harder to get up for each day's performance. Damn it — Trish had known what getting that part had meant to both of them. How could she risk it over something like a limo and food? She must know that Rett would have gladly walked backward to get there.

That was enough to be mad about. Enough to fire Trish. Could she fire Trish and stay lovers with her?

God, what was she going to do?

"I don't know what to say," she finally managed.

Naomi finished her drink. "You don't have to say anything. I'm sorry, Rett. I didn't want to do this —"

"I understand your point of view, Naomi." Naomi was rarely wrong about business, Rett reminded herself. Your career is going in a direction she wants no part of and that should scare the shit out of you.

She stared into her drink, feeling battered and confused and beyond words. Naomi just stared at the ceiling. Rett appreciated the time to think. Naomi had known her a long time now. Her mind reluctantly did the math. It wasn't ten years, but fifteen. Both of them were getting older than Rett wanted them to. Naomi knew that when Rett needed to think it was best to just stay out of the way. Trish tended to natter at her when she needed to make a decision.

If you're going to do this, she told herself, do it for the right reasons. Not because you're mad or because you're still hurt about the things she said. Fire her because she's a fuckup. And break up with her because there's just no love there anymore.

She was unwillingly remembering what she'd found

in a stack of bills three weeks ago. Breaking up with Trish because of that would be hypocritical. They'd agreed to an open relationship. Back when she'd been head over heels in love she'd agreed that the whole patriarchal monogamy head trip wasn't for them. What mattered was respecting each other. It wasn't supposed to hurt that Trish's flings were all probably half her age with buns of steel, or that most of them were after Trish in the hopes of connecting with someone, anyone, who could get them an audition somewhere.

As for her own flings, there were none. That wasn't Trish's fault. She wasn't wired for sex the same way Trish was. She could get lost in sex, and had with Trish way back when, but it wasn't something she did easily, or could do for just one night.

Three weeks ago she'd happened across a stack of bills waiting to be paid. Trish took care of all of that and Rett wouldn't have given it another glance except that the very first item on the American Express statement caught her eye: Sheraton Grande, Los Angeles. Two hundred and fifteen dollars and some change. Amex included copies of the charge slips and the charge was for one overnight stay and breakfast room service. She'd mentally reviewed her calendar. She'd been home that week. That was the night Trish had gone to an all-night party. Rett had suspected she was with someone, but she wasn't supposed to care so she didn't ask Trish about the party when she got home late the next morning.

She had shoved the knowledge of the hotel bill out of her head. It had taken a lot of effort. She didn't want to think about it. Couldn't think about it. She wasn't supposed to care if Trish had been with someone, but was it okay to care that Rett Jamison, Inc. was footing the bill? Was she cutting corners on her expenses so Trish could throw money around on other women? Was she more upset about the money than the lovers on the side?

She wanted to break up for mature reasons, but all the hurt she'd been bottling up was now at the surface. Hurt and angry — it was the wrong state to be in when such a serious decision was needed. She tried to stop thinking about the other women. She told herself they didn't matter.

They did matter, they mattered deeply. What an idiot she'd been. She'd founded their relationship on a lie and the karma was back in full.

All the little and not-so-little things that had been bothering her had been laid bare by this fiasco with Disney. If she didn't fire Trish over that she'd lose her self-respect. But she'd be lying to herself if she tried to believe it was the only reason. It was just the catalyst. She thought about Trish's unkindness, the other women and the money.

Her thoughts were reeling in all directions, but they kept circling back to the money. Through the corporation and Rett's personal account, all of Trish's living expenses, including a leased Lexus, were paid for. Now she was paying for Trish's hotel rooms and morning-after breakfasts. Meanwhile, Trish complained that cash flow was tight while she pocketed her 15 percent of whatever Rett made. Not one dime of it ever came back to the household expenses that Rett could see. Trish must have a pretty big nest egg, Rett thought. At the same time it seemed to her that her investment balances — the money that would tide her over in hard times or at retirement — were never really any larger.

Rett paid for everything and yet made none of the decisions. How long had it been since she'd been the one to say if she'd take a gig or not? Too long. Far too long.

The list of what was wrong between them was lengthy, but if money was at the top, then she couldn't really love Trish much anymore, could she? It would hurt to be lonely again, to go back to hanging out in clubs and going to parties hoping to meet someone with a brain and a heart.

"Do you think I'm a loyal person — wait, don't answer that." Rett finished her drink and then wished she hadn't. Her stomach was feeling queasy as she contemplated what was going to happen when she got home. "You're not a therapist."

Naomi didn't seem startled by Rett's sudden return to animation. "I try not to be. I should have said something sooner, maybe."

Rett shook her head. "No, you shouldn't have. This — this is a pretty big thing. Anything less than this and I'd have chosen her."

Naomi blinked. "And now?"

"Got time to manage an old friend again?"

Not even a ghost of a smile touched Naomi's thin lips. "I thought you'd never ask."

"I am *so* fucked."

"I'm sorry, Rett. Really sorry."

"Not your fault." Rett pressed her lips together. She could feel her throat tightening and she talked around the clenched muscles. "Just hard to be single again."

"You think she'll leave?"

"I think she'll have to when I change the locks." Rett tried to laugh but she clearly didn't fool Naomi.

"I'll take you on home, then."

Rett tried to find some courage by running the words to "I Will Survive" through her head, but it didn't work. What had been a pretty day now seemed gray and foreboding. Naomi let her out at the lobby of the small condominium complex two blocks from the Santa Monica Promenade, just off Idaho and Second. It had been Trish's advice to buy the place and she'd been right for once. It had appreciated nearly 50 percent in the last three years. The building and apartments were as bland as could be, but location was everything. So far none of the neighbors had objected to her two-hour practice stints in the morning, which made it as good a place to live as any.

She glimpsed Trish's car in the underground lot, parked next to hers, and tried breathing exercises to calm her racing heart. What should she say? Should she just get right into it? Should she try to pretend everything was normal except that Trish was fired and could Trish please move out ASAP?

Her hand was shaking so hard she pushed the wrong floor button and got off before she realized her mistake. She had to wait for the elevator to come back for her, so she tried more deep breathing. She was still trying to calm herself when she let herself into the apartment.

Traces of Trish were everywhere. Clothes on the floor, dirty dishes on the counter and dining room table. She glanced at her watch and realized she hadn't reset it for local time. Her body clock said four p.m., but it was only one here. Trish might be asleep if she'd been out last night. The cheese and cracker remains on the table were Trish's favorite up-till-dawn snack.

She stood in the bedroom doorway and cursed herself for not noticing that there were two of everything on the table. Two wine glasses, two plates. There were two pairs of slacks on the floor next to the bed.

She didn't want to look. Trish knew she was coming home. She was maybe an hour ahead of schedule, which meant that Trish hadn't planned on clearing up her little fling before Rett got home. The pants that weren't Trish's looked like a size minus-three.

Her suitcase slipped out of her numb fingers and the thud stirred the bed's two occupants. Trish's eyes opened first; she glanced in Rett's direction.

"Shit!" She threw off the covers and sat up. The flat-stomached, firm-bosomed, long-legged features of her companion were also revealed. "What time is it?"

"Time for you to get out of my life."

"Don't be that way. I didn't mean for this to happen."

The other woman was awake now, her Kewpie doll mouth open in surprise, but otherwise she lacked any expression of chagrin. If anything, she looked triumphant.

It was then, over the woman's shoulder, that Rett saw the mirror, razor and remnants of white powder. The realization hit her harder than anything else that had happened, and it literally knocked the breath out of her.

Trish knew how she felt about drugs. Trish supposedly felt the same. Drugs were for losers on a one-way trip to Loserville. Trish had agreed.

Everything she's ever told me was a lie, Rett thought. Even that she loved me.

She struggled to find enough breath to speak. "I'm serious, Trish. It's over."

"Rett, honey, you don't mean that. I've embarrassed you. You're upset."

"Embarrassed me?"

The other woman spoke up. "I'm so sorry to be the bone of contention —"

"Don't flatter yourself." Rett didn't want to look at the woman, let alone talk to her. "Now's a good time to get dressed and get out, because this doesn't concern you."

Trish nodded when the woman looked at her. They waited while she dressed. Rett did not fail to notice that Trish mouthed, "I'll call you," at the woman as she left.

Trish began to get dressed herself while Rett stood in the doorway. After Trish pulled a tight muscle shirt over her head she looked up at Rett. "Have you eaten?"

Rett's laugh was incredulous. "We're not done."

"Yes, we are." Trish tidied her short hair with her fingers and then met Rett's gaze in the mirror. "God, I've missed you."

No, she thought, I'm not going to let this happen. Traitor body — how could she still want Trish?

Trish turned from the mirror, all muscled legs and shoulders. "I think I got dressed too soon."

She was letting Trish get too close. Trish's breath was whispering over her ear. She could smell . . . she could smell sex and couldn't help her own response. To get in their bed where Trish had been with someone else, to make Trish prove how much she still loved her by obliterating the memory of another woman — she was dizzy with the temptation.

Trish lightly touched her lips with one finger and Rett wanted to nibble at it.

I am not my mother. I will not make her mistakes. Rett had carried that litany with her from the moment she had left home, and yet she knew she was on the verge of making one of her mother's mistakes — settling for any kind of love as better than none at all.

She stepped back and whispered, "No."

Trish looked dumbfounded. Her sexy air faded and her voice was like steel. "Am I going to get a reason?"

Rett had to clear her throat. "You know the reason."

"I'm sorry Cheri was still here."

"This is not about whoever that was or any of them. It's about Disney." Cheri — cute little name to go with her cute little ass.

"We got the callback, babe. I'm just waiting to find out when. It was going to be a surprise."

"They canceled, *babe.* Because I'm a pain in the ass to work with. Because Rett Nobody Jamison demands limos and buffets."

"Those shits! They do that for the person who walks Mariah Carey's dog. It was a perfectly reasonable request."

Rett shook her head in disbelief. "This was the biggest break of my career and you don't seem to realize that you fucked it up."

"We don't need them if they don't know how to treat us." Trish shrugged as if that was all that needed to be said.

Rett's voice was squeaky with anger. "*I* need them.

I needed this job. This isn't about how they treat *us*, it's about *me* getting the break of a lifetime. You fucked it up — why? Was Cheri coming along for the ride as foreplay? Were you going to introduce her to me as a fresh, young voice who needed the invaluable experience of seeing a working studio?"

"You're jealous of Cheri and you shouldn't be." Trish was turning up the pheromones again. "You know how I feel about you."

I am not my mother and I will not make her mistakes. Rett took a deep breath. "I know what you want me to think. But it's over. You've fucked up my career and you've brought drugs into the house."

"That?" Trish rolled her eyes. "It's Cheri's. Though it wouldn't hurt you to try it. It would let your hair down a little."

"It's over, Trish." Rett felt as if she was looking at a stranger. "I don't know you anymore. I don't trust you to handle my business anymore. I don't respect you anymore."

Trish's expression was mulish. How had she ever mistaken it for sultry? "You're from nowhere and heading back there on the fast track. Who the fuck are you to throw me out?"

It was like her mother's voice out of the past. Rett gritted her teeth. "I'm the owner of this apartment. The one who pays the bills. The one with a career that now needs some major repair. I'm taking the career back to Naomi and I'm looking forward to one person in my bed, not three."

"That bitch — I knew she was behind this. She's had it in for me since the start. She tells you lies and you have a hysterical fit!"

Rett's anger made her feel intensely calm. "I've

realized I trust Naomi more than I'll ever trust you. Naomi doesn't use me. I know that we agreed no monogamy. But that doesn't mean that I don't see the hotel charge receipts on the credit card I pay for. Five-star hotels for you for a roll in the hay, but I'm always at Motel 6 when I'm working."

"This is all about money." Trish lounged against the wall in the leave-me-alone-come-get-me manner that had brought Rett running four years ago. Rett thought it viciously unfair that those dark eyes still made her weak in the knees.

"You know, I've just realized that it is. It's all about how much money I can make to keep you in the style you're accustomed to. You don't spend a dime of your percentage on anything related to me and our home or your car." She waved a hand at the paraphernalia on the bedstand. "For all I know, you've been putting it all up your nose. It doesn't matter. The free ride is over."

"You don't have a problem living the good life."

Rett's lips tightened. Her voice fell to its deepest level. "I'm the one with the three-octave vocal range and a flawless memory. I'm the one who does the actual work that pays the bills. I'm the one who spends two hours a day practicing. I'm done with your making everything my fault. I'm not taking the blame for your arrogance. The only thing I've done wrong is let this go on too long."

Trish ran one elegant hand through her short, dark hair. She looked at Rett through her lashes and said nothing. Rett could sense the pheromones again. Her body reminded her how much she had been looking forward to being with Trish. The feel of Trish inside her and her mouth finding the places that she

23

knew would make Trish tremble . . . it would be very easy to say yes.

I am not my mother. I will not make her mistakes. Rett stood stock-still, afraid even the slightest motion would betray her unwanted desires. The rest of her life was more important than a quick fuck. Otherwise what was the point of working so hard for a future?

When the silence got too hard to bear, Rett dragged one of Trish's suitcases out of the closet. It wouldn't hold all of Trish's things, of course, but the significance was important. She filled it with polo shirts, underwear and chinos, put Trish's toothbrush on top, zipped it shut, then crossed the room to hold it out to Trish.

Trish stared at the case as if it were a snake. "You don't really mean this."

"I do."

Trish moved so quickly that Rett couldn't do more than let out a startled yelp. She knocked the suitcase from Rett's hand and seized her, pulling her into a tight embrace.

Rett arched her neck back so she could look into Trish's eyes. She found her most scathing tone. "Is this where we clinch and I forgive everything? You're not macho enough for this move." She knew that Trish could feel how hard she was shaking. She was still angry and now the electricity of Trish's touch was threatening to change anger to lust.

Trish was looking down at her with an expression that Rett didn't recognize. Was it contempt? Did Trish really feel so little for her? Had she been mistaking contempt for love all along?

For several heartbeats Trish just held her tightly, then she put her mouth on Rett's. Rett turned her head away as far as she could, trying to not dignify Trish's caveman tactics by struggling.

"Let go of me. This is ridiculous."

"Who are you to dump me?" Rett glanced back into Trish's eyes and didn't recognize what she saw there. In that instant, Trish shoved her into the wall so viciously that Rett saw stars. Just as her muddled vision cleared, Trish slapped her, hard.

In that instant, Rett was sixteen again, hearing the crack of some boyfriend's hand across her mother's face. *I will not be a victim. I am not my mother.*

All her rage boiled to the surface. She did what she had learned to do when the kids picked on you because your mom was a lush and you had no idea who your father was. Didn't include you because you dressed in garage sale clothes, because you weren't interested in boys or getting drunk. Called you names because, even in strange clothes and with a tramp of a mom and not liking boys and never getting drunk, you could still sing the national anthem and bring the crowd to its feet on the word *free* all without a microphone. She grabbed Trish by the back of her hair and pushed her face into the wall hard enough to bruise.

"If you ever, *ever* touch me again, you'll need a plastic surgeon. What did you think — I'd crumple up and cry and beg you to forgive me? I'm nobody's victim. It won't work anymore!"

"Let go of me!"

Rett let go and stumbled back several feet. Her tunnel vision was receding and so was the adrenaline rush. The hand she put to her slapped face was shaking.

Trish had her hand on her face, too. "I know you

plenty well. So you can sing. You're still trash. You don't get the big gigs because everyone knows it."

"You hit me and *I'm* the trash?"

She saw Trish swallow hard. "I'm sorry. I . . . lost my temper. I should be punching Naomi."

"As if this is her fault. As if punching someone could settle anything. Naomi was ready to walk away from me, you know that? Your fucking up my reputation was more than she could bear to watch."

"Well, you're not going to listen to anything I say. Four years and that's it."

Rett was stricken with guilt, then she stiffened her spine. How did Trish do that? Trish had slapped her and degraded her and somehow ended up making her feel like the guilty one. "You don't love me. I don't love you. What's the point of it anymore? What could you say that could possibly change that?"

"You'll never know, will you? I'll be back for the rest of my stuff." Trish snatched up the suitcase.

Rett followed her to the door. For what, she didn't know. A tender good-bye after that exchange of violence? Just to be sure she was gone?

Trish turned from the open door. "By the way, if you think what we had was love, think again."

"If it wasn't love at the beginning, what was it?"

"A means to an end. After that, it was just pathetic."

"You're half of that story," Rett said hoarsely. Emotion and exhaustion had taken their toll on her throat. "If it was pathetic then you get half the blame."

"Sorry, sweetie." Rett wondered distantly if Trish knew just how unattractive that sneer was, and how much worse it would be if she ripped Trish's face apart with her bare hands. "I was the one who laughed about your sad little libido with other women. Lots of them."

Rett closed her eyes for a moment, not wanting Trish to see the knife going in. Then she fixed Trish with an unwavering gaze. "And *I'm* the trash?"

Trish didn't answer. She swung her suitcase as she went through the door, knocking over a little table laden with mail and papers. She slammed the door behind her and a picture nearby slipped off its nail and shattered on the tile.

In pieces. Rett gasped for breath. She struggled against the tears. Crying ruined her voice and her face. Then she remembered she wasn't singing in the near future.

She cried about loving and not loving Trish, and for losing the woman she had thought Trish was. She cried because she wasn't who she had hoped she'd be by now and she wasn't sure she was strong enough to start over. She cried because she could.

2

"How come you won't go out with the boys who hang around here? You too good for them?"

"I don't like boys, Mama. It's none of your business anyway! You bring enough men into the house for both of us!"

"Don't you talk to me that way, young lady. I can still pull you over my knee and I don't care if you are Miss Artsy Fartsy in your third-rate school play . . ."

Rett woke up on the couch. The VCR clock blinked 8:30. For a minute she was too disoriented to know if that was A.M. or P.M. It was P.M., the same miserable day. The echo of her mother's voice hissed in her ears.

She reached for the phone to call Naomi, then stopped herself before the call went through. What was she going to do? Dump her mess on Naomi's lap and expect her to pick up the pieces? That was weak and unprincipled. She thought of old friends she could call for comfort. Friends she'd let drift away because Trish didn't like them. She couldn't call them just because she suddenly could use a good shoulder — she was not going to be one of those people that used friends as stand-ins between lovers.

Today, Rett vowed, she was done with being weak. Maybe Trish was a manipulative bitch, but as Eleanor Roosevelt had discerned, no one can make you feel inferior without your help. She shoved all thoughts of her mother into a mental closet and visualized padlocks on the door — that was where she belonged.

She glanced at her ravaged face in the mirror. She could still feel the sting of Trish's slap. Tears threatened. You're no Eleanor Roosevelt, she told herself. But you're going to have to try harder. You gotta be strong, you gotta be tough, you gotta be wiser.

She felt a little less hollow after a large glass of milk and some ibuprofen. A hot shower removed the sticky airplane feeling and the unclean aura of the scene with Trish. She threw away the paraphernalia, stripped the bed and put the sheets in the washer, then dug around until she found her old ratty chenille robe. She'd always liked it better than the silk kimono Trish had given her one Christmas. She wandered into the den that served as her home office. She wasted an hour playing Myst, then clicked onto the Internet to check her mail. It was then that she realized this was the first problem she had to confront. Trish had her passwords, and Trish's screen name account was through Rett's online membership.

She changed her password and then sent Trish a terse e-mail to the effect that her screen name would be canceled in two days. She clicked for return receipt acknowledgment so she would have proof that Trish read it.

Another thought occurred to her, even more chilling. Trish had all the passwords and privileges to Rett's bank and investment accounts, electronic wallet passwords to order merchandise at dozens of eShopping sites, and ATM and credit cards that gave out cash. In a panic, Rett used her master setup privileges to limit Trish's activity to sending and receiving mail. But that wouldn't stop Trish from accessing the Web through the nearest Internet café or a 50-hours free access CD-ROM.

She started clicking through Web pages to change access passwords. When she got to the checking account page, she saw that a thousand dollars, the daily maximum, had been withdrawn that day. She clicked to a credit card interim statement site — a cash advance had been made that day for another two thousand dollars. Shit.

Frantically, she dug through the credit card file folders until she found the company they paid to keep track of all the cards and insure against theft. When Trish's wallet had been stolen it had saved them a small fortune and a tremendous amount of time. One phone call and all the credit accounts were closed with new cards to be reissued in her name only.

It was almost midnight before she finished faxing letters to all the various brokerage houses and mutual funds to rescind Trish's access. Trish would certainly still be up at this hour, and Rett realized that at midnight she would be able to withdraw another thousand from the checking account using the ATM card. She didn't know what kind of treatment she would get from the big bank — she had started out with a small local that had been bought up several times since. But someone answered the 800 help number.

"I need to cancel ATM privileges for my account and remove an authorized person from the account records. It's urgent."

"I can help you with that," the soft-spoken man on the end of the line assured her. He asked her a few questions to prove her identity. She could hear tapping in the background as he made a note about removing Trish from the account. "Your ATM cards are now invalid. I'll put a flag on your account right now for a supervisor's review of all transactions processed later today — it's just after midnight now so that an in-person cash withdrawal will be impossible unless it's you. You need to go into a branch tomorrow, as early as possible, and sign a new account application and signature cards. That's crucial."

She promised she would be there in the morning and hung up, feeling a little more secure. She would be able to turn things over to Naomi a little less messed up and with a promise to stay more involved. She shouldn't be letting someone make so many decisions for her. It was lazy and irresponsible. It was the same as tattooing *sucker* on her forehead. Until she'd opened the file cabinet she hadn't known they had accounts at so many different companies. She wasn't even sure if that was good or bad.

She fished a diet Coke from the back of the refrigerator and took it out onto the small balcony. The night air was refreshing and the never-ending hubbub from the Promenade reminded her she wasn't alone. During infrequent lulls in both traffic on the Pacific Coast Highway and raucous pedestrians and rollerbladers on Ocean Avenue, she could just make out the quiet brush of surf against sand along Santa Monica Beach. She was okay. She would be okay tomorrow, too. Keep singing that tune, she told herself. You might begin to believe it.

The bank was crowded but otherwise uneventful. She stopped at the market for fresh milk and bagels, then went home to practice.

She preferred to practice in the bedroom. The vaulted ceiling had slightly better acoustics. She found her Casio keyboard under the unwashed laundry Trish had left and played herself a little Mozart fanfare to get going.

She faced the mirror over the dresser and closed her eyes. *Feel your feet on the ground,* she thought. *Feel your feet on the carpet on the ground. Feel your feet in your sandals on the carpet on the ground. Where is your center? Make it quiet . . .*

Inhale . . . expanding ribs and stomach, feeling the muscles around her diaphragm pulling for even more air . . . *Don't raise your shoulders. Exhale* . . . muscles working reverse, letting the air go as slowly as possible, but all of it go out in the end to make all possible room for fresh. *Inhale . . . exhale.*

Just above a whisper she vocalized a round "ah" at middle C and holding, then increased volume to full voice. C became D, whisper to full voice and back again. She worked her lower range first, pushing on the D below middle C to keep it accessible. There were not a lot of women who could hit and hold a note that low. All warmed up, her throat was a musical instrument that ran scales, flipped between upper- and lower-range notes and slid two octaves like butter. It sounded as good at nearly forty as it had at nineteen. Heck, it sounded better.

She forgot all about Trish in the lush beauty of the B-flat that opened a short French art song. Love, flowers, blue skies all ended at that B-flat again. The world was her voice.

She flipped on an accompaniment recorded on a CD and ran through several standards she always had ready: "Rainy Days and Mondays," "Love for Sale," "Are You Lonesome Tonight?" "The Air That I Breathe." She spent another half hour trying out a new song, "When She Believed in Me," for the jazz festival where she would perform with David Benoit. It would be great exposure, and she owed the gig to Naomi's perseverance with the recording label that represented Benoit. It was possible the live gig would lead to another recording chance, even if it was on someone else's project. The song originally had been written for and recorded by Kenny Loggins, but she pushed the memory of his voice out of her ear and found her own inflections.

Singing jazz for a week in New York had made her lax with her phrasing. It always did. Phrasing mattered less with jazz, where the rhythm and harmonies were what the other musicians counted on. She made her vocal muscles remember better habits by running through some lengthy pieces, including Sting's "Fields of Gold" and Loreena McKennitt's "Lady of Shalott." They both required concentration on phrasing and memory. When she finished she felt back to normal. Her voice was still her rock. Nothing could bother her now.

Fuck you, Trish.

Replenished with a bottle of water and a bagel slathered with cream cheese, she headed for the office and discovered a series of faxes waiting — various waivers and forms to close or restrict accounts. She also discovered an e-mail from Trish saying that closing off her access to the checking account had been breach of contract since fees were due her for work Rett had performed.

Rett sent back a short missive. *At her earliest convenience, Naomi will account for your unpaid percentage from which she'll deduct the funds and cash advances you withdrew yesterday. Please keep her informed as to your location since this e-mail address will go away tomorrow.* She didn't add that the credit cards were all canceled. Let Trish find that out for herself, and please, Goddess of Retribution on Faithless Lovers, let it be in the most embarrassing setting possible.

The thought of credit card bills made her realize the mail was due. She found Mrs. Bernstein in the lobby trying to ferry her groceries from the parking garage to the elevator. Mrs. Bernstein wouldn't admit to being a day over seventy, but Rett suspected eighty was closer to the truth.

"I'll carry those if you'll get the mail," Rett bargained. Mrs. Bernstein treasured her independence.

"I must admit they seem uncommonly heavy today. Thank you, dear." Once Rett had taken the bags, Mrs. Bernstein removed her gloves and tucked them into the matching leather bag.

"Of course I might insist on a cup of your coffee." The delicious Viennese blend would lift her spirits considerably.

"You won't have to twist my arm. I have some ginger cookies my granddaughter made me if you're so inclined."

The elevator chugged its way upward while Mrs. Bernstein talked about the weather and the smog. She would discuss nothing personal until she was inside her four walls, where, as she had once told Rett with a sour glance at her neighbor's door, she knew no one was listening to her private business.

Once inside Mrs. Bernstein made deliberate haste to the kitchen. "I'll make us both a cup, dear. Here's your mail. Looks like something nice is right on top. I'll have nothing but bills."

The "something nice" was a hand-addressed gray envelope — no doubt an invitation of some sort. There was no return address on the front, so she turned it over.

Time shivered to a halt.

She had not thought about Cinny Keilor consciously for years, although her fantasies had been known to include a lissome blonde with tanned legs and a tight sweater — pink and fluffy. Cinny Keilor.

It was unreasonable that her heart beat faster. She

could hear Cinny's soft soprano in her head, singing one of the ditzy high school chorus songs they'd learned. Cinny's voice in her ear, crooning, "Rett, I need you. Rett, I can't believe you make me feel this way. Rett, I want you to . . ."

She could almost taste Cinny's lip gloss and smell the herbal shampoo in her hair. Just the sight of her name and Rett was in the rear seat of Cinny's brother's car and Cinny was slowly sliding onto her back.

"Rett, I can't help it. That feels so good, Rett." An aching whisper, "Please, Rett, please. Please, Rett, stop. Stop it, Rett!"

Rett snapped out of her reverie when Mrs. Bernstein set down a delicate saucer and cup and a plate of ginger cookies. Cinny Keilor had been good at saying yes and even better at saying no.

"Looks like a party invitation," Mrs. Bernstein observed. She settled onto the barstool next to Rett and sipped from her steaming cup.

Rett pulled a card and a folded sheet of paper out of the envelope. "Oh my God — my twenty-fifth high school reunion. Unbelievable."

"Twenty-five years? Did you graduate when you were sixteen or have you been fibbing about your age?" Mrs. Bernstein sounded disapproving, but the faded gray eyes behind the thick lenses twinkled.

Rett set the papers down as if not touching them would help her not remember the silk of Cinny Keilor's skin. "Actually for me it's twenty-three years. Our high school was really small the years I was there. There was a lot of talk of closing it and combining it with Greenleaf High, even though they are homecoming rivals. God, I haven't thought about that in years. Homecoming."

Rett caught herself before she said "shit." Homecoming was not a pleasant memory.

"Anyway," she continued, "there were less than twenty in my graduating class. So the tradition is to have a reunion every five years and invite everybody who graduated in that five-year range. So it's exactly twenty-five for some and two years more or less for everyone else. I haven't gone to any of the earlier ones, though." Rett inhaled the bracing aroma of the coffee, then delicately sipped. Very nice.

"But you'll go this time — just think of showing everyone what a success you've become."

Rett started to protest that she was not a big success as success was measured in the music world, but then she realized that she was about as big a success as anyone from Woton, Minnesota, had probably ever been. It was not an unpleasant realization. Trish might call her trash, but in Woton she would be a star. That is, as long as her mother wasn't around to remind everyone that Rett would never amount to anything.

Mrs. Bernstein asked all about New York and they talked through two cups of the Viennese coffee. She accepted with equanimity Rett's news that Trish was no longer living with her. All the while Cinny Keilor's name seemed to glow on the paper in front of Rett and a ludicrous flutter of breathless anxiety flitted in the pit of her stomach.

Mrs. Bernstein settled in front of her favorite soap as Rett went back to her apartment. When she opened the door she remembered that Trish could still get in. There was no sign of her, though. A quick flip through the yellow pages had a locksmith on the way.

She studied the reunion invitation for a long time.

There were a variety of parties and get-togethers over the one-week period preceding the official reunion set for the third Saturday in August. August in Minnesota — the humidity didn't get any higher and the mosquitoes didn't get any bigger than August in Minnesota.

Cinny was chairing the reunion committee — that was typical of her. Head cheerleader, organizer of the student prayer group, secretary of the student council . . . the list went on and on. Cinny had handwritten her name on the back of the envelope as Cinny Keilor, but in the official announcement she was Cinny Keilor-Johnson. So she'd married. That was hardly a surprise.

There was a reservation card included and when Rett unfolded it, she found a note. *I hope you'll come, Rett. I'd love to see you again. Hugs, Cinny.*

It was just an innocent little note, Rett told herself. Cinny would have long forgotten their code. Whenever they'd ended up in each other's arms Cinny referred to it later as "seeing" each other. Cinny had always initiated their encounters by asking for a hug.

It was easy to slip into memories of Cinny Keilor. One hot, humid summer night she had nibbled Cinny's neck and nuzzled her earlobe for the first time. Cinny's breathing was shallow and ragged.

She had whispered, "I want to, Rett. You know I do."

Rett had been beyond words. Cinny's top was half-unbuttoned and Cinny was clutching Rett's mouth against her breast with desperate intent. Rett knew what she wanted. Had known that was she wanted for what seemed like all her life.

"Yes," Cinny whispered. She gasped when Rett's

tongue found her nipple. "That feels so good when you do it."

Rett was on the verge of tears. She had no words, just pent-up need. She wanted to be inside Cinny, to be everything to her. Her hand was sliding down the tight front of Cinny's jeans. Cinny had never let her get so far before. Instead of nuzzling through her shirt and bra, her mouth was exploring Cinny's breasts. Her searching fingertips found silky hair and Cinny let out a hard groan. She was arching, trying to give Rett more room for her hand.

"Oh, Rett, oh my lord. I can't believe the way you make me feel . . ."

She couldn't get her hand any farther down the tight jeans. She pulled it out and fumbled with the snap and zipper.

Cinny's hand captured hers, then Cinny was trying to sit up. "I can't . . . Rett, I can't do it."

Rett bent her head to Cinny's breasts again and for a moment, when Cinny sighed and offered them, she thought Cinny would relent.

"I really want to, but . . . I just can't, Rett."

She found enough voice to mumble, "I can make it really good for you, I promise."

"I know you could . . . but I can't . . ."

Cinny's voice faded into memory and Rett put a hand on her stomach. She had begged Cinny until Cinny got mean. Rett had tried more than once to leave Cinny alone. After a week or two Cinny would always suggest they "see" each other and then she would ask for a hug to show they were friends again. A hug always led to kisses, kisses to touching, touching to Rett's sexual frustration. All through their junior and senior years in high school they'd repeated the dance. Even when Rett knew Cinny was going all the way with her steady boyfriend, she would still come running when Cinny wanted to see her. Cinny always said yes, then Cinny always said no. It had been pathetic.

Rett shook herself out of her self-condemnation. How was she supposed to have known any better? She was the pervert, and perverts didn't deserve to get laid — or so she had thought then. It had been easy when she'd left Woton to think of Cinny as a manipulative tease, but all these years later it occurred to Rett that Cinny probably just hadn't been able to cope with her own sexuality. Proving to herself that she could say no to Rett had probably bolstered Cinny's desperate need to believe she wasn't gay. She couldn't blame Cinny for being confused and afraid, not when "lesbo" was a worse insult than "slut."

Begging for sex — Cinny was the last time Rett had ever done that. Then Trish had almost manipulated her into that place again. It had felt rotten at seventeen, and even worse at thirty-nine.

Now Cinny was married. Rett wondered what would happen if... No, she thought. There's no point to that what-if scenario. Finding out was not worth at least a week in August, temperature and humidity at ninety-nine and mosquitoes the size of sparrows. It would mean almost certainly having to see her mother and endure God only knew what kind of verbal abuse for the sake of nonexistent filial devotion.

She pushed the invitation to the back of her sock drawer. All dealt with, she thought. No need to think about it anymore.

3

The next week passed too slowly and Rett got too much rest, practiced too little and spent too much time thinking. She imagined going to the gym more than she actually went and discovered the comforting properties of fettucine Alfredo takeout from a nearby restaurant.

Her first meeting with Naomi as her manager again had been depressing. She graduated from the Alfredo to carbonara della casa. Even after the steps she'd taken to clean up some of the financial mess, Naomi had said she would have to pull in an accountant to make heads or tails of it all. The worst news was that Trish had moved her investment accounts around a lot and Rett had paid and repaid load charges. The accounts had earned nothing for the last two years as a result. Naomi had also reminded her about the car Trish was still driving. Rett sent a short e-mail requesting its return within five days.

Trish never called, not that Rett wanted her to. She didn't even call to arrange to pick up the rest of her stuff. So Rett spent all of one day boxing up Trish's clothes and odds and ends. She put the boxes in the guest bedroom where she didn't have to look at them.

She exhausted herself moving furniture around and didn't like the results. She ate far too many Snackwells, knowing full well that low in fat did not mean low in calories. She broke every promise she made to herself about going to the gym. Thank goodness she had a gig that night. She felt unwanted, unappreciated, unloved and just plain unhappy.

It did not matter that the gig was completely volunteer, "starring" at a Friday night karaoke event at Monica's, a women's coffeehouse by day and bar by night. It was a good deed combined with an opportunity to perform with a live audience. She had her own karaoke CD for her numbers. It had cost a bundle but in the end was far cheaper than hiring a keyboardist to accompany her every time she needed live practice. Her ego could certainly use an appreciative crowd.

She could have driven to the bar — many Angelinos would have preferred a four-block drive and then a skirmish for parking that cost nine dollars an hour and still meant a two-block walk to the final destination. But she knew the short walk would clear her mind and cast off the self-pitying blues refrain she'd been hearing in her head.

Within a few minutes she was glad she was on foot. Fabulous hibiscus the size of dinner plates hung over walls like springtime flags. Roses were blooming all along the boulevard, leaving the night drenched with their heady scent. The cool air was bringing out the heavy aroma of watered soil and greenery. Nights like these made her forget that most of Los Angeles was a concrete freeway. By the time she got to Monica's she felt less like she had been put through an emotional meat grinder. *Ob-la-di, ob-la-da.*

"Rett, you doll!" Monica Green hugged with her whole body. Given her size and tendency to wear flowing caftans, it was always an enveloping experience. Rett emerged from the fluttering fabric slightly mussed and smelling of rosewater. "How do you want things to go tonight? Like the last time?"

"Well, I thought you could —"

"About forty minutes for the amateurs, right?" Monica pushed her yellow-blond curls out of her eyes. The fix lasted no more than a second. "Then a set for you — thirty minutes. Is that too long? I think you went longer than that last time."

"No, I —"

"Then amateurs for the rest of the night. Could you host the first part? You know, sing along when people chicken out, that sort of thing?"

"I was planning to —"

"Then we're all set." Monica was beaming. "I have room-temperature water set aside for you. I'd have

43

never known how important it was if you hadn't told me. I'd have thought iced water was better. Is it for your throat or your vocal cords?"

"I'm not sure, it just works —"

"This is Camille Masterson. She's the D.J. and she'll be more than happy to help jolly people up, won't you?"

Camille just nodded. Rett decided Camille knew that actually talking to Monica took more energy than any one person could maintain. Rett nodded back and added a belated smile. Camille was all in black with short-cropped white hair and a body that looked like she spent half of each day doing Tae-Bo workouts. Just looking at her made Rett feel slovenly and overdressed in her jeans, denim vest and what now seemed like an ultra-femme linen shirt with poetically full sleeves. If she was looking for a diversion, Rett was sure Camille could make her forget all about Trish.

Yeah, that would be a good step, she thought. A little meaningless sex so you can feel guilty for weeks for not calling and then avoid all places where D.J.s might hang out. Better yet, move to another city just to avoid any chance encounter. That would put your life back on the right track.

The seats were starting to fill and Rett felt the familiar rush of anxiety and adrenaline that always accompanied a performance. This space of time was when Trish would do something to distract her — chat about nothing in particular, or discuss some minor business matter. It took the edge off, but was a piss-poor reason to start missing Trish.

"Your disc is in the machine." Camille was lounging next to her control panel. "Do the numbers cue by themselves or should I do it?"

"I prefer to have them cue automatically, but if you could stand by to pause if necessary, that would be great." She had forgotten to give Camille the selection numbers. So much for her head being on what she was doing. "Thanks for reminding me, though. There's a few tracks I don't want to cue up." Like "Lost Without Your Love." She wasn't going to sing any come-back-to-me, I-can't-survive-without-you songs tonight.

The cabaret area of the bar was standing-room-only and Monica flitted about scattering song lists to people. Camille cranked up "We Are Family" for background until Monica clambered onto the low stage and waved her arms for silence.

"We are so lucky tonight to have Rett Jamison hosting our evening. She's going to do her own set, too!" Monica paused and the crowd oohed on cue. "Thank you all for coming. Part of tonight's cover charge is going to the Santa Monica women's shelter program." Monica fluttered into the audience so Rett took that for her cue.

There was appreciative applause, which Rett let subside before she breathed into the mike in her sultriest voice. "Ladies ... someone has to go first. Tonight you can be a ... virgin. So come out, come out, wherever you are."

Thankfully, a quartet of tipsy friends was willing to start. They gave a rendition of "Ain't No Mountain High Enough" that made up in enthusiasm what it lacked in pitch. The next forty minutes was a blur of pop hits and laughter. The crowd was in good spirits — whenever someone faltered everyone would join in to finish the piece. Rett didn't have much to do except chatter while Camille cued up the next song. She kept to easy topics: Xena, Ellen and Anne, and women's sports.

"Okay, ladies. We've reached that point in the evening where you should refill your beverage of choice and set for a spell." Rett adjusted the standing mike to her height and nodded to Camille. The gentle opening piano work of "Color My World" flowed out of the speakers. Rett nodded appreciatively when someone turned down the lights.

The energy was good and the clatter from the bar didn't overly intrude as she worked from a low, dreamy beginning to "The First Time Ever I Saw Your Face," then picked up a little with "Superstar" and another Carpenters hit, "Top of the World." She stayed in a light country mood for "Back to Georgia," then segued to a husky version of "So in Love," a favorite Cole Porter number. She kept up the trick of making eye contact with two or three women, which made the rest of the audience feel as if they were making eye contact as well.

She was sinking into the deep, final "my love, am I" when she realized that the tiny dark-haired woman she was singing to looked familiar. Just a little. Like someone she'd maybe sat next to on an airplane — but not recently. Her hair might have been longer. The momentary distraction was annoying, so she redoubled her concentration for the opening of "Are You Lonesome Tonight?"

Her concentration was broken again when she heard Trish's voice just to the left of the stage. As the song reached for its climax she could just make out phrases like "not as sharp as it used to be" and "possessive is an understatement" and "willing to work hard or you'll end up singing in places like this."

The crowd was friendly enough to whistle and cheer as she ended the song, though Rett could not remember the last time she'd sung in such a distracted state.

She tried to empty her mind of the refrain "bitch, bitch, you bitch," but it wasn't working. The intro to the next song was already starting. Fine, she thought. *If I can't get you out of my head, then I'll sing this one for you.*

The song was "Unchained Melody," and Rett felt the tickle of a smile as she sang about hunger and need and the power of a touch. As she sang she thought about all the love and devotion she had to give. Trish had wanted the sex and the life, but never all of her. All this passion and desire could have been hers, but now Rett would have to save it for someone else.

Her voice was resonating in her chest and sending prickles all along her arms and back. Suddenly it was easy to forget about Trish. She sang for the someone she hadn't yet met, the someone who would treasure what Rett had to give. In the throes of the closing verse, she sang for the audience. She gave it her all. *You didn't know I'd been holding back, did you? Here it is, everything I have to give.* She infused all the emotional power she could command into the final lines, then let her moaning voice fall to a whisper as the orchestration faded away.

She was aware that the noise from the bar had stopped and the silence, even as brief as it was, rewarded her for what she'd given into the song. The

47

room erupted into hoots and hollers as Rett stepped back from the microphone and bowed.

As the applause died down, Rett stepped up to the mike again and said, "That concludes my portion of the evening —" and was gratified by the ensuing groans and calls of "Encore!"

Camille leaned into the mike's range and said, "I think we're owed at least one more."

Rett wrinkled her nose and opened her mouth to give a token protest when someone said loudly, "I've heard plenty."

Bitch, Rett thought. She saw Camille's surprise at the rudeness, so she covered the mike and said, "My ex, as of last week."

Camille glanced in Trish's direction. "The she-woman type, I see." She pursed her lips for a split second, then said, "Let me handle this. Just follow my lead."

Camille favored the room with a conspiratorial grin. "I think what we need now is a little competition. D.J. — that would be me — versus songbird — that would be her. Loser buys winner a beer."

"Hey," Rett said loudly. "I didn't agree to this." Her feigned outrage drew a few chuckles from the crowd.

"What can I say? I'm thirsty," Camille said. "So I'm going to pick a song and if she doesn't know the words, I win."

"That's not fair," Rett protested, even though she realized she had an advantage Camille knew nothing about. "You could pick anything."

Camille muttered, "It's a small price for you to pay

for what you get to do next." To the room she said, "Are there any boot-wearing girls out there?" There was a loud hoot of yeses. "Well, if you know the boot scoot line dance, I want you down front, 'cause Miz Rett is gonna sing us a boot tune."

"Don't I even get to know the title?"

"Nnnnnope."

A half-dozen women slid into a line in front of the stage as Rett shrugged at the crowd. "I guess she's making all the rules."

"Like I said, I'm thirsty." Camille's fingers played over the karaoke machine's control panel.

Rett put her mouth so close to the mike her lips brushed it. Her voice boomed, "Would now be a bad time to tell her I have a photographic memory?" Camille's heartfelt "shit" was lost in the crowd's laughter. Rett instantly recognized the opening notes and she laughed into the mike. "Oh, I know this one really well. Been singing it to myself recently." She'd buy Camille a beer anyway. She was going to sing "These Boots Were Made for Walking," start to finish, and enjoy every minute.

The line dancers immediately got into the rhythm and their stamp-claps punctuated the number and brought appreciative cheers from the crowd. Every time the chorus got to "gonna walk all over you," the crowd boisterously sang along. It was a romp.

After that it was easy to encourage women from the audience to take a turn at the microphone to finish the evening. Rett relaxed and faded into the background. From her vantage point on the other end of the stage from where Trish was sitting, she could see a pair of long legs entwined around Trish's. The legs emerged from a miniskirt that left thighs of steel in plain sight. Toothpick Legs, a.k.a. Cheri, was getting up; they were leaving. Thank God. Thinking catty thoughts about whomever Trish was with was not going to help her do that letting-go-moving-on thing.

As they disappeared from view she thought that Calista Flockhart only wished she were that thin.

Rett sighed, realizing she was both tired and loath to go home. It was cold and empty there. Dark and lonely. She let herself be coaxed into a couple of duets and hammed up background vocals when courage failed a few of the singers. The night was still going to end all too soon. When Camille turned off the karaoke machine she knew she had to face going home. Alone.

"I owe you a beer," Camille said.

"I owe you — that was a lot of fun."

"I won't argue. Make it a Corona with a lime."

Monica was bubbling with glee at the evening's success. "You were sensational, both of you!" Rett submitted to another rosewater hug. "Rett, I can't believe you aren't turning out number one hits right and left. How come you don't have a record out?"

"I'd do them if anyone asked —"

"I hear voices coming out of the radio I wouldn't pay two cents to hear live, and here you can give me goosebumps singing a song I've heard a thousand times. Why do you think that is?"

"Goosebumps or —"

"It's just amazing. You're a delight." Monica waved

at someone who was leaving, then dashed in that direction, pausing briefly to thank and envelop Camille.

The bartender handed over the beers with a wink. "They're on Monica. It's the least she can do."

Rett clinked her bottle to Camille's and they settled onto the barstools. After several quick swallows, she felt revived enough to sit back a little and relax.

"Why don't you have a CD?" Camille was blunt. "You ought to be recording."

"My top octave is my weakest," Rett said honestly. "I need someone who's willing to arrange for a contralto. Karen Carpenter had her brother's talent to overcome an unfashionably low voice." It was her standard answer and the one closest to the truth. "I've recorded on backups with a couple of people, but I didn't get very much exposure. Not like when Paula Cole toured with Peter Gabriel. Now she's big-time herself — deservedly so. She writes her own songs, too, and I just don't have the talent for that. I tried."

"It does help if you can write for yourself," Camille agreed. "The charts have been taken over by women who have complete artistic control because they write and produce their own stuff."

"I just did a week in New York with a band — jazz standards with updated arrangements. I think it's pigeonholed as 'soft adult contemporary,' whatever the hell that means. They might get a record deal. They said they'd call me for one or two vocal tracks if they did. It could still happen. But I have no complaints." Rett dug down deep for something positive to say about her career at the moment. "I'm busy all the time." She took another swig from her beer. "How about you?"

"Running a karaoke machine is just weekend work," Camille said. "I started doing it to make extra money in college, and I never got rid of the machine. Now I do it mostly because it's fun and for good causes. Nine to five I'm in P.R. Sort of. Paying my dues with scut work, big-time." A thirty-something redhead was approaching and Camille hopped down from the barstool. "Gotta go. It was really great backing you up."

"And thanks again — my ex used to be my manager, too. That song was very satisfying."

Camille kissed the redhead on the cheek by way of greeting and said, "You missed all the fun." They began to walk toward the door when Camille paused to slap her pockets. "I thought I had — I do." She fished for a moment, then came up with a business card. "Just so you can remember my name. I might someday have enough power to actually do us both some good."

Rett took the card with a confused smile and waved good-bye. It took a few moments to register that Camille was an assistant talent coordinator and her business card was emblazoned with the Disney logo.

A new voice startled her. "You look like you just won the lottery."

It was the dark-haired woman who had seemed familiar. "I might have." This was one phone call she would make, all proper and business-like, first thing Monday morning. Maybe Camille could pass her name on to someone who could tell someone who knew someone that Rett Jamison was *not* a pain in the ass to work with. Even if that didn't fix the problem, it might help repair the damage her reputation had suffered. She realized the dark-haired woman had taken the barstool Camille had vacated. She indicated the card before she pocketed it. "A good contact — a bonus for the evening's work."

"You were great," she said. Rett had the oddest impression that she was being laughed at, not unkindly, but something she was doing was amusing this woman to no end.

Something in the deep brown eyes was familiar but she could hardly say, "Don't I know you from somewhere?" in a bar. It would sound too much like a pickup line. So she settled for, "Thanks. It's always good to have an appreciative audience."

The woman gestured at the empty beer bottle. "Can I get you another? Or something else? You must be feeling dehydrated."

"I'll take another beer, thank you." Rett instantly regretted accepting — it wasn't like her, actually. She usually would have refused. Usually, she would have been halfway home by now. She didn't want to go home. "Even though water would be better for me, you're right."

"I knew a singer once who was a fanatic about drinking water." The woman waved the empty beer bottle at the bartender and held up two fingers. She rearranged herself so she was sitting on her leg, then leaned comfortably on the bar. "They never make these things for the height-impaired."

Someone called, " 'Night, Angel!" and the woman waved.

"It was a coworker's fortieth tonight. We didn't

expect such a nice evening of music. We just wanted to embarrass her into a public display of her Diana Ross impression."

Rett guessed Angel was about her age. She was just making conversation when she said, "I hope someone will take me out on my fortieth," then realized it was a major-league depressing thought. It was only a week and a half away, and no one would be taking her out. Forty. Forty and alone. Not even a brother or sister to tease her mercilessly.

Angel's lips twitched. "I sincerely doubt you'll have any trouble finding someone to do that for you."

"You'd be surprised." *Shut up, Rett.* God, was there anything more pathetic than pouring out one's troubles to strangers in bars? The beers were delivered and she took a long swallow and sought frantically for something cheerful to say.

"Spoken like someone on the rebound," Angel remarked. "Sorry, that's really personal," she added quickly. "I just recognized the tone of voice from my own recent experience."

They shared a wry, mutually sympathetic smile and more beer. Someone turned up the jukebox and the noise somehow made it easier to talk. Rett offered to buy another round but Angel demurred.

"Two is my limit — goes right to my head. I do impulsive but usually wrong things." She was looking at Rett when she said it, and that small gleam of amusement was back.

"I only have a walk home," Rett said. "So I think I will have one more."

"Feel free, please. I hope I didn't sound preachy. Everybody tells me I tend to do that."

Rett laughed. "Friends are so supportive, aren't they?"

"Colleagues are even worse, especially when they have one more master's degree than you."

Yikes, Rett thought. Angel was some sort of brain. "What do you do?"

"I'm a research fellow at UCLA. DNA, human immune system, cancer, those sorts of things."

Rett could tell that Angel had dumbed down the subject for her. She wasn't that backward. "That must be fascinating."

"Fascinating and frustrating. I also do a little bit of teaching, but mostly it's research. Petri dishes, microscopes and genetic sampling." She munched on a pretzel. "We isolated the gene that creates the predisposition for uterine cancer. That was exciting, to say the least. Then our funding got cut in half. The life of a researcher in a nutshell."

"You have it almost as bad as a performer."

"Gluttons for punishment. A performer's career has a pretty big upside, you must admit."

"If there is an up."

"I hear that." Angel's eyes flickered with intensity. "There's a pretty big up for a researcher if you're in it for the love of the project. I want to be there when we unlock the last code. I know there's no chance of that — it's going to take more years than I've got left. But think of it — unlocking the secret of what makes us human instead of chimpanzees. How we think, what part of us laughs."

"What about why we think and laugh? Is all our behavior part of our code? Or is there room for improvisation?"

Angel took the question more seriously than Rett intended. "The mystery of what we can do is there, written on our genes."

It sounded too much like predestination to Rett. "But can't a building be more than its blueprint? Isn't that what art is all about?"

"What may seem like improvisation may really be growth. Finding the potential of your personal code. Doing things you didn't think you could do." Angel took a quick breath and her deep brown eyes never left Rett's. "Getting in touch with the parts of your code you ignore, or thought weren't even there."

Rett swallowed hard. Why did it seem like Angel was talking about something else entirely? Or was she just hearing something that wasn't there? "So spontaneity is just doing something you could have done all along?"

Angel reached for Rett's half-finished beer and at Rett's nod, took a quick swig. "Doing things that aren't typically you. Like this."

The kiss was quick but supercharged. Rett felt the zing through her spine and thighs.

Angel had her hand over her mouth. "I don't know what made me do that. I mean, I do know. But I'm sorry."

Rett wanted to say, "Don't be," but she was too startled by her physical response to have much ability for speech left. She found herself staring at Angel's lips while all the things she should have said, like "I'm not ready for this" and "Shouldn't we get to know each other better?" failed to come out of her mouth. She had never done what Trish referred to as "kiss and boff." Trish had been the quickest to get her into bed — and it had taken three dates. Trish had blamed Rett's prudish sex mores on a Minnesotan upbringing, but then Trish didn't know her mother's proclivities, and Rett had never enlightened her. Yet no matter how hard she tried, she couldn't stop looking at Angel's lips. She was short of breath and a prickle of sweat dampened the back of her neck.

"I think it's time for me to head home. It's a bit of a drive," Angel said. "Maybe . . . maybe I could give you my number."

Rett's mouth outstripped the rest of her body's opinions. "No, I mean yes. I mean it would be okay, you don't have to go —"

"I think I should. This is crazy." Angel laughed nervously. The hand that was writing her number on the bar napkin was shaking. "If you ever want to get together, give me a call."

"Okay," Rett said. She was already kicking herself for having blown the moment.

Angel slid the napkin toward her and Rett pocketed it without taking her gaze from Angel's. Lovely brown eyes, clear and topazy.

"I'll call." Rett meant it. She turned to her empty beer as Angel walked toward the door, but looked up when she realized Angel was coming back.

"An incentive," Angel said huskily, and she pulled Rett's mouth down to hers again.

Rett gasped and returned the kiss with more fervor than she had been willing to admit she could feel. Had she cared about Trish so little in the end that it had taken only a week to get over wanting her? You'd left her a while ago, Rett reminded herself, just as she'd left you. That you were living under the same roof is beside the point.

Angel's hands cupped her face as their kiss continued. Any rational woman would stop it here, Rett thought. *I must be crazy.* It felt too good to stop. She closed her eyes. In a minute, she promised.

A minute turned to two and her hands were on Angel's waist. She opened her mouth to Angel's eager exploration and then bit the fingers that Angel slipped between their lips.

Angel was the one with the sense to stop. Rett was breathing hard into Angel's shoulder, dizzy from all the blood draining out of her head to other places that were doing all the thinking.

"I think you got my message," Angel said into Rett's ear. "Maybe I could walk you to your car?"

Rett managed to lift her head, though she had to grip the bar to keep from appearing unsteady. "I walked, remember? I don't live very far from here."

Angel's tongue flicked over her upper lip as she digested that information. "My car is right outside. I could drive you home at least. No expectations."

"I think you know that if you did I wouldn't say no," Rett said. She managed to make eye contact, which was hard when she felt so emotionally naked. "Though I . . . I would rather not go to my place."

Angel's mouth opened as if she was going to kiss Rett again, then she glanced down at their entwined hands. "It's forty-five minutes to my apartment even at this hour and I think I know what you mean. Home is still too full of someone else." She squeezed Rett's hands. "Maybe we both need a little more time."

From far away, through the dizzying desire and the roar of her pulse, Rett heard herself say, "There are a couple of motels just down Santa Monica Boulevard."

Angel caught her breath. "Yes, that would work."

Rett just stared at Angel, unable to say that she needed Angel to make the decisions right now.

"Let's go," Angel whispered.

They were in Angel's car heading quickly toward the motels when Angel said, "I'm not like this all the time."

The vacancy signs swam into Rett's vision. "You decide, I can't."

She watched Angel walk into the lobby of the motel they'd come to first. It was all she could do to breathe. Angel was back with a key in a few minutes and she drove them toward the back of the building. After she turned the engine off they sat there in silence.

Angel took a deep breath. " I think I might like to get to know you. I mean, I don't know very much about you, really." Her voice was raw. "But not tonight."

Rett looked at her in confusion.

"Tonight I just want to . . ." Angel gazed at her in the dim light. "I just want to . . ."

"It's okay," Rett repeated. She managed to open her door, but her steps toward the door Angel was unlocking were unsteady.

Rett's only awareness was Angel inside of her. At some point she had taken off her clothes and found her way to the bed, but she didn't remembering doing so. Angel had her wrists pinned over her head with one hand while the other satisfied Rett's need. Angel's tongue and teeth were making her breasts burn with desire for more.

More, more — Rett was aching with raw want, feeling alive and hungry and wanton and consumed. Her climax left the sheets and Angel's hand drenched, then Angel was straddling her, pinning her wrists with both hands while she hungrily kissed Rett's mouth. Rett was still trembling as Angel trailed feather-light kisses along her jaw and neck. She felt completely exposed.

"I knew," Angel whispered as she sat up. "I knew it would be like this."

"How did you know?" Rett pulled her wrists free and raised herself on her elbows so she could kiss Angel's shoulders. The wet heat on her stomach brought her trembling hunger back and she sat up all the way.

Angel tipped her hips to welcome Rett's fingers and with a luxuriant sigh drew Rett's mouth to her breasts. They were still for a moment. Rett almost didn't want to move — the sensation of holding this woman tight to her, the whisper of her hair and brush of her skin was like the pause between notes of a song. The rest of the world was in its place. Everything else was perfect. Her entire being was focused on the next inevitable note, the next sensation.

Angel broke their fierce stillness with a barely audible "Rett."

It was slower than when Angel had been in her. Her fingers stroked inside and out, learning every receptive place, knowing what pleasured because her fingers told her so and because her sensitive ear heard the rise and fall of Angel's breath as a melody of need.

Faster now, faster because Angel was breathing

more loudly, her hips moving more frantically. Like that, yes, but harder.

From touch to taste, to more exploration with fingers tangled in hair and shoulders bruised with kisses. Finally an exhausted completeness overwhelmed Rett and made her beg for a rest.

Angel settled beside her in the dark. Rett liked the smell of her skin. It was enough for a while to just breathe it in. She was going to fall asleep, she realized.

She managed to mumble, "How did you know it would be like this?"

She had to be asleep when Angel answered because what she thought she heard made no sense. "I've always known. You never did."

4

Rett woke up alone. Brilliant sunlight was trying to creep past the closed motel curtains — she'd slept late into the morning. Little wonder, she thought. All that exertion on top of some serious mental stress.

She wished Angel had woken her, though. It was Saturday, after all. They could have had breakfast, made plans to see each other again. Surely Angel would want to see her again.

Rett put her head on her knees, not wanting to look for a note in case there wasn't one. She wasn't that bad a judge of character. Angel hadn't just been putting on a line. There was nothing smooth about her, not the way Trish was smooth.

But what if she had been an experiment? What if last night had just been Angel trying to escape her own code? They'd certainly escaped Rett's. She buried her head in the pillows, wondering how pathetic it was to be going-on-forty and experiencing what could be her very first one-night stand.

She knew what Trish would say. What Trish would say no longer mattered to her. Hiding in bed in case there wasn't a note was pretty pathetic, she decided.

There was a note. It wasn't a one-night stand after all. In almost illegible script it read, "I had a Saturday Symposium I couldn't miss. You were very asleep. Call me later." At the bottom there was a scribble of such flair that it was probably her initials, but there was no telling where an *A* or anything else might begin or end.

Greatly relieved, she hummed "Isn't She Lovely" as she showered and dressed. She went through the embarrassing process of asking if the bill needed to be settled. The clerk had a nasty smirk as he told her the "other party" had taken care of it. She would have to pay Angel back. She caught a cruising cab and headed for home.

As she turned out of the elevator toward her door she ran smack-dab into a fuming Trish.

"Where the hell have you been?"

"None the hell of your business," Rett shot back. She felt the red flush start in her neck and spread upward.

"Still in last night's clothes — don't tell me you finally figured out how to get fucked?"

From down the hall she heard a snicker and took

note of two burly guys and Toothpick Legs all outside her door.

"You're as tasteful as always," Rett said. She was still reeling from last night's delectable passion and unprepared for Trish's brand of cruelty. "If you wanted your stuff a phone call would have helped. I could have been here then."

"How was I to know you changed the locks? And I hardly expected you to be just getting home from last night."

"I know — that's your usual style." She brushed past Trish and headed for the door. "I put all your things in the spare room."

Toothpick Legs favored her with a mock sympathetic glance. "I know this isn't easy for you," she said breathily.

"Watch how it's done," Rett said sweetly. "Because someday you'll get to play my part."

The men were strong and efficient and cleared the room in short order. There was a little ugliness over a wall hanging they had bought together. Reminding Trish that Rett had paid for all of it made Trish claim it had been a gift.

"Take it, then," Rett said. "Whatever you think, this is not all about money."

"Kiss my ass," Trish snapped.

"I don't like standing in lines."

"Class act as always, Rett. Oh, and here's the keys to that piece-of-shit car." Trish tossed them on the couch, then turned her back.

"Naomi needs your address. If you want a check, that is."

"I'll give it to her myself." Trish looked slyly over her shoulder. "Unless you're interested."

Rett managed a serene smile. "Not in the least." She couldn't help herself. She gestured at Toothpick Legs. "But I'm assuming her parents aren't letting you stay at their house."

Toothpick Legs stammered indignantly, "I have my own place now!"

"Shut up, Cheri, she's just baiting you because you're half her age."

Rett gestured at the door. "All done? That's the way out. Feel free to slam it if it makes you feel better."

Apparently it did. After the thudding echo died, Rett locked the door and murmured, "Out of sight, out of mind." Trish had no hold on her. Great sex had therapeutic value, apparently. Wouldn't that make an interesting infomercial, she thought. Forget pills, forget therapy — lesbian sex is the cure to what ails you.

Angel. She wanted to call her now. She wanted to see her tonight.

She wrapped her arms around herself and grinned dopily in the mirror. What a night, she thought. The stuff that love songs are made of. She burst into "I Feel the Earth Move" and went to change her clothes.

She tossed the jeans in the hamper before realizing she hadn't taken out the napkin with Angel's number. She dumped out the hamper and put her fingers into the pocket.

She found her keys, billfold, the note Angel had written this morning, the remains of the twenty she'd paid the cabbie with, Camille's business card and some prehistoric lint. No cocktail napkin. It was her only pocket. It had to be there.

She turned the pocket inside out, all the while

cursing herself for not actually looking at the napkin. If she'd looked she wouldn't need it — Angel's number would be right there in her memory. What was the point of a photographic memory if she didn't use it? She fumbled through the entire laundry pile, just in case. No note.

"Stupid, stupid, stupid," she chanted to herself. She quickly dressed and dashed down to the street to see if the napkin was at the curb where she'd paid the cab.

She found it half-smashed by a tire tread in the gutter. All she could make out was the last two digits.

She stood at the curb for a long time feeling like this bad universal joke was being played on someone else. What on earth had she done to deserve this?

If she didn't call, Angel would surely consign her to the realm of cads and bounders. She could call UCLA's science department and see if she could get a last name for a professor named Angel. Angel had said there was some sort of symposium today. Maybe the office was open.

She tried every number for UCLA in the phone book and there were a lot of them. The only ones that answered had recordings telling her when she should call back to reach a live body. She heard the phrase, "If you know your party's extension," about fifty times.

The second to last number, "Public Affairs," turned out to be an event listing. It was lengthy and at no time did the words "symposium," "cancer" or "DNA" come into play. Of course she'd assumed that because Angel worked at UCLA that's where the symposium was, but it could be at USC, or dozens of other campuses. It could even be at a hospital. Hell, the symposium could be about anything, not just Angel's field of research. Damn. She would have to wait until Monday. Driving out to UCLA and walking up and down the science building halls hoping to stumble across an office door with Angel's name on it was just too desperate. Out of the question.

She would try it this afternoon. She would also call Monica and ask if she'd ever met the mysterious Angel. That is, if Monica let her get a word in edgewise.

She put Camille's business card next to the phone. That call she would do first thing Monday morning. She found herself humming "Calling All Angels." She'd never been to the UCLA campus. It would be a . . . cultural outing. Nothing desperate about trying to better oneself.

The fax machine rang and whirred into action, then the phone rang.

As she said, "Rett Jamison," her cell phone beeped. The cellular's digital readout said Naomi was the caller.

"Thank God you're there. It's Tamla. Naomi's been trying to get you all morning." Tamla had been Naomi's assistant for the last two years.

"Naomi is calling me on my cell phone."

Tamla laughed. "Answer it, please."

"Naomi, I'm talking to Tamla on the phone."

"Tell Tamla to hang up — wait . . ."

Through the phone and the cellular lines she could hear Naomi in stereo. "Tamla, I got her. Call Jerry Orland back."

" 'Bye, Rett." Tamla hung up and Rett walked out to the living room with the cell phone cradled on her shoulder.

"Something urgent, Naomi?" The fax machine spat out a page and Rett flipped it over to read it. Huge block letters read, "Call Naomi!"

"Pack a bag. Fancy, big band stuff. Grab it and head for the airport, now. I'll tell you more when you call back to say you're in a cab."

Rett hurried into the bedroom. "I can do that and talk at the same time. Cab? I'm going to be away a while? Who's sick? Where am I going?"

"No one is sick, but someone is canned. You're going to San Francisco, Portland, Seattle and Vancouver. Besides, you don't have time to deal with parking a car or a shuttle schedule. Just take a cab — believe me, you can now afford it."

"Who am I going to be traveling with?"

Naomi announced triumphantly, "The one and only Henry Connors Orchestra."

"Lordy, lordy!" It was fabulous news. "What happened to Gilda Bransen?"

"Henry finally snapped — she had one missed rehearsal after another all the way from New York to here, three months of them. I told Jerry Orland they should have picked you from the beginning and he admitted that Gilda's big name did not make up for the agony of working with her."

Rett quickly chose four formal dresses. She'd sung with the Henry Connors Orchestra at a pop festival last summer and knew what would work. She'd been seriously bummed not to get the touring job. "Tell Jerry I'm sorry that being a lesbian is not as notorious as sleeping with a presidential candidate. I refuse to seduce any of them to get a gig."

"You say that now, but what if Ellen DeGeneres was the candidate?"

"For those eyes, I'd consider it." The phone slipped off her shoulder when she bent over to get her garment bag. "Sorry about that. When's the first performance?"

"Tonight, of course! So get a move on. Call me from the cab and I'll give you the info on your flight."

"Moving on," Rett said. She threw matching shoes, her always packed stage makeup case and some day clothes into a suitcase, then carefully arranged her dresses in the garment bag. Both pieces were small enough to carry on, which would save a lot of time on both ends of the flight.

The jeans and polo shirt she'd pulled on to look outside for Angel's napkin would have to suffice. She shrugged into a Berber jacket and traded her flats for black Adidas. A few minutes later she slipped a note into Mrs. Bernstein's mailbox saying she'd be gone for several weeks, put a forwarding notice in her own box for her mail to be sent to Naomi's office, then headed around the corner toward the many Promenade eateries where cabs were always cruising.

She speed-dialed Naomi. "I'm on the way to LAX," Rett reported.

Naomi told her the airline and flight number and then the six songs she would be singing. "Someone will meet you at the gate, probably have your name on a card or something. There's a big, fat bonus for your trouble. I told Jerry it was only fair, which he already knew. Not to beat a dead horse, he also told me — I didn't ask — he was glad he only had to work with me and not Trish."

"I'll let you know when I want you to stop beating it — she gave me back the car keys this morning, by the way."

"Are they somewhere that Tamla could find them? She'll be dropping by to make sure your place is okay, pick up any mail or parcels that get left."

"I'm glad I sent you the new front door key already. I put the car keys on my desk. They're on a Lexus key ring along with the security remote."

"Tamla will drop the car off at the dealer, then. Good — I'm glad that's all wrapped up. She's gone for good?"

"Took all her stuff and some of mine, but she's gone. And you know what? I don't miss her at all." Angel came readily to mind and Rett lost some of what Naomi said to the memory of Angel's skin.

"— look before you go leaping again, okay?"

"Yeah, sure," Rett said absently. Shit, she thought. She was leaving town and hadn't called. She doubted she'd be able to call in the next forty-eight hours. And if she could find out who Angel was on Monday what would she say? Sorry I didn't call for two days and guess what, I'm gone for the next three weeks, but this isn't a brush-off? Sure, Angel would believe that.

She had no choice but to push thoughts of Angel into the background. The plane ride was only an hour or so, barely enough time to mentally review the numbers she would be performing. Her mind might remember every word and her ear might remember every note, but her vocal cords were far more fallible.

She knew enough about Henry Connors' style to know there would be a chance to rehearse each song at least once. But time wouldn't allow for much more than that. They would all be counting on her ability to do it perfectly. Pedal hits the metal, she told herself.

Jerry Orland himself picked her up at SFO. He'd

been Henry Connors' promoter for a number of years. His short, dark hair was tipped with more gray, but his charm was just the same as the last time they'd met. "Rett, you are a darling to get here so fast." He embraced her with a peck on the cheek. "I've got a car waiting."

The airport was a mess — construction everywhere and only two lanes circling the pickup area. Jerry's driver was idling in the parking lot just outside the elevators and Jerry ushered her into the back seat, then joined her. They both flipped open their cell phones.

"I made it, Naomi. Jerry picked me up."

"I'm looking right at her, Henry, in the flesh. So you can relax. We'll be there in thirty-five minutes." Jerry glanced at her. "You don't need to go to the hotel first, do you?"

Obviously, the only acceptable answer was no, so that was the answer Rett gave. To Naomi she said, "I think you can relax now. Keep an eye out for reviews. I can always hope." She switched off the phone and took a deep, calming breath.

"She's being a real sport," Jerry reported. He clicked the phone shut and heaved a sigh of relief. "I've been wanting to dump Gilda since Chicago. I can handle high-strung, but she was a purebred poodle."

Rett laughed politely. "What does that make me?"

"If you had red hair, I'd say a beautiful, talented, sensitive Irish setter. But you've got that sort of blondey-brownie thing going on. Beautiful, talented and sensitive will have to do."

Rett knew when she was being flattered and she certainly didn't mind. After the horrible past few weeks, flattery was more than welcome. "Oh, stop," she said insincerely. "Why, it'll go right to my beautiful, talented, sensitive head."

Jerry grinned. "I think this is where I have to admit I was the one who threw you over in favor of Gilda. *Mea culpa.*"

"Then I hate you," Rett said pleasantly.

"Anything I can do to change that?"

Rett sucked in her cheeks. "Well-l-l-l, the body part responsible for the Gilda decision on a silver platter would be nice."

"Ha ha," Jerry said in a flat tone. His expression grew mischievous. "You don't have a silver platter big enough." He let Rett's scoffing protest go by, then added, "And you'd need fireplace tongs to handle it."

"Oh, oh, as if tweezers wouldn't do the job."

"I thought you were a nice girl."

"I am a nice girl. A not-nice girl would have brought a knife and the platter with her."

They sparred and talked about the performance for the rest of the drive. It had been a while since Rett had been to San Francisco. There were more tall buildings and a new ballpark between the freeway off-ramp and the water. Fog was blowing over the hills that separated the downtown area from the ocean, making Rett glad of her jacket.

The driver let them off at the stage door to the Fillmore. Rett had only heard about the legendary venue and was eager to see the inside. Jerry took charge of her bags and delivered them into the keeping of the dresser, who bemoaned the wrinkles in Rett's gowns.

She also met the woman who did hair and makeup for the featured performers. The elderly woman studied Rett for a moment, clucked with some distress and announced that she would have to think of something to fix the shape of Rett's eyes. Rett had never noticed that the left was slightly larger than the right. She wasn't sure she could tell now, even though it had been pointed out in no uncertain terms. The stylist muttered about her "case of the blahs" hair as she walked away, and Rett had to smile. There was nothing like backstage people to remind you that you were imperfect.

The orchestra was in the middle of a high-energy salsa number Rett hadn't heard before. It sounded terrific.

Jerry drew her onto the stage as the number ended. Several of the musicians hurrahed while Henry gave her a huge hug.

"Delightful, just delightful. I know we'll pull this off." Henry Connors had to be her age, Rett thought, but he still had a boyish quality that infused his music with vigor and charm. "Let's do 'Blue Moon' first."

"I haven't warmed up," Rett protested.

"Oh." Henry looked crestfallen. "Okay, we'll do another number. Go warm up."

Four minutes, Rett thought, at the most. Stage right was deserted, so she ducked into a dark corner and sang scales in half and full voice. She shook her arms to release tension and felt a quiver of nerves. Pedal to the metal, she reminded herself. This is what it's all about. This is what makes you a professional.

"It's going to sound a little tight because I didn't have time for breathing exercises," she warned Henry. She glanced at the well-lit house. The ceiling soared to allow for two balconies. The concave structure had fabulous acoustics.

"Don't waste full voice if you need to keep it for tonight."

"I'll take it easy," she promised. She liked the old-fashioned, oversized standing microphone Henry preferred. It set the mood of an earlier era. Portable mikes left her wondering what she should do with her feet, and the power pack on her back always rubbed the wrong way.

The stage manager pointed out her entrance and mark. A sorrowful clarinet heralded the number and Rett let herself sway into the slow rhythm. She'd learned over the years that singing an old standard like 'Blue Moon' only pleased a crowd when they heard what they expected. The opening verse she presented in straightforward style, every note true and on beat.

A soulful clarinet solo bridged back to her entrance, accompanied by glittering guitar. She recognized Cleetus Washington's golden touch immediately. She took more liberties with the phrasing, keeping an eye on Henry the whole time. At one point he emphasized a downbeat in her direction and she brought her rhythm back to the standard. He smiled, clearly relieved, at her quick adjustment, and Rett felt about half the tension in her body drain away. The rapport they'd found so smoothly at the concert last year hadn't been a fluke.

The stage manager and Jerry Orland applauded loudly when they were done. "That was wonderful. Henry, I'll be back in a bit."

"Very nice indeed," Henry said. "Let's move on to 'I Told You I Love You, Now Get Out.'"

They ran through the song three times because Rett hadn't performed it for quite a while. The humor of the song needed good timing. They decided to have Rett continue talking over the orchestra's closing.

"You'll remember the order?"

"But of course," Rett said. " 'Today. I mean it. Go. Now,' three beats, then 'get out' with the final two downbeats."

"We don't have time to do it again, but I had a feeling we'd be best served spending time there. The rest of the songs we did last year. Let's do them in order. 'Candy,' everybody."

By the time they ended rehearsal, Rett was glad she'd kept her Adidas on. She had about ninety minutes to get to her hotel, have a bite to eat, do her breathing exercises for relaxation and then return to the dresser's ministrations. The other musicians were all quickly leaving, though many waved and said they'd catch up after the show. Time was too short for chitchat at the moment, which Rett certainly understood. She picked up her luggage, lighter for the gowns, shoes and cosmetics removed by the dresser, and headed into the misty late-afternoon sunshine.

The hotel was just down Geary, off Union Square. She dodged street musicians and sidewalk vendors, then ducked into a deli for a ham sandwich and an uncarbonated fruit drink. Her room was tiny, but the accoutrements were a definite step up from the clean but sparse shoebox she'd slept in while in New York. Food consumed, clothes hung up, she kicked off her shoes and stretched out on the bed.

Forget about not having enough underwear, she told herself. Forget about forgetting an extra bra. Forget about the little details. Breathe in . . . out.

Her deep breathing exercises calmed her nerves. She floated for a few minutes in restful ease. Her mind was still — then a shivering memory of Angel intruded. Rett could almost feel the silk of her thighs as she'd straddled Rett's stomach. Instead of peaceful relaxation, Rett found her heart racing and her palms damp.

Annoyed with herself, she sat up. She caught a glimpse of herself in the mirrored-closet door. "Look," she said to her reflection. "You're over Trish. This is not a good time to obsess about someone new. This is not a good time for someone you don't even know if you'll ever see again to come between you and the biggest break you've had in years."

She made a face, then stood up to swing her arms and stretch her back.

"So it was fabulous sex. Certainly the best in a long time. So she seemed like someone you could talk to, someone with her own life that sounded kind of interesting. In two hours, savvy music-lovers in a packed house are going to expect you to take the place of Gilda Bransen. They're expecting Gilda. The critics in this town were hoping to get their chance to review her. You have to be great. You can sing circles around her, but if you aren't fabulous the reviews will crucify you for not being Gilda."

She continued her pep talk as she brushed her teeth and combed her hair, which seemed rattier than usual. Back at the concert hall, she was glad she'd invested no time in her hair. The stylist slathered it with gel, then scraped it back and quickly wove in a well-matched plop of curls. Rett was glad she couldn't really see them — curls had never been her thing. Cinny Keilor had had the curly hair.

What on earth was she doing thinking about Cinny Keilor? Earth to Rett, she thought. Hello! Performance coming!

The stylist sprayed the whole arrangement with red tinting, then set about lining Rett's eyes with more makeup than Rett would have chosen to wear in a year.

"The red is nice," she admitted, when she finally had a chance to assess the entire look. She didn't know about the curly hairpiece on the back. It was sophisticated, a quality she didn't necessarily cultivate most of the time. Still, she needed to fit in with the tuxes the orchestra would be wearing.

"The spray will wash out tonight. I'll do highlights for you tomorrow morning, if you like. It'll save time every night and look more natural."

Rett considered it. "Okay. Something new." The dresser appeared with one of Rett's formal gowns over one arm and various undergarments over the other.

Rett refused the pantyhose with built-in girdle until she saw her silhouette in the glittering blue sheath. She hadn't had the dress on for at least nine months. She put her hand on her tummy. "My God. Stop going to the gym and look what happens."

The dresser made an "I told you so" face and handed over the girdle contraption. It made the difference, though Rett could tell she would have to work harder to breathe in fully. Three-quarter-length white gloves completed the torture, but when she studied herself in the full-length mirror, she was pleased. She looked good. So she was turning forty — she looked good. She was not in the glamorous Gilda's league, but her voice would make up the difference. If she sang well, it would make up the difference with plenty to spare.

"You need more bosom," the dresser announced. "I could cut this down across here." She traced a line across Rett's chest that would expose considerably more skin. "You think anyone was looking at Marilyn Monroe's stomach?"

"We'll see," Rett said. Sit-ups, she promised herself.

She stood in the darkened wings and waited for her entrance. Her two three-song sets came about eleven minutes into each half of the evening. She concentrated and kept to steady, normal breathing as she waited. She was abruptly aware that Jerry Orland was standing near her.

"I didn't want to break your concentration," he said.

"It's okay. A little distraction is good."

"You're going to be terrific. The crowd knows it's you — there were signs at the doors. They got a few returned tickets and that's all. I had enlargements of the review from last year put around the foyer, so the audience should have pleasant expectations. You'll knock 'em dead. And you look like a million bucks."

"Nothing that two women working for forty minutes couldn't achieve."

"No kidding, Rett." Jerry appeared to be serious. "I met you — what? Late 'eighties, that club in Detroit? You look and sound better now than you did then. Your career is just starting. Some singers peak early and are never heard from again — you're going to mature magnificently."

She wanted to believe every word. "Like a good Irish setter?" Her cue was approaching.

Jerry tweaked her chin as if she were a child. "I like the red hair. But no. You're like a painting created by a master."

"Flatterer." It was exactly what she needed to hear.

"Break a leg."

The floodlights blinded her to the audience, but she took in the polite applause. Thank God the first number was the familiar "Blue Moon." Nothing fancy, she reminded herself. Pour the notes like syrup, like you've poured them out of your throat a thousand times before.

The musicians seemed in top form. The clarinet echoed the smooth flow of Rett's voice, picking up her last note to start the solo as if they were one and the same. The guitar work that followed sparkled, and Henry moved to the music like a dancer, letting his enjoyment of the sound show in the way he cued and directed.

The applause was a mite better than polite and Rett launched into "I Told You I Love You" with confidence that let the humor come through effortlessly, earning audible chuckles and enthusiastic applause at the end of the number. When she finished "Candy" and took a bow it wasn't hard to tell that the audience would be glad to see her in the second half of the program.

The rest of the concert was the smooth, glittering performance anybody could have wanted. Henry brought Rett out after the band's encore and whispered, "I should have thought of an encore for you."

"It's okay," she answered through a brilliant stage smile. To her elation, the audience kept clapping as if they expected something. "We needed to get through the planned songs."

"Could you do 'Just the Way You Are'?" Henry drew her into another bow.

Rett was sure of it. They'd done it last year and it was an easy sing.

"We only took it out because Gilda hated it." He gave the audience one of his patented crooked smiles and waved Rett to the microphone. He picked up his baton from the first violinist's music stand as he told him the number they were going to do, then joined Rett briefly. The audience fell into an expectant hush. Rett could hear the song being whispered from musician to musician.

"We'll do one more," he said, "so you can have a chance to hear the fabulous Rett Jamison one more time." He was interrupted by applause and Rett's heart flew to the balcony. It was like a dream. "This is completely unrehearsed, but you've been a great audience and I'll know you'll forgive us if we flub."

Laughter, applause, the opening notes. Rett realized Henry had forgotten to key it down for her, but her voice was well-limbered and the high notes wouldn't be a problem. Her verses gave way to a sexy but light saxophone solo, which handed off to the arrangement of strings that set Henry's version apart from Billy Joel's. Rett came back on her cue and found the high notes after the key change no difficulty at all. She was taking a bow with Henry and the saxophonist — another woman, which pleased Rett — when Jerry Orland stepped on stage to give her an enormous bundle of white roses.

"Thanks for being you," he whispered in her ear.

Backstage was awash with high spirits. Rett was hugged, kissed and squeezed by the other performers, then flattered and schmoozed by the press and VIPs. In her life she'd never had a night quite like it.

She looked at her glowing face in the mirror and thought, *I get paid for this, too. Pinch me.* The roses festooned the dressing table and their light scent added another layer of memory to a night she knew she would never forget.

Henry's compliments came in a form Rett could not dispute. "We're going to add another song for you in the second half and find a showier encore. But not until the Tuesday night show. There's no rehearsal tomorrow because of the matinee. Everybody's off Monday, then we have a longer rehearsal on Tuesday morning."

"I'm really glad this is going to work out," Rett told him. "I keep telling myself it's just my ego that thinks I've got a special sound that works for you, but I'm right, aren't I?"

"I wanted you all along, but Jerry thought Gilda had the box office draw. Which she did, he was right about that."

"I already confessed that," Jerry said. He leaned into the dressing room. "I just got a message from Gilda's agent. He must have been at the performance and could not have been at all pleased at what he heard."

"Tell him to fly the proverbial kite," Henry said.

"I will," Jerry said. "Meanwhile, I'm going to walk back to the hotel and I'll see everyone in the morning."

"I'll walk with you," Henry said. "It's great that

we're so close by." He kissed Rett on the cheek. "Go celebrate — I know there's a gang headed somewhere fun."

Rett watched the two men leave and her gaydar went off the scale. It had never occurred to her before, but she hadn't spent that much time with them. She'd never heard even a rumor about Henry, but it didn't take much deduction to know why he stayed in the closet, if indeed she was right about him and Jerry. Though the Henry Connors Orchestra was well-known and could fill venues coast-to-coast, including several weeks in Las Vegas twice a year, his reputation as a fine musician and conductor wasn't so secure that he could risk losing audience and venues because he was gay. Michael Tilson Thomas could be out, but he was in so-called "serious" music, and in his case, genius had silenced any critics. Henry hadn't proven his genius at that level — and sticking with the popular music he loved he might never be able to do it.

She was interrupted from her musings by the dresser, who stripped her of her clothes in a no-nonsense fashion. Over her protests that she could do it herself, the stylist scrubbed her face free of makeup. She removed the hairpiece and, when Rett said she was probably going out, moussed Rett's hair into an asymmetrical wedge. They set a time for the red highlights in the morning and then musicians started dropping off their tuxes for dry cleaning.

As Henry had thought, a group was going out to find a bar with food. Zuni's was suggested, but it would take a cab to get there. Then someone said Tommy's Joint, which was met with general agreement, and they set out up Geary. Fog had obscured the stars and she huddled in her jacket.

She found herself shoulder-to-shoulder with the saxophonist who had soloed during the encore. Rett searched her memory for the woman's name — Zip Curtis, that was it.

"You sounded really great tonight." Zip had the same crooked smile as Henry. It was so charming that Rett was reminded of Marilyn Monroe's dire warnings about saxophone players in *Some Like It Hot*.

"I was just going to say the same thing," Rett admitted. "How long have you been with Henry?"

"About five years now. You can't beat the steady pay and I like the way Henry treats me. Women sax players don't get a whole lot of respect."

"I was just thinking that," Rett said. "I think he's one of the few big bands I know of that has women players."

Cleetus Washington, whose golden guitar work was going to someday help him form a band of his own, had slowed down from the front of the group to walk alongside them. "Henry knows quality." He flashed a grin. "That's why he keeps bribing me to come back every year."

"I was surprised to see you," Rett said. "I thought for sure you'd be headlining Vegas."

"Henry makes it worth my while. Besides, I'm not into the headaches — after what he went through with Gilda I have no interest in running a band."

"Henry hates to dump people," Zip added. "But she pushed him to the brink."

"Anyone who tells me my fingering is sloppy can kiss the cement from the third story as far as I'm concerned." There was a murmur of agreement from the musicians in front of them. Cleetus made a fist. "I'm a lover, not a fighter, but I swear I was going to pop her one — Hey, this place is jumping."

The group slowed as they came abreast of a bar that was, as Cleetus had observed, jumping. Dance music pulsed from the open door. A short line of twenty-something women waited outside, next to a crudely painted sign reading "Ladeez Nite."

The trumpeter cracked his knuckles and said, "The clientele is just my speed."

Zip snorted. "Sorry, hon. I don't think you're their type. Know what?" She addressed everyone more generally. "I think I'll hang here."

Cleetus protested. "Zip, honey, you know it won't be the same without you."

"Hey," she said without heat. "I went to that disgusting straight-guy bar with you all in Salt Lake City. This is my kind of place now. It's Saturday night in San Francisco! See ya later, gator."

Zip had a major point, Rett suddenly thought. There were going to be lots of nights spent in nondescript bars after performances. Turning down a Saturday night in San Francisco in a bar packed with lesbians was beyond stupid. "I think I'll hang with Zip," she announced.

Cleetus put his hand on his heart. "You too? You're breaking my heart, here. Are there any straight women left in this world?"

Two violinists, who Rett now noticed were holding hands, joined her and Zip in the line. One blew Cleetus a kiss. "Sorry, sugar."

The only remaining women in the group abandoned the men as well. Cleetus tried one last protest. "I don't think they let straight women into places like this."

"So we'll be gay for the night," one said with a shrug.

"Now you're going to give me wet dreams," he said.

"Ewww!" Zip put her hands over her ears. "TMI, TMI!"

"Way too much information," Rett echoed.

The bereft men slunk into the night amidst mutterings about the sad lot of straight men in today's world.

Thinking of the bonus her bank account would soon receive, Rett tipped the very butch woman at the door to get them in quickly, and another generous tip landed them a table not far from the dance floor. The violinists never made it to the table — they lip- and hip-locked on the dance floor and Rett guessed she wouldn't see them again until tomorrow.

"Let me buy the first round," Zip shouted. They all agreed on beer and she disappeared in the direction of the crowded bar.

The two other women were new to Rett, so she asked their names, and they managed to share backgrounds over the relentless tom-tom beat of the music. Mary was from Cleveland and Jan was from Detroit. Rett compared old stomping grounds from her years in Detroit and learned that most of the clubs she'd first made her way in were still hanging on.

Zip returned with four amber bottles. After she was seated, she raised her bottle. "Good-bye, Gilda, and hello, Rett!"

"Hear, hear." Bottles clinked around the table.

"I have to ask," Rett said after she had taken a cooling swallow from the bottle. "What exactly did she do?"

Zip rolled her eyes. "She doesn't show for rehearsals until the final fifteen minutes, that is, if she showed at all. Then she stops in the middle of her numbers to criticize everyone else's performance — I mean she really did tell Cleetus, Cleetus of all people, that his fingering was sloppy."

Jan leaned over the table so she could be heard. "She was the most insecure performer I've ever seen. It was actually pretty rare when she criticized one of the guys, but she had no compunction at all about ripping one of the girls to pieces."

Mary was nodding. "She was convinced that the only way she could be top banana was on the backs of the other women. Henry didn't like it one bit."

"Well, Henry's a New Age, sensitive guy," Zip said. She tapped Rett's hand. "Let's dance."

They wedged themselves into the mass of moving bodies. Necessity put them breast-to-breast and thigh-to-thigh. Cher's "Believe" had Rett singing along. She believed, oh she believed in life after love. She felt alive and whole for the first time since everything had fallen apart. The music segued to Madonna's "Nothing Really Matters" and it seemed perfectly natural to have her arms around Zip. Kisses were a logical development, though Rett felt no real jolt of passion. It was just kind of nice to hold her and be held.

When she and Zip returned to the table, Mary and Jan took their leave. There was no sign of the violinists. She and Zip finished their beers and danced again.

Zip said into her ear, "Wanna go to bed?"

"To sleep, yes," Rett answered.

"Crud — oh, I remember. Last year you were with tall, dark and muscles."

"That was last year," Rett said.

"Oh, so you're just rejecting me for no reason at all." Zip sighed into her ear. "Then what the hell am I dancing with you for?"

"Solidarity among musicians?"

Zip laughed. "I have to admit this feels pretty nice." She lifted her head from Rett's shoulder to kiss her nose. "But I actually don't have any compulsion to go any further. I mean, if you had said yes, I'm sure I would have managed to fake it —"

Rett guffawed. "Saxophone players are all alike."

"That hurts," Zip protested, though her eyes were dancing. "Okay, let's go back to the hotel. I bet you even have your own room — it would have been so cool."

It was inevitable as she was trying to go to sleep that Rett would think of the motel bed she'd been in just last night. With the performance behind her and nothing but roses in the future she unfolded the memory of Angel like a treasure map, and followed it from beginning to end. Shoulders, neck, ears — sensuous memories that flared her desire for more.

When she tried to visualize Angel's face, however, the image was a little blurry. Eyes, lips, cheekbones — they were all there, but the whole picture didn't come together. Rett remembered that at the outset Angel had seemed just a little familiar and now she couldn't recall precisely what she looked like. How vexing.

For the moment, images of breasts and the curve of hips would have to do. As she fell asleep, "Calling All Angels" was in her head again.

5

The overnight reviews were enthusiastic and as Rett's week in San Francisco progressed, none of the notices failed to mention her as the perfect addition to the Henry Connors Orchestra. Naomi faxed up the text of a short review by a syndicated reviewer posted on the E! Entertainment Watch Web site that ended with the question, "Gilda who?"

Rett felt like she was walking on air. Everyone was so nice to her. Even the dresser had a kind word. When they packed up for Portland Rett no longer felt like every performance was an audition.

She had remembered Monday morning to call Camille. Camille had promised that if she got the chance to mention what a swell singer and fine human being Rett Jamison was she'd certainly do so. She cautioned, however, that she was stuck doing grunt work in the television studios and wasn't likely to escape to the movie studios anytime soon.

The call to Monica was a dead end. Monica swore the only angel she knew was her chiropractor. The call to UCLA was even more frustrating.

"I'm trying to get in touch with a professor there," she'd told the science department secretary. "I only remember her first name, Angel."

The woman had popped her gum, then announced in a voice muffled by too much in her mouth, "I dunno everyone by name yet. I'm new. Lemme look at the list. When id you meed her?"

Rett decided that the truth would needlessly embarrass Angel. "At a symposium on Saturday."

"The list sorted by firs' name would be easier," she complained, just as if Rett was the one who had given her the list. "Arnold — nope. Ann, anudder Ann. Here's an Angelique."

"That could be her." Rett's heart leapt. "Very petite, dark-haired. Late thirties?"

"I dunno. She's on sabbatical." Pop, snap.

"The woman I'm looking for participates in ovarian cancer research."

The secretary's tone grew slightly impatient. "There are over fifty researchers here, another hunnerd faculty and assistant perfessors, teaching assistants, yadda yadda yadda. I dunno them all."

"Well, what is her last name?"

"Sinson." Snap, pop.

"Anyone else?"

"I don' think so." Chew, pop.

"Well, can I leave Angelique Sinson a message?"

"Like I said, she's on sabbatical. I can put a note in 'er box, I guess."

Don't strain yourself, honey, Rett had wanted to say. "Please say that Rett Jamison called and had to go out of town unexpectedly. She should call me though. Here's my number." She thought a moment, then added her cell phone number. "She should leave a message and I'll call again."

"Brett James, I got it."

"No B. And it's Jam-i-son."

"No B?"

"Rett. Short for Loretta."

"Should I say Loretta?" Snap, snap, pop.

God forbid. "She knows me by Rett."

"Rrrrrett Jamison, I goddit."

She made the secretary repeat the numbers and hung up with a sinking feeling that she was never going to hear from Angel. She had serious doubts that her Angel and Angelique Sinson were even the same woman — she was not that lucky. With one day off a week for the next three weeks, flying home to go out to UCLA seemed extravagantly obsessive. By the time she got back to L.A., classes would be over for the summer. It was very frustrating.

Maybe she'll call me. Maybe she'll ask Monica for my number. I'm in the book — maybe she'll look me up. Rett crossed her fingers briefly

From San Francisco they went to Portland for three weeknight performances, then on to Seattle to open Friday night and appear through the following Sunday, just as they had in San Francisco. Vancouver was after that, for appearances Thursday through Sunday.

The time flew by. There wasn't enough time to explore every city in any depth, but in Seattle almost everyone made the effort to see the new Jimi Hendrix museum. The building alone was amazing — it was sculpted like Hendrix's guitar and the Seattle monorail went right through it.

She and Zip spent a lot of time together. It was Zip's considered opinion that Angel had been a ship in the night and that Rett really ought to go to her high school reunion and boff the prom queen so Rett could get on with her life.

"It's too short to worry about what you could have done or should have done." Rett sprawled on the bed and Zip looked up from cleaning her sax. "Sex is sex and love is love. They're not the same thing, never were, never will be."

"You're wrong," Rett answered.

"Prove it. Sleep with me and we'll see if it's just sex or really L-O-V-E."

Rett had rolled her eyes. "One of these days you're going to fall in love and you'll find out it's not as clear-cut as you think."

"Yes, Mother." She easily ducked the pillow Rett threw at her.

Their last performance came too quickly. Rett could hardly believe it. The sophisticated stage outfits were second nature and she continued to marvel at how nice everyone was. She studied her reflection after she drew on her gloves.

They think you're a star on the rise, she thought

suddenly. The idea was seductive. Don't you go thinking that way, she warned herself, then stopped. Was that the voice of her mother, telling her she could never amount to anything? That she would never be a star?

The muffled sound of her cell phone ringing interrupted her thoughts. Naomi was the only person who had called her lately. Angel had never called.

"I just had the most interesting discussion with Jerry Orland," Naomi said.

"He's right across the hall, I think."

"Probably telling Henry what I told him." Naomi sounded excited in a guarded way.

"Which was?"

"That if he wants you to sign for the next three years touring *and* any recording *and* the Vegas gigs, they'll have to come up with a signing bonus."

Rett dropped into the chair at the makeup table. She thought for a moment she would faint. Finally, she managed, "Could you repeat that?"

"Happy birthday, sweetie!" Naomi was exultant. "Henry Connors wants you, Rett, wants you lock, stock and barrel. He wants to incorporate Rett Jamison's vocals into his entire sound. 'Featuring Rett Jamison' sounds pretty damned nice, I must say."

"Holy shit," Rett breathed.

"Vancouver and Seattle were sellouts after you joined on. I think I made an excellent case for your box-office appeal because of the critical push. You're a serious musician, not some lightweight bimbo using her assets to cover a lack of talent. If you start doing interviews with Henry, get some feature press in the mags — you'll be a very positive draw. Jerry knows it and he wants to sign you now before someone else figures out how good you are and offers you the moon."

"Maybe I'll just walk over there and ask for a pen." Rett's head was swimming.

"You'll do nothing of the kind," Naomi commanded. "You don't sign anything I haven't read." She softened her tone. "Jerry and Henry are fairly honorable for this business, though. You can give them a verbal. Pending the details being worked out between Jerry and me, you're in."

"I'm in," Rett echoed. "Naomi, I'm shaking like a leaf. It doesn't seem real." She was glad she was alone.

"This is the last time I'll say it, because we can forget all about it forever after: Trish was holding you back. She didn't have the contacts or the moxie. What she had was major attitude."

"I know. The moment I got her out of my life everything turned around." Except finding Angel again.

"Jerry and Henry are probably talking about a reasonable signing bonus. Don't you go talking money with them."

"Not me," Rett promised. She finally remembered what she'd been meaning to ask Naomi since San Francisco. She was still alone, but lowered her voice anyway. "Jerry and Henry — is there, uh . . ." She heard voices outside the door so she let her voice trail away.

"I think so," Naomi said. "I wouldn't know for sure. I would say that the orchestra is their lives and has been ever since the beginning — what, twenty years ago?"

"Henry started the orchestra when he was twenty?"

"More like thirty. I think he turned fifty last year."

Rett was shocked. "He doesn't look a day over thirty-five."

"Neither did Robert Redford for the longest time. It's the little boy in him. Anyway, given their careers, I'd guess that Henry and Jerry are from the Rock Hudson and Raymond Burr school of gay identity — they have each other and don't see any reason to tell the world about it when they would much rather tell the world about the music."

"S'alright," Rett said. "I just wondered if I was imagining things."

"I don't think so," Naomi said. "Let's go over the numbers Jerry ran by me. The money is great. You should give yourself a hell of a birthday party."

"The concert starts in about twenty minutes," Rett reminded her.

"I'll be quick."

Her mind still reeling from the enormity of her changed fortunes, Rett found Henry just before the curtain went up.

"Jerry and Naomi have to work it out, but I'm in."

They shared a heartfelt hug that didn't jeopardize their stage makeup.

"I'm so glad," Henry said. "It's been magic working with you. I feel fresh inspiration."

"I'm overwhelmed," Rett admitted. They separated and she smiled at him fondly. "I want this to work, you have my promise."

"I didn't need it," Henry said, but his eyes crinkled as if he was extremely pleased.

The after-tour party at the hotel went on until daybreak. Rett kept the fact that it was her fortieth birthday to herself. She'd been trying not to think about it for the past year and now that it had come she didn't hate it the way she thought she would. Maybe because she had finally achieved a measure of success. She wasn't forty and still nobody. Earlier in the night the other musicians had received the news of her tentative return the following year with cheers. It was enough of a birthday present.

Rett found herself in her room at six A.M., giddy from Champagne and praise. She set the clock radio to wake her at noon and poured herself into bed. Is this what it feels like to be a star? she wondered. She was the vocalist for the Henry Connors Orchestra. She wasn't a household name, but when she signed the contract there would be a notice in the trades.

She felt so lucky that she turned the light back on and checked her messages — just in case Angel had called. Now *that* would be a birthday present.

She had one new message. The voice made her body reflexively shudder, but it wasn't Angel's.

"I'm hoping you remember me, Rett. I'd be flattered if you did. It's Cinny Keilor. Well, it's Cinny Johnson now. I found your number through the online white pages and just had to call to see if I could convince you to come to the reunion. I would love to see you again. It's just going to be a super week. Almost everyone is coming. Tell me what I have to do to convince you. I would really love to see you again. Call me if you have the time."

The breathy, slightly excited voice trailed away after giving her number. Rett replayed the message, then lay in bed trying to ignore her tingling body.

That voice — her head was full of it now. "Rett, I want you to touch me there."

Cinny was in a tight pink formal gown. The senior class homecoming queen's tiara had slipped onto the backseat floor of her brother's car.

Rett tasted Cinny's lips again. "I want to show you how good it can be."

Cinny was helping pull her dress up. Rett had one knee between Cinny's thighs. She tugged one shoulder of the gown down and ran her tongue along the top of Cinny's breasts. She kissed the firm column of Cinny's throat while her hand smoothed Cinny's hips.

"I'm ready," Cinny had whispered. "I want you so much."

Her fingertips pressed into the crotch of Cinny's pantyhose. Cinny groaned. Rett kissed the groan away and in one swift motion, not waiting for further permission, pulled the hose down and tangled her fingers under the fabric.

The same hot wetness that Cinny generated in her was coating her fingertips. She pressed where she knew it would feel good and let her slick fingers find the way.

Cinny breathed out, "My God."

"I told you." Rett kissed her again, then murmured, "I always knew it would be like this."

Cinny's legs were opening wider. Rett was trembling. "That feels so good."

Just as Rett's fingers poised to take her, Cinny twisted to one side, panting. "I can't, I can't."

"Don't do this to me."

"Please stop, Rett. You know I want to, but I can't. It's wrong."

Rett had flung herself to the other end of the backseat. "I can't go through another year of this."

"I'm sorry," she said sadly. She pulled down her dress. "We shouldn't see each other again."

"I guess not," Rett said. She didn't want Cinny to see her cry again, so she got out of the car. Her own secondhand dress was crumpled. She wouldn't go back to the dance. She'd only come because Cinny had asked her to be there.

She went to the gymnasium bathroom and sat in a stall for a long time to calm down before starting the long walk home. As she walked through the parking lot she passed Cinny's brother's car, and hated herself for being so weak that she would take any chance to bump into Cinny again. She prayed that if Cinny saw her again, she'd say, "Rett, I was wrong. I can't go on this way. Make love to me."

Her weakness got what it deserved. Cinny was in the car, but her boyfriend was there, too. All she saw was his back and her legs, and all she heard was his groaned-out, "You're so hot tonight."

She felt punched in the stomach. She wouldn't talk to Cinny for weeks after that and would never tell her why. Then one afternoon Cinny had slipped a note into her locker, asking Rett to "see" her after school at the creek beyond the old Gefferson place. She'd gone, all the while rehearsing the speech where she told Cinny to go to hell.

Cinny had said she missed Rett's friendship. She'd asked for a hug to make up whatever it was that was bothering Rett. The hungry, bruising kisses that followed had led to another rejection, and not the last one. Her entire senior year, from homecoming to prom night, she'd still followed Cinny around like a desperate lapdog, hoping for any castoff caress that might come her way.

That voice — that breathy, hungry voice. Rett rolled over in bed and wrapped her arms over her stomach. After all these years that voice made her shiver.

Even as sleep threatened, she was asking herself if she should go to the reunion, just to tie things up with Cinny. Just to see if Cinny would be willing to talk about it. Just to see if Cinny would be willing... Don't finish that thought, Rett warned herself. If you go you'll have to see your mother.

Four weeks ago she couldn't even contemplate that. Four weeks ago she would have had no real proof that she was successful as a singer, something her mother had repeatedly told her she would never achieve. But now she was the vocalist for the Henry Connors Orchestra. Now she had a handful of reviews. Now she could walk into Woton a new, more sophisticated Rett Jamison, and no longer feel like a failure or an imposter.

I'll go, she promised herself sleepily. Not because Cinny asked, and only if her schedule was clear. Then she'd go, maybe...

The first few days home were hectic. Naomi had her financial affairs back in order and a slew of papers for her to sign, including the Henry Connors Orchestra contract. She caught up on her mail and undertook to learn the financial software Naomi was using so she could look at her reports via Naomi's secure Web site. Online banking coordinated with it so her transactions would automatically be forwarded to Naomi's accountant.

She put the furniture back where it was when Trish had lived there and didn't mind that it was the best arrangement. She had bought a new wall hanging in Seattle and had it shipped home. It filled the hole left by the one Trish had taken. That was that.

When the contract signing was reported in the trades she did two phone interviews for biographical sketches. Naomi sent her out to three different studio assignments, all to do vocals for commercials, which were always easy work and lucrative. One Wednesday afternoon, after a lunch with Naomi and a casting agent from Fox, she dug out the reunion invitation from the back of her sock drawer.

She stared at it for the longest time, then found her keys and got in the car.

Chet Baker crooned to her all the way to UCLA. School was out, she told herself. It was a completely wasted trip. Maybe she could take in a movie in Westwood so it wouldn't be all a waste. But she had to try. It was the strangest thing — she felt like she couldn't say yes to the reunion, yes to seeing Cinny Keilor again, until she'd made sure that Angel was gone beyond reach.

Just finding the science part of the campus was daunting. There were several buildings, all multi-storied, and judging from the first one she entered, the faculty offices were scattered all over. Maybe an in-person appeal to the gum-chewing department secretary would work.

It took her nearly thirty minutes to find the department office. Gum Chewer didn't appear to remember their earlier conversation and she let Rett peruse the staff directory on the condition that Rett wouldn't tell anyone. That she was obviously breaking the rules would have bothered Rett more if she hadn't felt this compelling urge to find Angel and find out if . . . if what had happened between them was just a one-time thing.

Angelique "Sinson" turned out to be Angelique Simpson, who had earned her graduate degree in 1971, about fifteen years before the fortyish Angel had probably earned hers. While it was possible that Angel was some sort of prodigy, Rett seriously doubted that this was the same woman. If only there were pictures. There was no Angel or variation on the list other than Angelique Simpson. It was a dead end.

She thanked the secretary for her help and went out into the hot sunshine to ponder her options.

Okay, she thought. There's hardly any students here, but researchers don't have a school year. Walk every floor and every hallway and you'll at least know you tried.

She was footsore by the time she finished, then discovered another science building beyond what she'd thought was the last one. White-coated figures were coming and going — scientists doing research, maybe?

Rett quickly discovered she needed a badge to go inside. There was no staff list or any such helpful information on the building door. Maybe if she sat on the bench just across the short stretch of grass she would see if Angel left at the end of the day. It was nearly five.

What are you going to do? she asked herself. How many days will you do this?

Too desperate. You tried. Get over it.

She turned on her heel and headed into the last building she'd walked through. Three white-coated figures carrying coffee mugs and armloads of paperwork were coming toward her. The one in the middle was Angel.

Angel stopped short. "Fancy meeting you here."

The other two people, a man and a woman, stopped as well.

"I was looking for you," Rett admitted.

"Really?" Angel's expression was cold. "I can't imagine why." To her companions she said, "If you want to go on ahead, I'll be along in just a minute."

They shrugged and left the building, leaving Rett and Angel in the momentarily empty hallway.

"I lost your number. I mean, it got smooshed," Rett said. "I left you a message."

Angel looked over her shoulder as several people came around the corner. "Let's go in here." She opened a door marked "Study Carrels" and turned on the lights.

Her expression was no less cold once the door was closed. "I have phone company voice mail. They don't lose messages."

"I mean I tried to leave you a message. With the department secretary. The only Angel she could find was Angelique Simpson."

"When did you leave this supposed message?"

Rett was feeling more than embarrassed. "That

Monday morning, as soon as the science department opened."

Angel's tone was exasperated. "First of all, I'm in biomedical research, not science. It's a separate department."

"How was I supposed to know that?"

"You wouldn't."

Rett felt as if she'd been found mentally wanting. "I tried."

"It takes you a month to do more than leave a message for someone you don't even know for sure is me?"

"I had to go out of town. Touring." She could see that Angel didn't want to believe her.

"Well, now that you're back, what exactly do you want?"

"I'd like to see you again."

"You mean you want to have sex again." Angel made up for her short stature by raising her chin.

Yes, Rett's body screamed. Her bra suddenly felt two sizes too small, and her thighs clenched. "Not only that."

"I can't believe you lost my number. I put it on the note."

"No, you didn't."

"I know I did."

"It's not there. I just had the napkin and it got all wet in the gutter. It fell out of my pocket."

"I know I wrote it on the note in the motel."

"I still have the note. I'll show it to you if you like." Rett did not care at all for the way their conversation was going. "Okay, I could have come looking a couple of days ago, but that was the absolute soonest." Rett was breathing hard now.

Angel's invoking the motel had stirred her memories even further. "This was a bad idea." She should have walked out, but she didn't. She didn't have enough Bette Davis in her to do it.

"I don't know what to think." Angel's eyes conveyed her anger and frustration, and Rett remembered how lovely those eyes were up close. "I felt really terrible when you didn't call. Like I was just a body to you."

"I don't have a collection," Rett snapped.

"How am I supposed to know that?" Angel appeared to be breathing hard, too.

"I'm sorry I bothered you." Rett realized that she had to go by Angel to get to the door. She stepped in that direction and Angel didn't move.

Rett was entirely too close to Angel now. She fumbled in her pocket for the business card she'd brought that gave Naomi as her agent and contact. Considering Angel's mood, she almost didn't give it to her. "I wrote my home and cell numbers on the back," she said. "The ball is in your court."

Angel put the card in her lab coat pocket without even looking at it. "I don't know what to think," she said. "I've been trying to forget all about you."

"Was it working?"

"No."

"Me neither," Rett said. "So call me if you feel like it." She strove to appear aloof, but inside she was praying that Angel would call, and soon.

Angel only gave way a few inches when Rett reached for the door. In a choked voice that sounded desperately unwilling, she said, "Is there an incentive?"

Rett failed miserably to maintain an aloof air when

she kissed Angel's upturned mouth. A sharp crackle of desire surged through her — it was just like their first night.

Angel broke away with a gasp. She set down her mug. "I'm late for a meeting." She dropped all the papers she was carrying and threw her arms around Rett's neck, bending her down for a kiss that held nothing back.

Rett's hands found their way under the lab coat. The blouse Angel wore was thin enough to let Rett revel in the heat of Angel's body.

Angel pushed her against the door and rested her head on Rett's breasts. "This is crazy."

"I know."

"What is it about you?" Angel dropped to her knees to pick up the folders and papers. "I'm late," she repeated.

Rett helped her gather everything up. All the while she felt as if invisible streamers of electricity joined her body to Angel's. "Call me?"

Angel clasped the papers in front of her like a shield. "I — yes. I guess so."

They went back into the hallway and Angel turned toward the exit to the research building. Angel was almost to the door.

Say something, she told herself. Ask her again to call.

No, her pride said. Don't beg.

As Angel opened the door, Rett found her voice. "What's your last name, anyway?"

Angel looked a little like she wanted to laugh and Rett remembered that she'd had the feeling Angel was laughing at her when they first met. Then Angel's expression was tinged with anger again, anger Rett suspected was directed at both of them. "What is it about you?"

Angel was gone before Rett could think of an answer.

Rett's first instinct was to follow her. Follow her and do what? Scamper about like a puppy begging for a treat? Reliving her tempestuous relationship with Cinny Keilor made Rett wary of doing anything remotely similar.

You got what you came here for, she told herself.

No, you didn't, a little voice answered.

She'd thought that seeing Angel would help her make up her mind about the wisdom of seeing Cinny Keilor again. Now it seemed very likely that she wouldn't see Angel and for the life of her she couldn't see how that had anything to do with a woman she hadn't seen in twenty-three-plus years.

Tears threatened. She clamped down on them the way she was clamping down on the still-raging desire to strip herself naked and throw herself at Angel's feet. She walked quickly to her car, replaced Chet Baker with Melissa Etheridge, and drove home in a state of steely calm.

What is it about me, Angel wanted to know. Well, what is it about her?

She pulled into the parking garage under her building and looked at herself in the rear view mirror as she turned off the engine. *She ignites you. She makes every nerve in your body dance.*

Rett swallowed hard. Their first encounter had not been a fluke — that much had been clear from the way Angel had kissed her today. She understood Angel's being mad about her not calling, but Angel seemed mad about something else. Maybe it had nothing to do with her. Angel had alluded to a breakup. Maybe she was still getting over it.

The days went by and Angel did not call. Rett's days were busy enough that remembering Angel's touch did not distract her unduly, but her nights were so empty that Angel invaded her dreams. Cinny Keilor troubled her sleep as well — tight pink sweaters and long, tanned legs got mixed in with the curve of Angel's back. The scent of candy lip gloss seemed as real as the smell of Angel had been on her hands.

If she couldn't get Angel out of her mind, then maybe getting Cinny out would help ease the empty ache she felt as she slid into bed every night.

Minnesota in August. Putting the ghost of Cinny Keilor to rest might be worth it. Maybe, after all these years, it would be worth it to give her mother one more chance to admit she'd made something of herself. Minnesota in August. Ugh.

6

The phone on the other end of the line rang once. Rett quickly hung up.

Her heart was pounding as if she'd just dashed up four flights of stairs.

This is ridiculous, she told herself. She dialed the number Cinny had left again.

After two rings, the phone was answered with a brisk, "Cinny Johnson."

Rett slammed her phone down and backed across the room.

"This is stupid!"

Twenty-three years. Twenty-three years and she was a breathless mess all over again.

She approached the phone as if it were a snake, then veered off, snatched up her keys and ran down to her car. She still had fifteen minutes before she really had to leave for the rehearsal with David Benoit, but you could never tell with traffic, she told herself. Every minute might count.

She was on the Santa Monica Freeway heading for Century City when she told herself that cowardice was an ugly trait and got out her cell phone. She dialed Cinny's number again and took a deep breath, remembering at the last second that Cinny had given an area code different from the old one. They were probably having the same endless changes in area codes that plagued Los Angeles.

"Cinny Johnson."

"Cinny?" Oh, that was brilliant. She'd just said so. "Yes?"

"I'm returning your call. It's Rett."

"Rett Jamison. My God."

A lengthy silence stretched out and Rett felt as if memories were pouring out of the satellite, into her cell phone and piercing her body. She forgot to get off the freeway, bit back a curse and swerved for the next off-ramp.

"Well, how the hell are you?" Cinny's voice was just the same. Firm, but edged with a touch of breathiness that had never failed to make Rett yearn to hear more.

"I'm great." In Minnesota-speak, anything less than "great" was an admission of terrible problems and as such was sharing way too much personal information over the phone. "How about you?"

"Just terrific. I can't believe you called me back. This whole reunion has me thinking about everybody, and remembering. I have such vivid memories of you."

"Ditto." Oh, what a wit you are, Rett scolded herself. What repartee.

"I hope you're calling to say that you're coming."

"I think I can make it. My agent says my calendar is free."

"Agent? Are you singing professionally? Really?"

"Really." So much for the absurd idea that Cinny might have heard her name recently. "I've been doing it all along."

"I just *knew* you could do it. We'll have several celebrities at the reunion."

Rett realized belatedly that the light ahead was yellow and probably had been for several seconds. She slammed on the brakes and lost hold of the cell phone.

"— won the National Science Award, can you imagine that?" Cinny laughed. "Just goes to show that girls who wear glasses get the last laugh. She spent an entire year at Cambridge — the one in England — and I've never been out of the country. And remember Bobby Johnson? The class ahead of us? He's an astronaut! We always knew he was an airhead. He's not coming, though — his excuse is being in outer space." Cinny laughed again and the sound of it flowed over Rett like warm sunshine on a cool day.

"I can't honestly say I remember Bobby." Rett tried — no one was clear in her memory but Cinny. Cinny saying yes, Cinny saying no. Cinny's shoulders, her breasts, her legs, her mouth —

"He was a ROTC geek — he and Natalie what's-her-name. Listen to me! All the slang came back to me . . . like you know?"

"Oh, yah," Rett intoned with a long-forgotten Minnesota inflection. She was bobbing her head as she said it. God, high school. She was nuts to go back.

"I'm really looking forward to seeing you again," Cinny was saying. Her voice was a little lower and her high spirits faded. "There have been times in the last twenty-three years that I've thought about you and thought, what if."

Rett did not know what to say. Her heart was racing again. "I haven't forgotten about you, either," she finally managed.

"That's flattering," Cinny said. "I hope you'll be here the whole week. So we have time to catch up."

"I'm not sure about that," Rett hedged. The lure of Cinny's voice flowing through the phone was a powerful inducement, but it was occurring to her that it would be hard not to revert to a Rett Jamison she didn't want to be.

"I'll send you the entire package, just in case. Lots of people are staying at the same resort and bringing their families. You'll remember it — Honey Lake Cabins."

"The place with the blue and yellow cabins next to the big lake?"

"That's the one. I know for a fact that they're sold out, though, so I'll put in the number for the motel up by Litchfield. It's a Best Western, so you know it's pretty good. It might fill up, so don't wait too long to book a room."

111

"I'll keep that in mind."

"If you come I think the rest of the Wiffenpoofs might be willing to work up a number or two."

Christ, the Woton Wiffenpoofs, or as they had often referred to themselves, the Wippenfoops. Their rehearsals and performances contained almost all of Rett's pleasant high school memories. "I guess that would be fun."

There was another long silence, then Cinny said hesitantly, "I have to ask you something, but I don't know how. I mean, I think it's, um, well, rude, but I have to know." Her voice sounded tight now and Rett remembered all the times Cinny had sounded that way when she was upset or excited.

"Ask. I won't answer if I think it's inappropriate."

"Are you still . . . you know."

Rett knew. She resented the question — from Cinny of all people. "I don't know."

"Gay."

"I'm still a lesbian, Cinny. Never found a cure, never looked for one."

"I knew it was rude. You're angry."

"Only a little."

"We'll have to hug and make up when you get here."

Rett pulled into a parking lot. She couldn't drive and have this conversation. Cinny was invoking potent memories. "Well, that does beg the question, doesn't it? Are you still . . . whatever it was you were?"

"I guess I deserve that. I'm not proud of the way I led you on." She laughed nervously. "You know, I think you're right. I'm still the way I was. But I think it's high time I made up my mind."

Shit. Rett was reeling with conflicting emotions.

Her first thought was that Cinny had yet to mention her husband, but it was quickly pushed aside by the possibility of finally being with Cinny, to finish what they'd begun so many times. It was so tempting. Still, she knew she was opening herself up for yet another rejection. The Rett Jamison with the voice the Vancouver *Sun* had termed "the stuff legends are made of" would not be destroyed by another of Cinny's rejections. But when she walked into Woton again it would be like stepping back in time. She could turn into the Rett Jamison who could be shattered by an unkind word or hostile glance. The more she talked to Cinny the more she remembered not just Cinny, but the excruciating awkwardness of not fitting in.

Come on, Rett, what do you care any more about how that town thinks of you? It's Cinny you want to get over. Cinny and your mother. No one else ever mattered.

"Are you still there?"

"Yes," Rett answered. "Sorry, I had to get off the freeway. I have a rehearsal to go to."

"I'll let you go, then. I have your address. You know that I found nearly half the people who moved out of town through the Internet?"

It hadn't occurred to Rett to wonder how Cinny had found her to begin with. She'd moved around a lot in the early years. "Technology has its definite upside."

"I'll put everything in the mail today. If you want to call before then, feel free."

"I'll remember."

" 'Bye, then. See you in about . . . five weeks?"

Christ, that was soon. As Rett finished the drive to

the rehearsal studio, she asked herself what she had let herself in for. All because Angel had never called and she was too chickenshit to get out of the house at night and find someone to date. Three trips a week to the gym hadn't found her anyone interesting either, but it had helped her waistline.

With a great deal of difficulty she put Cinny out of her mind. David Benoit had slots for his CDs in most music stores, and living up to a well-known recording artist's standards was just a teensy bit important career-wise. Her contract with Henry was not exclusive except for the dates specified throughout the course of the year. Nothing prevented her from performing with David at the Newport Jazz Festival as she had previously contracted, or from recording with him, should she impress him sufficiently. As with Henry's dealings with Cleetus Washington and the rest of the featured musicians, what was good for them could only be good for Henry's box office.

Having that contract with Henry was not just a financial blessing — it took all the pressure off. Pressure led to stress led to tight vocal cords. Henry's confidence in her made her a trusted commodity who had proven her professionalism.

The rehearsal was made up of just a few principals and David himself. A full stage rehearsal would take place the day before the festival opened. It went smoothly from start to finish. Rett was amazed at the difference it made to have someone as gifted as David arranging the entire sound around the qualities of her voice. Henry hadn't yet had a chance to do that. Yee-gods, she thought. If she sounded good without that, just think how she'd sound when Henry did arrange for her.

As she left, David said, "Now I know why Henry Connors snapped you up before I heard you."

Rett felt herself flush slightly. It was just show biz flattery, she knew, but it was pleasant to hear all the same. "Feel free to tell me anything along those lines whenever the mood strikes you. I can take it."

He laughed pleasantly and Rett was more than halfway home before she even thought of Cinny Keilor. When she did, however, it was with a trembling, butterflies-in-the-stomach sensation that was more unwelcome than welcome.

Cinny obviously had some expectation that they would take up where they left off. Rett considered that she had had those expectations, too. But they couldn't — she was not the same confused, put-up-with-anything lesbian she'd been back then. She was not going to go back to being that person. There was also a husband in the picture somewhere.

On the other hand, that Cinny could move her so powerfully was a strong indication that indeed they had unfinished business. Until she had talked to Cinny she'd thought it was just sex. But there was more than that. She needed to face Cinny as the woman she was today.

She needed to do the same thing with her mother. If she was even alive. Rett guessed she had to be or someone would have notified her. Her mother had sent a Christmas card as usual, which was the sum total of their annual contact over the past twenty-odd years. The handwriting was increasingly spidery. It was hard to imagine her mother old — she'd always seemed too hard to age. But there was no doubt in Rett's mind that otherwise her mother was unchanged — she'd be half-plastered, bitter and critical about everything from Rett's hair to her figure to her failures in life.

If her mother treated her exactly the same way she had when she was a teenager, then Rett would know in her heart what she knew intellectually — the verbal abuse and poison hadn't been her fault. She hadn't deserved it then and would not tolerate it now.

She had lots of unfinished business, and she hadn't really been aware of it until the invitation to the reunion had arrived. Of course, letting things go from not good to bad to worse with Trish proved she tended to put off dealing with unpleasant things.

So. She would face her past and confront the future differently. She would overcome the limitations of her genetic code.

Damn. She was thinking about Angel again.

"Can't you do anything right? You walk like a horse."

"I'm leaving, Mama. My stuff's in my car. I won't be back."

Her mother spat out a bit of tobacco that had made it past the cigarette filter. "You'll be back. You won't make it any farther than I did."

Rett put a check on the counter. "That's the last of my pay I'm giving you. I'm going to need every dime for myself."

"What am I supposed to do now?"

"Work harder for tips?" Rett had shrugged and

clamped down on the rage that threatened to break to the surface. "I'll have my own bills to pay, Mama. Maybe all I'll ever do is wait tables, but just keeping a steady job will mean I made it farther than you ever did."

"You ungrateful little snot . . ."

The captain was saying, "Let's be grateful for that smooth ride and an early gate arrival."

Rett felt as if she had to claw her way up from sleep. The past week had been a restless one. She knew her memories of her mother's ravaged face and smoker's hack were overblown, but the fear was real.

She'd read the words, "Guest artists like chanteuse Rett Jamison enlivened the David Benoit performance. Jamison in particular shone in a special arrangement that highlighted a deep, melodic voice." She'd read them and had a rare, focused insight. She could not be the person the reviewer described if she was afraid to face her mother and put the past to rest. The self-doubt that her mother had engendered in her from birth was still there. She had a chance to let it go before her mother died. Given her mother's vices, it was amazing she was still alive. If Rhett waited too much longer she might never get the chance to look fear in the face and put it behind her.

Minneapolis was spread out below her. She was coming home for a mixed bag of reasons, none of them untroubled or easily resolved.

As the plane taxied, she reminded herself about the humidity in August. You break into a sweat the instant you step onto the jetway, she'd complained to Mrs. Bernstein only yesterday. You feel like a flower in a microwave before you even get your rental car.

The moment the airplane door opened and the first

whoosh of local air swept in, Rett broke into a sweat.
She already felt like a flower in a microwave on the
jetway. At the car rental counter she felt a chill from
the heavy-duty air-conditioning. Back into the thick
air she went, dragging her suitcase behind her,
clutching her contract and keys. She wished she was
wearing shorts.

"Shitty weather," she mumbled. The car was midnight blue, a color guaranteed to absorb and amplify
every pulse of sunlight. The cheap vinyl seats were
perfect for creating an instant perspiration slick.

She cranked the air-conditioning to maximum. She
felt like a pot roast in a pressure cooker.

Minneapolis had changed. It was not the city she
remembered — she doubted Mary Richards would
recognize it either. She'd been prepared for the shock
of more than a few tall buildings, and yet the sight
left her sadly nostalgic. At one bend of Highway 52
she expected to glimpse the Mississippi River, but the
view was now blocked by skyscrapers. When she
finally did see the magnificent waterway, it seemed
dwarfed by St. Paul's towering financial district.

Even knowing her way around the basic street
layout of the city didn't save her from getting lost on
the way to the Top Hat Club. One-way streets loomed
out of nowhere and twice she thought she had found
her left turn only to discover that at this hour of the
day she couldn't go that way. She missed the university district entirely and wasn't able to turn around
until she crossed the river into St. Paul.

It seemed impossible, then, that the Top Hat Club

looked exactly the same. Even the fading facade was no less and no more impressive than it had been twenty-odd years ago. The marquee, however, was freshly done. "Two Nights Only — Rett Jamison!"

She liked it, including the exclamation point. Naomi's finding her this gig helped defray some of the cost of the trip, but that was a secondary consideration. It let her arrive home as a professional singer. The reviews from the Newport Jazz Festival had been terrific and Naomi was trying to get Rett a copy of the feed that had been taped for cable broadcast. If that wasn't enough to bolster her self-esteem, any time she wanted to she could replay in her head David Benoit's comment that he might be able to use Rett's unique voice in an upcoming recording project. It staved off the specter of the terrified, desperate girl she had been when she'd left Woton for the Twin Cities looking for work and a place to sing.

The club was smaller than she remembered — maybe that was just because she was older. She was certain that Woton High would seem smaller, too. She'd tried most of the time to be small, inconspicuous — it kept her out of her mother's way. It was her first voice teacher who had helped her get over that. "You're as big as your voice," Mrs. Raguzzo had snapped. "Stand up straight, take up space. The bigger you feel, the bigger your voice will be."

Though every day she used almost all of what she'd learned from Mrs. Raguzzo, she hadn't thought about the elderly woman in quite a while. She'd died five, no . . . at least ten years ago, not long after Rett had moved to L.A. She wished Mrs. Raguzzo could know that her hard work with Rett hadn't gone to waste.

She stood just inside the club door. None of the people, including the owner, were familiar from the old days, but the rickety tables, the scarred bar and tiny stage were the same. She shook off the feeling of stepping into the past. Bad place to go, she warned herself. You have to dance with the past while you're here, but you don't have to take it home.

The club's house band was kicking back with beers while they waited for her, but the five of them — all men — got down to business readily enough. They quickly agreed on a song list. Like the jazz group she'd sung with in New York, they were focused on the improvisation and musical rapport.

The unofficial leader, Dave Clark — no relation, he said quickly — wrote down the songs they chose on a bar napkin. Rett would never trust important information to a bar napkin again.

"We've been working on some killer solos and waiting for a vocalist — you willing to do 'Me and Mrs. Jones'?"

Rett fluttered her eyelashes. "Mrs. Jones, yes. You — sorry."

The other musicians snickered.

Dave grinned. "I guess that's a yes — just wondered if you'd be up for singing about a hot affair with another woman. It's not the same sung as 'Mr. Jones.'"

"If you think the audience won't go Jerry Falwell on us, I'd love to sing it." It was a bluesy, moody piece that worked into an all-out fever. Yes, she was in the mood for a song like that.

The bass player hissed air through his teeth and said, "This may be a rundown firetrap, but I'll give it one thing. The people are here for the music."

"Great. You want to try a couple of numbers? I have to check into my motel and change, but that can wait an hour or two."

Keyboards, bass, guitar, drums and sax. They were well-balanced, and Rett found a low, even tone that brought a smile to Dave's face. They grooved through "You'll Never Find" and "Fever," then turned to "Me and Mrs. Jones." The sax moaned and the bass player took the beat into definite pelvic regions. The keyboard and guitar teased each other while Rett sank into the mood of the song. Improvisation let her draw out "we got a thing goin' on" so that all the emphasis was on "thing." Her voice, husky and low, communicated that this "thing" was consuming and physical. She closed her eyes. Angel was there behind her lids, then Angel became Cinny and she let memories shade her phrasing and tone, holding back a little of the passion for the evening.

The song ended with a brush on the snare drum and Rett sighed.

"Oh, yeah," the sax player said. "I knew with the right vocal that would be sweet." The bartender looked approving, which was more than most bartenders ever conveyed.

They rehearsed a few more numbers, then Rett took her leave until later that evening. She checked into her motel and went in search of dinner. She was tempted by a Mexican restaurant off the freeway, but she doubted that it would compare to what she was used to on Olivera Street in L.A. When she'd left Minnesota the favorite spice was Miracle Whip.

She ended up at White Castle, a real trip down memory lane. The burgers and fries tasted just the same, with all the artery-clogging fat and grease she remembered packed into a Chiclet-sized burger. Delectable, even in small quantities — she didn't want to get full. She had to take an antacid while she was dressing, but it was a small price to pay.

Having seen that the club was very much the same as it always had been, she felt perfectly comfortable in the jumpsuit she'd been planning to wear. The electric purple looked even better with the red highlights she'd decided to keep in her hair. She remembered Henry's dresser's comments about nobody looking at Marilyn Monroe's stomach and left the zipper down a little bit lower than she normally would have. It was hard to sing sexy songs zipped up like a church organist.

With the owner's permission she parked behind the club and let herself in the rear door. The club was still only half-full, but it wasn't quite nine yet. The band was just fooling around as a way of warming up. The owner was affable and assured her that a friend from the *Star Tribune* was going to stop in to do a review.

Smoky, smelling of beer, sawdust and musty air-conditioning, the place did take Rett back. She didn't, however, feel like a girl barely out of high school lying about her age to get a chance to sing. Confidence was a wonderful feeling. Only a few months ago, she had thought this sense of competence would elude her forever in spite of all her hard work. Now it seemed like she'd found Patti LaBelle's "new attitude" — a sense of self that allowed her to deftly find and hold a sultrier stage presence than she was usually comfortable with.

The dim, filtered light added to the mood. They entered torch song territory with "Fever" and the first set climaxed with "Me and Mrs. Jones." Rett found herself thinking about Angel again — it was that kind of thing goin' on. Two meetings and both seething with desire. The jumpsuit felt too small; the lights were too hot. "Me and Missus, Missus, Missus Jones" became an "oh-whoa" moan and she let the note go to the saxophone, which soared upward to a full-out wail as Rett moved into the shadows.

She sipped from the bottle of water she'd stashed behind the stage and fanned herself. Thinking about Angel left her feeling lightheaded. The solos would take as long as ten minutes, given the slow, aching mood everyone seemed to be in — enough time to pull herself together, certainly.

Out of the lights it was possible to see more of the seating area. The Top Hat used to court a seasoned jazz crowd, but the average age was now on the young side, Rett noticed. Most looked like university students in basic black T-shirts and jeans. They were good music fans — they all seemed into the sound, moving with the beat.

A flash of hot pink caught her eye. The shoulders and back the pink blouse was clinging to were curvaceous enough to motivate Rett to lean out a little to see if she could see the whole woman.

All she could think was, I should have anticipated this.

Cinny Keilor looked as if she hadn't aged a day. Nothing on her body appeared to have moved southward. Her blonde curls were caught back with a Barbie-type bandeau in hot pink that matched her blouse. Her mouth . . . Time was stopping for Rett. Her throat was dry and a quick sip of water made no difference at all.

Cinny was at a table with other women — no sign

of the husband. The woman next to her had to be Bunny Gustafson — she and Cinny had both been cheerleaders and at the very top of the best clique in school. God, it looked like a group of Woton High grads had come to see her.

I should have anticipated this, she told herself again. She was desperately glad that she had not, however. The idea of singing all these bluesy, lovesick songs in front of Cinny would have been too distracting. The only thing that would have been worse was if Angel had been . . .

. . . it couldn't be.

Angel leaned into view between Bunny and someone else who looked familiar. *Angel.*

Angel.

Longer hair. Add glasses.

Angelica Martinetta.

She hadn't changed that much. No wonder she had been peeved — Rett knew she should have recognized her. Besides Cinny, Angel was the only other girl she'd ever kissed in high school. How could she have forgotten — the night of the senior prom had been the lowest point of all in her non-relationship with Cinny. Angel had been one of the group of kids sitting on the hill behind the school pretending they were too cool to go to a stupid prom. Rett had tried to be cool that night, tried to get drunk for once. She had failed as usual and stayed on the fringe of the group, nursing a single beer.

One of the boys, under the cover of darkness, said loudly, "They don't let lesbos go to dances, do they?"

Rett didn't recognize the voice, but it didn't matter. They all said pretty much the same thing.

Equally loudly she said, "Does anyone know if a small dick makes you stupid?"

"Shut your pie hole, Jamison."

"Just an innocent question." She rolled over onto her stomach and looked down at the brightly lit gymnasium with "Stairway to Heaven" theme banners for the dance. Every once in a while music would drift up to her, but it all sounded the same.

The memories, once tapped, came back vividly. They came back several months too late.

"Stairway to fucking heaven," she had muttered.

"They're morons. Just ignore them."

Angel had been sitting just far enough away for Rett not to have noticed her sooner. She was wearing cutoffs and an old T-shirt. Her glasses occasionally reflected the lights below. She drained her beer and tossed the empty bottle into the growing pile near the trash can.

"I think there's more beer in that cooler over there."

"Two's my limit," Angel answered. "Otherwise I do things I regret." She scooted down the slope toward Rett, stopping when their shoulders were level.

Rett had barely looked at Angel from the depths of her depression. Cinny was at the prom, of course, wearing a low-cut, backless formal that her boyfriend would get to remove later. They were probably down there getting chosen King and Queen of the fucking Prom. "Oh yah? Like what?"

"Like this."

Angel kissed her and Rett kissed her back, wishing Angel were Cinny. She had never stopped to wonder about Angel's feelings at that moment.

"You could stop thinking about her," Angel said.

"I can't."

Angel looked as if she wanted to cry. "We're all going to graduate in a month. Maybe we'll never see each other again. I'm going to Cal Poly."

"I'm getting the hell out of this town."

"She won't go with you."

Rett drained her beer. "What do you know about it, anyway?"

Angel's anger flashed in the night. "She's a phony and you're a fool, Rett Jamison. You don't know the real thing when you see it." She had flounced off into the night and Rett had truly never given her another thought.

Angel had been right. Cinny had refused to leave Woton the day after they graduated. Rett had scrimped and saved for a car and with her mother's invectives ringing in her ears she'd driven east to Minneapolis, which had seemed a world away. She'd spent much of the first year on her own thinking about Cinny until other women had come into her life. But she'd never remembered that Angel even existed.

How could she have been so blind?

Belatedly she heard the guitar winding into the melody for the verse and she hurried back to the microphone as the crowd applauded the soloists.

She had to clear her throat. She'd been using the memories of Angel and Cinny to get into the music, but now she used the music to push Angel and Cinny out of her head. She'd never get through the song otherwise. She closed her eyes and found the words somewhere in the tumult of her mind. Her vocal cords remembered and she found her way back into the mood. Her hesitation gave way to more skillful intonation. Think about anything else, she told herself — think about Trish if you have to — just pull yourself together.

The song and set were over, finally. Rett was perspiring and feeling dizzy when she beat it for the storage room in the back that doubled as a dressing room.

She'd recovered somewhat when the bartender leaned in. "There's a group out front who say they're old friends if you want to say hello."

It was what she had been dreading. Now she had to meet Cinny again in front of Angel, and look at Angel and somehow not want her and hold it all together in front of Bunny and the others.

"I don't know what I've ever done to deserve this." She didn't realize she'd spoken out loud until the bartender gave her an odd look, shrugged and walked away.

Deep breath. Calm, cool, collected, she repeated to herself. *Dee-ee-eep breath.* She had to actually put her hand on her abdomen and breathe in until it inflated to fill her lungs completely. Her nerves steadied a little. She walked toward the table with Chopin's *Funeral March* playing in her head.

Cinny saw her first and hopped to her feet with a bounce worthy of a seventeen-year-old.

"Rett!" She threw her arms around Rett's neck. "You were amazing! God, it's good to see you."

Rett hugged her back, feeling none of the taut passion she'd been expecting at this moment. Her lack of response might have had something to do with the mocking glance Angel gave her over Cinny's shoulder. Then Angel looked away.

"I know you'll remember the old cheerleading

squad," Cinny said when she let Rett go. "Bunny and Lisa and Mary and Kate. I'm sure you remember Angel-the-brain, too."

"It's been a long time," Bunny said as she hugged Rett by way of greeting.

Rett agreed, then waved at the others across the table. "Sit, sit. It's too crowded." Thank God, she thought. She didn't know what would happen if she touched Angel.

Yes, she did. She'd make it plain to everyone that she wanted to double-aardvark on the floor all night.

There was no chair for Rett, so Cinny slid to the edge of hers and invited Rett to join her.

Cinny's thighs were still excellent, Rett noticed. "Is this where we all lie and say none of us have changed a bit?"

Mary looked down at her chest. "Three kids — I know I've changed."

"You don't wear glasses anymore." Rett looked right at Angel.

"The miracle of contact lenses." Angel's voice was husky. She glanced down at her drink, then back at Rett. Her gaze was like a flame and Rett did not care if it was anger or lust. The heat went right through her and she moved on the chair, realizing too late that it was Cinny's thigh she was rubbing her hip against.

The others seemed blissfully unaware of the undercurrent, though how they could have missed the fact that the temperature at the table had gone up ten degrees was beyond Rett.

Cinny twisted a little on the chair and put her arm around the back to keep from falling off. Under the cover of "do you remember" conversation, Cinny's thumb smoothed Rett's shoulder blade.

It should not have felt as good as it did. Rett prayed that Angel was unaware of it.

"So we decided it was high time for ladies' night out. I'm so glad we came," Bunny said. "Cinny saw the notice in the paper."

"My agent sort of pulled it out of the hat. A friend of a friend knows the owner. The place is packed, so I guess it's worth his while."

Rett was suddenly acutely aware that the zipper on the front of the jumpsuit had slipped down a bit lower somewhere along the way. Cleavage is not a crime, she told herself, though you might want to escape before you expose your belly button. With a sigh of relief she heard the sax player tuning up and she made her excuses.

"We're going to see you at the picnic on Sunday, right?" Bunny shouted over the sudden twang of the guitar. "There's going to be a pajama party at my house Friday night. No boys."

"Sounds fun," Rett lied. Right, a sleepover. Sure, why not just have her roll a sleeping bag out between Cinny and Angel. That would be conducive to sleep.

"Oh, it will be. I'll be making some of my world-famous rum punch. The kids are staying at my mom's all weekend and I'm going to par-tay."

Rett went into the next set feeling as if she'd landed on another planet. Her thigh was hot where it had been up against Cinny's, and Angel's fiery topaz gaze had left her breathless. Cool, calm, professional Rett Jamison was long gone. She wasn't the Rett

Jamison she'd been in high school — oh no — this was a new Rett Jamison who couldn't think past her libido.

The mood in the second half was definitely lighter as they moved away from blues toward jazzy, contemporary numbers. Most were songs she could sing in her sleep, and she was able to put her turmoil aside and enjoy the music. Well, almost. When the performance was over and she had escaped to the back room she wondered how she'd avoid going out front again.

Angel was already there.

Rett found herself so tongue-tied she couldn't even say hello.

"I'm sorry." Angel looked more approachable now. "I should have called. A few days after we saw each other I left for summer vacation, but I could have called first."

"I really did lose your number."

Angel's lips twitched. "I believe you. I was being childish, and sometimes I can't help myself. Anyway, I had the feeling I'd be seeing you here."

"How did you know I was going to come?"

"Cinny told me she had you just about persuaded. We talked because she wanted me to do a guest lecture while I was here."

"So you didn't call me, but you did check up on me because you knew who I was."

Angel colored slightly. "I know it sounds a little homeroom, but Cinny offered the information. I didn't ask."

"Oh, I feel so much better." Rett didn't know quite what to feel aside from the pulsing ache in several increasingly influential parts of her body.

"I hadn't forgotten how good she was at persuading you to do things." Angel waved a hand. "I'm sorry, I didn't mean to say that."

Rett liked Angel's forthrightness, but the remark stung. "Yes, you did."

"You're right. I did." Angel looked at her steadily. "I didn't call because I knew there was a chance she would be in the way again. I don't know who you've become over the years, and I didn't know if she would still —" Angel hesitated. "I just didn't want to go down that road again. What happened over twenty years ago seems like it shouldn't have anything to do with right now, you and me. But it does."

"It does," Rett admitted. "I've been looking forward to and dreading this."

Angel bit her lip. "Then don't talk to me until she's out of your system, one way or another."

"Who says she's in my system —"

"I'm serious, Rett. It took me a long time to stop looking for you in every woman I met, but I did it." She rubbed her face with her hands and then ran her fingers through her hair. "I think it's pretty obvious that you could become very important to me all over again. I'm not going to let that happen if there's no chance of my being happy."

Rett wanted to pounce on Angel and it made following the conversation very hard. "So we're playing by your rules."

"I'm sorry if it seems that way. I just don't want to play by *her* rules." Angel half-smiled, then stared at the floor. "The funny thing is, I'm finding that I like this Cinny a lot. She deserves her own chance."

"I feel like some sort of door prize."

Angel looked up at her then. "Do you really not

know? I think half the girls in our class were half in love with you. There was something about you, there still is —"

"I remember the name-calling, I remember the fights. I don't remember much in the way of love, half or whole."

"That's because you were only looking at her for it. Why do you think some of the boys had it in for you? The finely honed teenage male intuition for competition made you dangerous. But there wasn't a girls' club you couldn't join."

It wasn't quite the way Rett remembered it. "I never thought of myself as popular. I didn't care."

"Oh, God." Angel put her hand on her stomach and Rett could see tears glittering in her eyes. "That it could matter so much after all this time. I've been around the world, endured twelve years of college, yet I think about high school and some things still hurt."

"You're not the only one. A lot of my memories can still hurt me." Far more than Rett was willing to admit, even to herself.

"I wanted to have a name that didn't end in a vowel. I wanted to be wanted, but I wasn't even welcome in the prayer group. I knew my Bible better than just about anyone else, but the unwritten rule was Lutherans only. I was the only Catholic, the only wop, the only one who preferred garlic to mayonnaise. I didn't want to be skipped forward a grade and always be the youngest. I didn't want to be the brain. I'd have given anything to have a fraction of what you had. And I wanted to love you."

Rett could find nothing more to say than, "I'm sorry. But that was then and this is now." She reached out for Angel's hand, but Angel stepped back.

"I can't ... no touching. I'll have no resolve at all."

Rett let her hand fall back to her side. "I can empathize, you know." She knew how awful she had felt, suffering what seemed like rejection after rejection and not being able to be with the one person she wanted. Her lips trembled and she struggled for control. "I'm sorry I didn't recognize you. I thought something was familiar, but —"

"She was in the way. She was so blonde, so tall, so beautiful. How does a short, Italian girl in glasses compete with everybody's dream?"

"You don't have to anymore."

"I don't believe you."

Rett took a step toward her, suddenly aware of the open door and the clatter of people in the hallway beyond. "Leave with me."

Angel shook her head. "I told you, I want you to confront how you feel about her —"

"I don't need to."

"I need you to."

"That's not fair. I'm not the one who has a problem with it."

"I don't believe you. I can't. I have too much at stake." She started to walk by Rett, but Rett grabbed her arm.

"Angel, don't do this." A spike of heat surged up her arm.

Angel was breathing hard. "I may be nearly forty, but my mother won't sleep until I walk in the door. If I call at this hour she'll think someone has died while she kills herself running for the phone."

"That's just an excuse." She was breathing hard, too.

Angel's lips parted and for a heartbeat she leaned

toward Rett, then she shook her head angrily. "Stop that, just stop it." She yanked her arm away. "I want you to deal with her. I'm sorry if that's not rational. You have no idea how badly you hurt me the first time around."

Angel was gone before Rett could stop her. Jesus H. Christ, she thought. She wanted to shout after Angel that it wasn't all her fault and that she was not going to be manipulated into a guiltfest. She hadn't hurt her on purpose, all those years ago.

She was shaking all over, feeling torn in too many directions. She wiped ineffectually at her stage make-up. The sudden entrance of a critic from the *Star Tribune* forced her to find some semblance of calm.

He was complimentary and inquisitive, first asking some simple questions about her background, then working around to her new relationship with Henry Connors. The few interviews she'd done in L.A. helped her sound casual. When he asked exactly what had happened between Henry Connors and Gilda Bransen, she had her answer ready. Naomi's first rule of interviews: Never gossip, it never pays.

"I wouldn't know." She shrugged. "I wasn't there. I just feel like the luckiest singer in the world that Henry remembered me."

Her pretense at calm was tested by Cinny's arrival. She made a "duty calls" gesture but Cinny remained just outside the door. The critic wrapped things up quickly and Rett hoped he wasn't too disappointed that she wouldn't give him some exclusive dish on Gilda Bransen. Cinny entered as he left.

"I just wanted to say a private hello," she said from just inside the doorway.

After a long moment, Rett managed, "So hello."

Cinny was moving toward her slowly. Damn Angel, anyway. *Damn her for making me want her and then leaving me with Cinny.* Inch by inch Rett felt Cinny's approach.

Cinny edged toward the dressing table, glanced in the mirror, then crossed the room to touch a chair. Every step brought her closer to Rett. That slow approach was maddening, and Rett remembered that was how Cinny had always been. Never a beeline for a kiss, always a slow dance, allowing Rett a long look at every inch of her.

Rett was remembering how slowly Cinny had slid across the car seat toward her, how she made it seem not deliberate and yet directly intimate. Just now, with Cinny's back almost to her, she could be the same girl Rett had sweated over, held, tried to love. Cinny idly examined an object on the dressing table again, then turned to face Rett. She was only a foot or so away. She was all breast and all waist and all hip and all leg.

Rett was seventeen again, and wanting to taste Cinny's skin. Or was she all grown up now, and aching for Angel in her arms again? Her head was pounding in keeping with her heart. She put a hand on her stomach. There was still magnetism between her and Cinny, but would the flame be leaping so high if Angel hadn't fanned it?

"Bunny and the carpool went home. I drove by myself because I had a house to show." Cinny swallowed, then added in a low voice, "I'm not in a hurry to get anywhere."

Rett tried to tell herself she knew better. She knew how she felt about Angel and yet her pulse was throbbing at Cinny's nearness. The rule she'd carved in stone about being with women who were in other relationships was melting away.

"I liked this better lower," Cinny whispered. It seemed an eternity as she raised her fingertips to the zipper front Rett had hastily pulled up when she'd gotten back to the stage. A gentle tug moved the zipper down. "I was such a fool."

"Cinny, please." The door's open, she wanted to say. You're married, she should have said. "I think I'm in love with Angel" was something she couldn't say, not with Cinny so near.

"Please what?" Cinny tugged on the zipper again, this time pulling Rett closer to her. "I can say please, too. Please kiss me."

The years were nothing. Cinny had been under her skin all this time and now her skin was on fire. She told herself that she was betraying no one, that she was giving in to what Angel insisted she had to face. She filled her arms with Cinny, felt the press of her breasts.

"What a fool I was," Cinny breathed. "All those times you touched me and I never let myself touch you back." Her fingers came back to the zipper and she pulled it lower still. "I still have dreams about you, Rett Jamison."

There was a flicker of motion at the door and all Rett saw was Angel's back.

7

Rett broke away from Cinny. "Shit."

"What did I do?"

"Nothing." Rett was reeling. What had Angel come back for? To dump more guilt on her or to apologize? To say she hadn't meant Rett to be with anyone but her? She'd acted childishly, Rett reminded herself. She'd let high school come between what could obviously grow into serious feelings for each other. "Just someone at the door."

"This isn't the best place to get reacquainted." Cinny pulled the bandeau from her hair and the thick white-gold curls cascaded around her shoulders. "Where are you staying?"

"It's not very far. Why don't you follow me?" She was perfectly free to ask Cinny to her motel. There were no strings on her. Angel wanted her to deal with the past? Fine.

"Okay." Cinny stepped closer. "One for the road."

Cinny's fingertips nestled in the exposed hollow between Rett's breasts as they kissed hungrily.

"I'm not going to take no for an answer," Rett said hoarsely.

"I'm not teasing," Cinny whispered, even as her fingertips slid to one side to brush Rett's nipple. The shock of her touch separated them and Rett shakily gathered up her things.

The warm night air didn't provide any relief to Rett's fever. As she drove toward her motel she kept an eye on Cinny's headlights and tried desperately not to ask herself what she thought she was doing. There might be no strings on her, but the same was not true of Cinny. There was a husband somewhere.

She held the door open until Cinny passed her, then switched on the light. Cinny put her purse and keys down on the table and turned to face her. "You look apprehensive."

"I don't know what we're playing at."

"I'm not playing. I knew the moment I saw you on stage that this was how it was going to be. It's as if no time has passed at all." Her deliberate approach made Rett's skin prickle. "But I know what I want this time."

Rett could hardly breathe as the zipper came down all the way, then Cinny's hands were under the fabric, on her skin, on her stomach, on her breasts. It was as if Cinny was experiencing the sensation of touch for the first time. She pushed the jumpsuit off Rett's shoulders and Rett gave in to the wave of desire and the vertigo that accompanied it. She dropped into the side chair next to the table.

"Good idea. Let me do this," Cinny whispered. She bent over Rett to tug the jumpsuit down, then knelt. "There's no substitute for this." Her tongue trailed lightly from Rett's belly button to her throat.

Rett's arms were tangled in her clothes, but she could still twine her fingers into Cinny's hair, holding Cinny to her breasts while she gasped for breath. Alarm bells were ringing. She should stop this before it was too late. It was already too late. She was trying to form the words, but her body was screaming at her to give in.

Cinny's lips were at her throat. Give in, the throb between her legs commanded. Her mouth was thirsty for the taste of Cinny's lips. Her breasts ached to be stroked and teased. Cinny's every move was un-raveling her. She was dizzy with a primal lust that made her head pound and legs open.

There wasn't enough air in the room. Rett found what little voice she had left. She formed the words "please fuck me" in her head but she heard her voice saying, "Stop. I can't."

Cinny's tongue trailed along Rett's jaw. "You don't mean that."

"I do." Rett was panting. "I mean it. Please stop."

Cinny looked stunned as she sat back on her haunches. "Is this some sort of payback? Not that I don't deserve it."

Rett shrugged back into her jumpsuit. A large part of her couldn't believe that she was trying to be less naked. "No — I'm sorry. I shouldn't have invited you back here. I have a rule. I've never broken it. You're married and I am not going to be the other woman."

Cinny looked as if Rett had slapped her. She swallowed hard. "You're serious, aren't you?"

"Very. I'm not going to lie and say I don't think I'm being a fool." She fumbled with the zipper and had no luck. "You're married and I think I'm —" She stopped. How to explain about Angel? They weren't even dating. They didn't even have an arrangement to see each other again. Angel had practically ordered Rett to get into bed with Cinny. It was inexplicable that she felt as if she was cheating on Angel. So instead of "I think I'm in love with Angel" she said, "I think I'm going to regret this."

Cinny slowly got to her feet. She leaned over Rett in the chair and said in a low voice, "I'd like to try to change your mind."

Rett shook her head. "It won't work. I swore a long time ago that I would not make my mother's mistakes."

Cinny straightened and Rett was dizzy all over again at the lush curves outlined by the clinging blouse. "You're hardly your mother, Rett."

"I don't want to be her or anything like her. You're in a relationship, a marriage. And that means no."

Cinny's voice trembled with tears. "I like Sam a lot. He's — In another world he'd be perfect for me. But I've never stopped wanting . . . women. I've only been married for four years. I dated women almost exclusively for a long, long time, but nobody since I got married."

"By that you mean you dated men just enough

over the years to pass for straight?" Lord, Rett thought, how tawdry was this scene? Cinny was just getting her lesbian sex fix before she ran back to her heterosexual world.

Cinny's eyes flashed. "You have no right to judge me. You have no idea how hard it is."

"I'm not going to be the woman who tides you over for a few more years."

"That is so unfair. You have no idea what it's like to be me."

"You're right, I don't." Rett struggled up from the chair, pulled up the zipper and stepped past Cinny to the air conditioner. She found the On switch and basked in the rush of icy air.

"I'm perfect."

Rett turned to look at Cinny. "I won't argue with that."

"I mean it, Rett. I'm perfect. I'm the all-American girl. Perfect tits, perfect ass, perfect nose. Homecoming queen, self-made businesswoman, always ready to work for charities. I even read books to kids at the library."

"Sounds like a good life." But part of it was a lie, she wanted to say.

"Sometimes I hate it so much I think about cutting my face open." Cinny was shaking. "I'm trapped in this perfect body, in this perfect little world, and you think I can just announce to the world that I'm a lesbian? That I would have a hope of going on with the life I've built? Who would buy real estate from me? I could have any man I wanted and so I must be really, really sick to want women instead. Who's going to let me be around their kids? I'd be a pariah. You, you could get away with it. You're the sexy outlaw everyone wants to screw. You and Angel — you get to be whatever you want, but I have to be fucking perfect!"

Rett was stunned at Cinny's vehemence. "You could move. You could start over."

"Leave my parents and my brothers and all my nieces and nephews? I've already disappointed them enough by not having kids. I have an obligation to the gene pool." She smoothed her blouse with shaking fingers. "There was a moment when I was chosen to be freshman homecoming queen — I wanted to say no. I knew even then that it was a trap. I knew that it meant I'd be on the cheerleading squad and everyone would expect me to date football players, and I didn't want to ride down Main Street on a goddamned tank. I was only sixteen. How was I suppose to know what I was agreeing to was everyone else's expectations for the rest of my life? How was I suppose to know it meant having to be perfect forever?"

Rett said softly, "I tried to get you out of the trap."

"You made me realize I was caught in it for life."

Tears spilled down Cinny's cheeks and Rett wanted to hold her. A hug — no, it would lead to kisses and kisses to frustration. She was not going down that road again and she didn't want to take Cinny down that road either. "It's never too late."

"I thought if I made things right with you I'd be able to let go of my regrets. I do love Sam in a way. He's a good husband. But when I'm with him I'm not. It's not fair to him."

"Why did you get married, then?"

Cinny dashed away tears. "There was someone, a woman. She wanted to live together. She wanted me to move to St. Paul and be a couple. Her church would have married us. I couldn't — I couldn't do it."

"Just like you couldn't come with me when I left?"

Cinny's tormented expression was tinged with nostalgia. "I'd forgotten you'd asked. I should have run then. It's too late now." She took a deep, shuddering breath. "It was the hardest thing I've ever done. I treated her so badly. I gave her up and married Sam. A girl's wedding is supposed to be the best day of her life. I had to take Valium to get through it. I can't just come out to everyone now that I've involved Sam in my life. I would mean I did it all for nothing."

Rett felt unexpectedly sad. First Angel and now Cinny was making her realize that high school hadn't been easy for any of them, and she had been too centered on her own misery to notice. "I'm sorry I seemed to judge you." She didn't condemn Henry for staying in the closet. She accepted that he understood better than she did the harsh realities he would face. Why couldn't she accept that Cinny knew her own realities just as well?

Cinny swayed slightly. "I can't tell you how many times I've wished with all my heart that I didn't feel this way."

"As far as I know, wishes and prayers don't make a difference. I am what I am." She gave Cinny a gentle smile. "You can learn to live beyond your code, you know."

"What the hell does that mean?"

"You can be more than you believe you can. Now that I think about it, I've only become truly comfortable with who I am and who I can be in the last few months. I finally realized that what I'd taken for the gospel was written by other people." Had she been better off, she wondered, having never questioned her sexuality, but instead having questioned her value as a singer and as a human being?

"I have to go." Cinny picked up her things, then turned back for a long look. "Please don't shut me out. The reunion has made me think — has made me realize . . . well. I have to go."

Rett was still searching for something meaningful to say when Cinny closed the door behind her.

Her body ached and nothing she did helped. She took a cool shower and found herself writhing against the pillows, her mind steeped in sex and her body as frustrated as it had ever been. Cinny's breasts, her mouth . . . no, Angel's mouth. Angel's legs around her, Angel begging please, Angel inside her.

She tossed and turned, but sleep eluded her. Sounds of some sort of blissful union in the next room made her reach for the TV's remote control.

It was almost noon when Rett opened her eyes. She'd fallen asleep around dawn, bleary from info-mercials and televangelists who hawked and preached the same formula for happiness — part with your money. She staggered through her shower feeling weak with hunger and strung out on emotion. With another night's performance at the Top Hat Club ahead, Rett decided she would not drive out to Woton today to see the old sites and perhaps her mother. Definitely not her mother — she could not cope with that today.

Instead, she navigated the drive-thru at the nearest

Mickey D's to stave off her grumbling stomach, then visited all the places she used to go when she'd lived in Minneapolis. If her own evening had been free she'd have gone to the Guthrie Theater, which was famous in the region for its repertory performances. Instead, she took the short drive to the Eloise Butler Sanctuary. When she'd been a starving artist, the free admission to the expanse of wildflowers and birds in the middle of endless city and suburb had been a blessing. Much to her surprise, she had missed the open skies and rolling hills and farmlands of Woton, and the sanctuary had helped conquer the homesickness.

Little had changed. Late-summer wildflowers carpeted sunny spots, while vibrant lady's slippers still bloomed in cooler, shady groves. Though the air was smoggier than she remembered, it was still bluer than anything she'd seen in L.A. in a long time. Even the humidity didn't seem as unbearable today. She put Angel and Cinny out of her mind and stared up through the green branches at the sky. She felt thoroughly refreshed after an hour, then headed for her next favorite place, the Sculpture Garden. From there she walked across Whitney Footbridge into Loring Park, then past the Orchestra Hall where she had once been lucky enough to get SRO tickets to hear Leonard Bernstein conduct.

Walking made her hungry again, so she treated herself to an early dinner of freshly caught lake trout. The long walk back to the car helped her digest the meal so that she would be singing on an empty stomach. Like many singers, she found it easier to maintain her breathing that way. She was at the club by eight-thirty, invigorated and ready to cope if Angel or Cinny showed up again. She could admit that she would be much happier if neither did. She felt caught between extremes she didn't fully understand and even the tiniest measure of control over the situation was nowhere to be found. The only place she was fully in control these days was on the stage.

The owner gleefully waved a glowing review in front of her — she'd forgotten to look for one. She told him to contact Naomi if he wanted her to do another two nights two weeks from now. She was willing to change her plane ticket home if he and Naomi came to an agreement. When he toddled away Rett quickly called Naomi at home.

"I should think he'd be glad to have you two more nights," Naomi said. "He got you at bargain-basement prices."

"Don't up the price too much — the margin has to be pretty thin. But they're turning people away out front and I'm guessing he's over the fire law maximum seating by twenty-five percent."

"So you're okay with next weekend?"

"No, it can't be next weekend. The one after that." She was having second thoughts. Another entire week in Minneapolis? What would she do with herself? "Next weekend is the big dance and I think I'm going to a slumber party. So it would have to be the weekend after that."

"How horrible for you." Rett knew Naomi was rolling her eyes. "How are you holding on?"

"I'm doing very well," Rett assured her. It wasn't that big of a lie. "Don't worry about me, okay?"

"Manager's prerogative. By the way, I settled with Trish. It was somewhat more than we owed her, but she was threatening to get a lawyer. She's signed a complete waiver of any claim on your future, which is what I wanted. The last thing we needed was her claiming some role in the Henry Connors deal."

"That's a relief, then. Out of my life for good."

"And I'd have paid more than I did. So knock 'em dead, sweets. I'll make you a good deal."

The band members greeted her enthusiastically and Rett went onstage to a greeting of anticipatory applause. There was no sign of anyone she knew and she slipped into the first song with a wave of relief.

The next morning she slept late again, but finally woke up refreshed. If she dawdled over Sunday brunch, she would be late enough for the picnic to have no time for driving by old haunts, or even her old home. She knew she was procrastinating about seeing her mother, but it was a long week ahead. There would be time some other day. No one said she had to get all the pain over with all at once. Angel and Cinny would surely both be at the picnic, which meant it was no picnic for Rett.

She managed to tune in the university channel on the feeble rental car radio and lucked into a worldbeat music program. She cranked up Jai Uttal as loud as the tinny speakers could stand. State Route 12 had two more lanes than she remembered, and she was in Litchfield before she knew it. St. Cloud — the real Lake Wobegon — was just to the north. The drive had seemed much longer way back when, and the Twin Cities had always been a faraway place visited are rare occasions. Now it seemed no longer a drive than what many Angelinos commuted every day.

147

There were tract homes clustered around the highway, but as she got closer to Greenleaf and Cedar Mills the rolling hills and farms seemed just the same. The grain silos and water towers bearing the names of their towns seemed as permanent a part of the landscape as the lakes and clusters of shady pines. The sameness made her feel better.

The back road into Woton was only wide enough to allow two small cars to pass. It would have been faster to go the front way from Strout, but not nearly as nostalgic. Here and there were short dirt roads where enterprising lovebirds could park out of sight. Rett knew several of them well — each one was a site where Cinny had said yes, then said no.

She could let it go now. Cinny had had conflicts she had never guessed at. She might not have made Cinny's choices, but she could understand that Cinny felt as if she had no choices at all. It was enough that they had both survived when it seemed that today so many kids like them did not.

She shook off that depressing thought as she turned onto Main Street, not surprised to find that almost nothing had changed. The main intersection of town was still a stop sign. The business district extended one block in all directions, then gave way to farms and the occasional grouping of houses. There were a couple of new names on the stores, and the Five and Dime looked like it had turned into a more upscale toy emporium. In ten minutes she knew the whole town again, but recognized no one.

The picnic at the park next to Mill Lake was already underway, but Rett doubled back through town in the opposite direction. Left on South Road, right on Road 167. Third house on the right. The last house of the group, separated from the others by a narrow creek.

She coasted to a halt and stared at the half-dead rosebushes and scraggly geraniums. The same broken outdoor chairs still rusted on what passed for a front lawn. A dinged and dented Grand Prix dripped oil in the driveway.

In a sudden panic she slammed the gearshift into reverse and backed hurriedly out of the dead-end road. So much for thinking she was ready. Nothing about the house had changed. The woman inside would not have changed either.

It was a relief to leave the panic and the sticky air of the car for the cool, deep shade of the Norway red pines surrounding the picnic area. A handmade banner read, "Welcome Woton High Grads!"

She saw Cinny before Cinny saw her. She had expected more pink, and possibly Capri pants or something equally feminine, but Cinny was wearing denim shorts and a tight black Dixie Chicks T-shirt.

When Cinny did see her, she hurried over with a hug and a my-name-is sticker. "I decided I hate pink," she whispered in Rett's ear. She slapped the sticker on Rett's chest. "Not that anyone will have forgotten you. Our class is that way." She pointed and then hurried off to greet someone Rett recognized as having been one or two years ahead of her.

There were at least twenty families in the group under their class banner, which meant just about a hundred percent turnout. Central grills were sizzling with hot dogs and burgers. Kids were dashing around with grilled corn on the cob on sticks. Her mouth watered — it had been a long time since she'd had right-off-the-stalk sweet corn. Underneath the aroma of barbecues was the ubiquitous tang of bug repellant. Summer in Minnesota. It wasn't as bad as she had thought it would be.

She abruptly realized she was probably the only person who had come alone. Everyone else had families to sit with. She was going to have to linger hopefully here and there until someone took her in. Gads — it *was* just like high school all over again.

"Hey, Rett's here," someone hollered.

She turned to see someone who had to be Tom Stoddard rushing toward her. Tom had been a member of their singing group, and was part of her small collection of happy memories.

His enthusiastic hug surprised her. "It's great to see you."

"It's nice to see you, too, Tom."

"Come say hello to Bunny again."

Bunny was married to Tom. Well, that made sense. So she was Bunny Stoddard now. They'd been even-keeled, serious steadies all through high school. Three teenagers milled about getting soda and defying their mother's edicts against more Rice Krispie treats.

"I'm glad you made it," Bunny said. "I told Tom he missed an incredible performance on Friday."

"She wouldn't let me come along." Tom settled onto the picnic table bench and opened the cooler at his feet. "Want a beer?"

"Actually, I'll take a soda for now. Anything diet."

"Listen to you, you always were a stick."

Rett popped open the diet Fresca, a soda she hadn't had in ages. She prodded her abdomen. "Forty means more here. I drink diet to make room for cheesecake."

"I hear that," Bunny said. "So Rett, what have

you been doing with yourself all these years? I was hoping you'd be back for one of the earlier reunions or home to see your mom and we could catch up."

Rett ignored the comment about her mother. "I lived in the Twin Cities for several years, until I got out of U of M. My degree was in music, surprise, surprise. But mostly I sang with bands and in clubs — anyone who would pay me. After I graduated I did what every aspiring artist does. New York."

Bunny's eyes were bright with curiosity. "Is that where you got your big break?"

"Not a chance. I didn't last three months." She sipped her Fresca, then nibbled on the Chex mix Tom proffered. "The cost-of-living was astronomical, even sharing a shoebox with two other girls. I lived on peanuts and day-old doughnuts and realized pretty quickly that I'd use up every penny I'd saved long before anyone even noticed me. Clubs were glutted with people who had been in theater productions, and they got any and all the singing gigs that ever opened up. I had no agent, no contacts at all. So I left before I got desperate." She'd seen what some of the young women her age had resorted to in order to survive, and she'd decided she'd go home to her mother before she'd sell herself or drugs.

"Where to? Here, have some potato salad — my favorite recipe."

The salad was like a slice of the past. Rett had forgotten how tasty basic, ordinary potato salad was. No curry, no fancy mustard sauce. Mayo and celery salt — what could be better? "Detroit. It was much, much cheaper to live there, and bartending jobs in clubs where I hoped one day to sing were actually pretty easy to come by. The music scene in Detroit is still thriving, even jazz, which everyone says is dead. They finally let me sing to shut me up and I worked steadily after that. After a couple of years I was comfortable. Regular singing dates, a steady and not-too-draining bartending job. Good tips, but I think the cigarette smoke probably took ten years off my voice."

"But you live in L.A. now. I think that's what Cinny said." Bunny hooked a runaway Frisbee with her foot and tossed it back to one of her sons.

"When I did get an agent she convinced me it was a better place to be, and she was right. No more bartending. I got a lot of voice-overs, commercial work —"

"Anything I'd know?"

"Probably not — local companies mostly." She cleared her throat and sang cheerfully, " 'Bea is choosy so you don't have to be!' "

Bunny laughed. "Oh that's funny. I never thought about who would be hired to sing just one line." She swatted a hand coming up from under the table toward the Rice Krispie treats without even looking in that direction. "So you tour all over now? What's the most interesting place you've ever been?"

Rett thought about it for a moment. "Denmark, I think. Old and classic and yet very modern." If Rett stopped to think about some of the women she'd known in Denmark she would blush. She rushed on. "I was touring with a jazz band that would have made it big if they hadn't had creative differences." She grinned. "That's a euphemism for the fact that everyone finally got on everyone else's nerves to the point of near-homicide. I was with that band for I think two years, and it ended up coming to nothing. Well, I learned a lot. But now I'm going to be touring with the Henry Connors Orchestra, and Henry goes all over the world. I think Hong Kong may be on next year's itinerary. I'm very excited."

"Let me meet you in some exotic city somewhere. I'm dying to get off this continent."

"Can I come along?" Tom's plaintive question made Bunny wrinkle her nose fondly.

"I s'pose."

Someone touched Rett's shoulder then sat down next to her. "Bet you don't remember me." The fair-skinned redhead covered her name badge with her hand.

"That's not fair." Rett protested. Her brain clicked and she came up with a name. "Natalie Gifford."

"Hey, you do remember. I'm flattered."

"You were one of the ROTC geeks." Rett grinned to make sure Natalie knew she was teasing.

"That's me. I just finished my twenty with the Army." Rett's gaydar was beeping madly, but she put it down to the abundance of taut muscles framed by Natalie's khaki tank top. The matching utilitarian shorts had to be Army issue, and she was willing to bet there were boxers under those shorts. "Can I drag you away from Bunny? Come say hi to my folks — they say they remember you vividly."

Rett let herself be carried off, amazed that Natalie's parents did indeed remember the songs she had performed in the senior class talent show. From there she chatted with several people she dimly remembered; then Mary, who had been a Wiffenpoof with Rett, was introducing her to her husband and pointing out her kids. A lot of people had kids who were too old to be coerced into attending their parent's stuffy reunion. One classmate was a grandmother. That information silenced Rett for a full minute.

Johnny Woodstrom stopped long enough to say that some of the old Wiffenpoofs were going to be brushing up some vocals at the far end of the trees for an impromptu concert, if Rett wanted to join them. Wayne Igorson had brought his guitar.

"I'd love to," Rett answered. "I was hoping we would get together. Those were really great times."

"I think you'll be surprised by how much we've all kept in practice. Wayne plays with the symphony sometimes. Of course, you're the only one who makes a living at it."

"It's nice work if you can get it. I'll be there — in an hour?" Johnny confirmed that and headed back to his family. Races and games were getting underway. Rett was not surprised when Natalie won the potato-sack race by a considerable margin. She gravitated back to Natalie's parents, who were very welcoming. Natalie's mother appeared to have the inside scoop on just about everyone. As Rett looked around she spotted the men who had once been the boys who'd taunted and teased her. Angel was right — it had always been some of the boys who'd had it in for her.

Rett provided the requisite details about her own past to add to Mrs. Gifford's storehouse. In return she learned tidbits of small-town gossip. Adam Ericson had done something mysterious and not entirely successful about his receding hairline. Nate and Jenny Hughes had been married to other people before realizing they'd always loved each other. Cinny Keilor had waited a very long time before settling down with Sam

Johnson, who had moved into town as a new manager at the Green Giant plant.

Rett looked when Mrs. Gifford pointed out Sam. He appeared to be nice enough. It was strange to watch him, though, and to know so much more about his wife than he might ever understand.

". . . won the National Science Award — her family's along that way — with the next class. I think they could have sat in three of the five class areas, what with her two brothers graduating just ahead of her and all."

"Who?" Rett now remembered hearing Cinny mention something about the National Science Award, too, but she'd missed it.

"Angelica Martinetta. That's *Doctor* Angelica Martinetta. She won it just last year — it was in the announcement. I've never been much of one for science talks, but I think I'll go to that thing Cinny arranged. Natalie showed it to me in the announcement materials. All the way into St. Cloud to the university extension there, but it *is* about women's types of cancers. At my age I should take an interest."

Angel's name had been in the announcement materials? Her identity had been sitting in Rett's mailbox and the bottom of her suitcase for at least three weeks? She'd only looked long enough to find the name of the motel, fill out the obligatory questionnaire about what she'd done since high school and write a check for the various events.

Thank you, Universe, thank you so bloody fucking much.

Rett could now see Angel in the midst of a large and boisterous family group. She remembered that Angel had had at least two older brothers who graduated in the two years ahead of them, and a younger sister who went to high school the year after they left. The Martinettas were having quite a family reunion, then.

I'm a moron.

"She put in her bio that she spends all day staring into microscopes, but there's plenty more than that to it, doncha think?"

It was hard to associate the fiery Angel with a career that required such patience, but then again, she had spoken of her work with a great deal of passion.

"I would think," she echoed lamely.

Angel caught her staring. All the animation left her face and Rett found herself mouthing, "I'm sorry." She was sorry about Cinny, sorry about the past. She wanted to move on.

Angel pressed her lips together, then she was distracted by a family member. She did not look in Rett's direction for the entire time Rett kept glancing her way.

The relentless game organizers were beating the crowd for participants in a saucer-stacking contest, and Rett knew it wouldn't be long until they found her with no other demands as an excuse. She ducked into the trees to walk down to the lake.

Pines shaded the grassy shore and reflected sunlight dazzled Rett's eyes. She kicked off her sandals and carried them as she waded into the cool water.

The murky sand caressed her feet. She let her toes sink in and swatted her first mosquito. Summer — it had been a long, long time since she'd felt summer like this. The buzz of insects, the slight headache from the brilliant sunshine, the certainty that she'd forgotten to put sunscreen on one earlobe — summer. She closed her eyes and her mind opened a memory of a day she had never willingly recalled before.

She had to be nine. They'd spread a picnic on a shore very much like this one — she wasn't sure which lake. It was her first picnic. Bruce had insisted. He'd been living with her mother for a couple of months and was the nicest man Rett had ever met.

"Sing something for us," he'd said.

Rett had been standing in the water, just as she was now, and she'd opened her arms to the sun and sung "Good Morning, Starshine" from the musical *Hair*. She'd heard a woman sing it on the *Mike Douglas Show* and she'd been practicing it on her own.

It was the kind of day when the expanse of lake was the perfect orchestra pit and Canada only the first balcony. When she finished she'd turned, flushed with success, to face Bruce and her mother.

Bruce applauded enthusiastically. "That was wonder —"

"Christ, Rett, you'd wake the dead," her mother snapped. "Everyone is staring. You're getting all wet. Don't think you can sit down on this blanket until you're dry."

People nearby *were* staring, and she'd blushed beet-red. Her memory told her they were smiling, but what lingered was her guilt for embarrassing her mother. Had that been the moment her spirit first chilled? She had certainly never sung in public that way again, not until she'd joined the choir and been encouraged by Mr. Barnwell, the music teacher.

Bruce hadn't lasted long. He'd been too nice.

" 'The earth says hello,' " she sang softly.

A quiet ripple in the water told her someone had

joined her. Cinny's sandals dangled from her fingers, too.

"A penny," she said.

"Just thinking about the past." Rett met Cinny's gaze as she found a wistful smile. "There's nothing like summer here."

Cinny swatted a mosquito. "Right now it's winter in Australia. That just fascinates me. That I could get on a plane and tomorrow walk into a snowstorm."

Rett went back to studying the pattern of light on the water. "Life can be like that without getting on a plane. I was standing here thinking about how warm and beautiful summer was when I remembered something cold."

"Not about me, I hope."

"No, nothing to do with you."

"How unflattering."

Rett glanced at Cinny again. Cinny had a teasing air, but her eyes were too serious. "I hope you're just joking."

"I wish I was."

"Cinny —"

Cinny's lips had a bitter twist. "I know. You were very plain. I've thought about little else since Friday night. I can't even look at Sam. I can't let him touch me."

"Cinny —"

"That's just the God's honest truth. I wish it weren't, damn it all."

"You don't have to be honest with me."

"You want me to lie to you?"

"No! I mean, I'm not the one who matters. You need to be honest with yourself."

Cinny's voice was choked, but with what emotion Rett couldn't discern. "I thought I was. For the past twenty-odd years I've been honest. I want women and I don't want the stigma of being a lesbian. Maybe that's not politically correct, but that's how I've always felt."

Rett didn't want to have this conversation again. What did Cinny expect her to say? "I'm not going to deny there's a stigma. It's hard enough to handle without generating homophobia from your own fears."

"This isn't all in my head!"

"Don't you think I know that? I was the one they called lesbo, remember? I just found a way to stare them down. A way to say, 'So what.' Jerry Knudsen called me that and tried to feel me up. I kneed him in the nuts so hard his whole family felt it. I don't know where I found the strength for it when everything else they called me hurt so much." The memory of Jerry Knudsen gasping for breath on the ground turned her frown into a smile. Thereafter he'd stuck with calling her names from a safe distance.

Cinny drew in a long, shaky breath. "I don't know what's happening to me. I was okay until I saw you. I was managing. I want you so much I can't think," she whispered. "I don't know what I'm going to do."

Rett knew that ache, and part of her wanted to comfort Cinny, but she knew it would be unwise to touch her. She had thought on the way to the reunion that she'd be happy if Cinny got just the tiniest taste of her own high-school medicine, but now it didn't please her at all. "I'm sorry, really." She could think of nothing else to say.

"So am I." Cinny waded back to shore and ran

over the grass, pausing in the trees to glance back briefly before slipping on her sandals to return to the picnic.

Poor Cinny, Rett thought. How do you take the cheerleader out of the all-American girl? She had not considered that Cinny had felt the weight of other people's hopes and expectations and had never learned to put them in the perspective of her own happiness. Rett wished that she could make it easier, somehow, but only Cinny could decide what to do with the choices she'd made.

She waded along the shore for a few minutes, stopping to hold one foot after the other out of the water to feel the sand drip off. Mosquitoes only plagued her in the deepest shade, so she waded out to the sunshine. It took her a few minutes to realize that someone on the shore was keeping pace with her.

From the way her body tightened and her heart pounded, she knew who it was before she fully registered the small, dark-haired woman. They stared at each other over the strip of water separating them.

"Mind if I walk with you?" Angel balanced like a flamingo to unstrap first one sandal, then the other. She waded into the water and it seemed to Rett that the water glowed where it was lucky enough to embrace Angel's calves.

"Not at all," she said in a belated squawk.

They waded along the shore for several minutes, then Angel finally said, "I have a lot of flaws."

Rett hadn't known what to expect but it certainly hadn't been that. "I don't think I should agree or disagree."

"Wise." Angel stepped closer to shore to avoid a submerged branch. "For one thing, I'm a neat freak —

unbelievably anal retentive. Felix Unger could take lessons from me."

"That's probably why you're so successful in your career."

"Yeah, well, I won't argue with that. I hate things that don't make sense and I'll pick at them until they do. I like things tidy." Angel stopped walking and Rett turned toward her. She wanted to step over the branch and get close enough to smell Angel's hair and study the color of her eyes. "I keep thinking that life can be neat and clean."

"It's not, usually. There's that old saying about doors closing so other ones can open, but usually the doors open before the others are closed." Rett had no idea where this philosophical discussion might be leading.

"I'm sorry. I'm sorry I made you pick her or me. It's not for me to force you to do anything."

"You were right, though. I did have to know what I'd do if she — you know." Rett was suddenly embarrassed, recalling the kiss that Angel had witnessed.

The words seemed to burst out of Angel. "I think we should slow down."

"Slow what down?" Rett raised her arms in appeal. "Date less? Oh wait, we've never had a date, so we can't do that. Besides —"

"You know what I mean."

"Besides," Rett continued, "nothing happened between Cinny and me. I mean, only a little bit happened." She felt her cheeks reddening again. "I mean I said no."

Angel blinked. "Why am I having a hard time believing that?"

Damn her, anyway, Rett thought. "That's the

second time you've thought I'm lying to you. I don't know why you would think that —"

"Because I don't know you —"

"Well, this slowing down thing is certainly going to change that."

"You don't have to shout!"

"What am I supposed to do? She's a married woman and I don't do that. What I felt for her, the leftover feelings, weren't so strong that I forgot who I was. I'm not my mother and I won't make her mistakes!"

Angel had obviously been going to retort something, but she closed her mouth and stared at Rett for a moment. "I didn't mean to imply that."

"I've never lied to you," Rett said more quietly. She muttered, "The damned napkin fell in the gutter."

Angel's face crumpled into a grin. "Okay, I believe you."

They walked again, this time close enough to hold hands if they'd tried. The water was over Angel's knees in places.

"Your mother didn't come today?"

"She doesn't know I'm here," Rett admitted.

"Oh." Angel was obviously surprised but was trying to sound nonjudgmental.

"In all these years, I've never been back to see her."

"I — I can't even imagine . . . I mean, I knew from little things you said that you didn't get along with her, but . . ."

"Twenty-three years of silence seems a bit extreme?" Rett knew how it looked. It did seem extreme. "We've exchanged Christmas cards every year. She's never asked me to visit. I've never suggested it, either. First it was five years, then another five. I never missed her. I never had any feeling that she missed me."

Angel didn't ask, but the question trembled around them.

Rett answered it anyway. "I thought I didn't come back because we never had any kind of mother-daughter love and I didn't need to have anything to do with her."

"What do you think now?"

Rett stopped walking and turned to look over the lake. She didn't want Angel to see the tremor in her lips. "I'm frightened. I'm not sure why. I've been frightened all along and yet I thought I was fine. But the closer I come to seeing her the more terrified I feel."

"What do you think is going to happen?" Angel's tone was soothing but concerned.

"I think that I told myself she never loved me and I still don't really believe it. I'm afraid I'll find out for sure that she never did love me. That was why she treated me the way she did."

"How was that?"

She liked that Angel didn't automatically protest that *of course* her mother had loved her. The only time she'd tried to tell someone about it her confidant had immediately assumed that maternal love conquered all. She risked a glance over her shoulder. "Are you playing therapist?"

"I'm not very good at it. I'm too opinionated to keep my mouth shut. But if you don't want to tell me, I won't ask again. Really."

"It's okay." She fixed her gaze on the distant shore, counting the cabins that lined the waterfront to distract her mind from the throat-choking tears that still threatened. "It could have been worse."

"She didn't — hurt you, did she?"

"Not physically," Rett said quickly. "Unless you can call neglect harm. As soon as I could open a can I made my own meals. I washed my own clothes, changed the sheets on my own bed — that is, after I realized that people did such things on a regular basis. But that wasn't — that only hurts a little. It did teach me to do for myself. It's just that from the day I was born she did everything she could to remind me I was nothing, and that the world would never let me be more than nothing, that I was her daughter and I'd end up just like her."

"None of that has come true."

She couldn't hold the tears back any longer, and she dashed them from her eyes. "Damn." Her voice would be tight and high when she got together with the Wiffenpoofs. She forced herself to take two deep breaths, exhaling slowly. "It didn't have to come true. For a lot of years I just accepted what life offered. I didn't think I deserved more. I lost a lot of time. I didn't think seeing her mattered, and it's scary to realize that it does. I thought I had gotten over feeling like a failure."

"I never realized. I'm sorry."

Rett suddenly couldn't take Angel's sympathy. It wasn't what she wanted from Angel. "The Wiffenpoofs are going to do a little rehearsing — they've probably already started." She turned back the way they'd come, surprised to see that it was so far to the trees.

"It's quicker on the path," Angel said. She sloshed to shore and headed for a barely discernible footpath into the pines.

Rett followed slowly, stopping to slip into her sandals once they reached the edge of the grass. Angel was some distance ahead of her, but she stopped when she realized Rett wasn't following.

"About this slowing-down thing," Rett said with most of her composure returned. "What exactly does that mean?"

Angel watched Rett's approach and bit her lower lip. "This is a difficult week. We're not ourselves. I don't think we should base anything on this week. I was wrong to try to put strings on you. You shouldn't feel —"

"What if I like those strings?"

Angel stared at her feet and shook her head. "I just don't think we can — a lot can happen."

"Is there someone else?"

"No," she said quickly. "No, but —"

"Then what?"

Angel backed up a step. "You'll kiss me and it'll be perfect, that's what."

"That's a problem?" Rett thirsted for kisses now.

"Yes, yes it is." Angel's arms were dusted with gooseflesh.

"You're going to have to share your hypothesis, Doctor Martinetta, because I'm confused by that statement." Rett made up the distance Angel had backed away.

"Stop it," she said, stepping back again.

"Stop what?" Rett kept closing the distance between them.

"Don't tease me."

"I don't exactly have teasing on my mind."

"I want to know the real Rett Jamison."

Rett patted her stomach. "This is she."

"Not a holiday Rett Jamison." Angel's backward steps were halted by a tree.

"There is no such character. Christ, Angel, I don't know what you expect to see. If you mean you want to wait until we're back in L.A. and we can do the dating thing and decide if we can stand each other's company outside of bed, then okay, we'll wait."

"That's what I mean." Angel was breathless. "I think it would be — wiser. I'm thinking too much about — about the girl I loved in high school. I want to get to know you as a grownup."

"Then we'll wait," Rett said softly. "But don't think I'm going to make it easy on you." She stood close enough to Angel to smell her hair. It was just like she remembered.

"Stop that." Angel cupped Rett's jaw and drew her head down. "Just stop it."

Even though Rett was prepared for the electric sensation of Angel's lips on hers, it still surprised her. The flash of it raised hair on the back of her neck, and butterflies flitted in her stomach and places to the south. She pressed Angel against the tree and they kissed until Rett's knees were weak and she felt deliciously dizzy.

"Is that how you wanted me to stop it?"

"Exactly how," Angel breathed. Her tongue brushed Rett's lower lip, then they were falling into each other again. Dappled water glittered behind Rett's closed lids; her head spun as if she'd been in the sun too long. She clung to Angel with a gasp, thrilling to the heat of Angel's fingers under her thin blouse.

A burst of guitar music not far away startled them apart. Rett swayed and Angel caught her hand to steady her.

"I like slowing down," Rett managed to say. "We'll definitely have to wait for anything else until we get back to L.A., then," she teased. She drew Angel's fingertips to her lips.

"Yes, we'll wait." Angel untangled her fingers and slipped out from between Rett and the tree. She strode somewhat unsteadily toward the picnic.

Rett stared after her in a sort of shock. Every step stretched the electric tendrils between them ever tauter until Rett's skin prickled. Angel couldn't be serious.

The guitar was playing the opening to "Four Strong Winds." The Wiffenpoofs were expecting her to sing alto.

8

Messenger ribonucleic acid (mRNA) indirectly transmits instructions for protein coding of genes after transcription between the nucleus and cellular cytoplasm. Messenger RNA can also be used to sythensize cDNA to aid the chromosome/autosome map. This information formed the first level of inquiry into chromosomal examination by light microscope to accomplish karyotype (JNCI Vol 89).The cDNA map provides further banding refinement with specific amplified DNA fragments . . .

Rett sat back in the library chair and tried to shake off the chill in her stomach.

She'd woken up feeling so good, too. After the Wiffenpoofs' impromptu concert she'd been invited to join the Martinetta clan for dinner and conversation.

"Angel told us she had run into you in L.A.," Angel's brother had said after he'd reminded Rett who he was.

"At a charity event," Rett had replied vaguely. She didn't know how much Angel had told her family and didn't want to put a foot wrong by saying, "At a lesbian bar."

"Mama wondered if you would be interested in strawberry shortcake with all the trimmings."

"You betcha," Rett said. "Is my memory correct? Are both you and your brother named Tony?"

"You got it — my big brother is Antony Michael, but we call him Big Tony and I'm Antony Carmine, which is also my father's name. That's where the Tony Junior comes from. But please, call me T.J. Everyone does."

Everyone had to. Nicknames abounded as some sort of family naming tradition involving grandmother and grandfather names made given names very confusing when introductions were made. Rett's near-perfect recall only worked when she got something fixed in her mind and she lost count of the Antonys, Angelicas and Carmellas. Not all of the grandchildren were present, either. The Martinetta exuberance was a little overwhelming, but she could certainly get used to it.

She had found herself sitting next to Angel and facing a plate of homemade shortcake with a heap of fresh strawberries and cream. "Angelica says that you met again in Los Angeles," Mrs. Martinetta commented. She was beaming at Rett with unnerving approval.

"A few months ago. The horrid truth is that I didn't recognize her."

"Out of context people can look different." Carmella, the youngest of the five siblings, was dishing out strawberries to the line of teenagers. "I don't think I'd have recognized half the people here if I saw them in Ann Arbor."

"That must explain it," Rett said. She liked that excuse. She smiled benignly at Angel, who had not ceased glowering at her from the moment she had walked up with T.J. Obviously the invitation to join them had not been Angel's idea. But it would have been rude to refuse.

"Did you see much of each other after that?" Mrs. Martinetta never paused in her continuous slicing of shortcake.

Angel took a deep, long-suffering breath. Carmella gave her a sympathetic glance while T.J. muttered, "Your turn, finally."

Things were moving too fast for Rett to figure it all out. She kept her answer simple. "No, I left on tour the next day. I was gone three weeks and have been incredibly busy ever since." She forbore mentioning that Angel had had her number and never called. She fluttered her eyelashes innocently at Angel.

"We didn't see each other again until just before I left on vacation, Mama." Angel's tone said she wanted the subject dropped.

"Angel tells me you sing professionally with a symphony."

"An orchestra, Mama." Angel's voice was almost inaudible.

"What's the difference?"

Rett chimed in. "I'm singing with a big band orchestra."

"I see. Angel said your voice is one of the finest she's ever heard."

Rett could feel Angel cringing. So Angel liked her voice — that was nice to know. Mrs. Martinetta was far more forthcoming than her daughter. "I'm flattered."

"You should come to dinner. Thursday night."

"Mama," Angel said weakly. She said something in Italian and the whole family laughed. Rett stole a look — Angel was blushing.

Ignoring her daughter's obvious discomfort, Mrs. Martinetta asked, "Do you like Italian food?"

"Say yes," several of the family said in unison.

"Just say yes." Angel had an air of resigned acceptance.

"I love Italian food," Rett said. "Give me a *spignotti e aglio* or *pollodora scallopine* and I'm in heaven."

Mrs. Martinetta glowed with satisfaction.

Angel was looking studiously at her plate. "It would seem you're coming to dinner."

"Yes, I think it's a date."

Angel turned to her in a panic. "Don't use that word. We'll be married between the tiramisu and the coffee."

Rett opened her mouth to ask for clarification but Mrs. Martinetta sighed loudly, looked at her eldest daughter and observed that Angel was her only child not yet settled down. Someday, maybe she would be lucky enough to know that all her children were happy. Angel's siblings snickered.

"Okay, I understand." Rett gave Angel a long, direct look, then said loudly enough to be overheard, "It's a date, then."

"You shit," Angel had muttered, but her lips had twitched.

It was a date. Meeting the whole family officially on their first date — Rett had sung to herself all the way home and awakened on Monday morning with a smile. She'd showered and dressed, grabbed the packet of reunion materials to read, finally, and headed for the nearest waffle restaurant. After that she had promised herself a long walk and at least an hour of practice. The Wiffenpoofs were going to do several selections at the reunion dance on Saturday night. A practice session was set for Wednesday at lunchtime. If she wanted to keep her voice in flex she needed a good practice.

She read every word about Angel in the materials, but the few short paragraphs only whetted her appetite. Angel's undergraduate biochemistry degree from Cal Poly had been followed by an M.D./Ph.D. from Johns Hopkins. Education alone accounted for nearly twelve of the past twenty-three years. After her medical residency, she'd gone on to be an investigator on the Human Genome Project, whatever that was. Then the short bio stated she'd been awarded the National Science Award for leading a team of UCLA researchers who had isolated the genetic sequence that created a predisposition for ovarian cancer.

Rett had nothing else to do with her time and any excuse to avoid seeing her mother was a welcome one.

Minnesotans had always prided themselves on their public library and school systems. With a phone call she discovered that the nearest library did indeed have Internet search engines available.

A search for "Martinetta, Angelica" had returned over a hundred hits. Twenty or so were from UCLA's Web site, another twenty from CNN news articles and the rest from other university and medical research sites. Rett scrolled down until she found a CNN article about the most recent National Science Award. The article was too sketchy to be of much help in understanding Angel the scientist or the woman, but it gave her a link to the *Journal of the National Cancer Institute*, which had published the paper that had led to the award.

She followed that link and found she had to subscribe to read the paper. She went back to the original hits and finally found her way to UCLA bios of some of its professors and even discovered a head shot of Angel. She cursed herself for not thinking of going to UCLA's Web site a couple of months ago, but the path to the pictures was a long and involved one that she probably wouldn't have known to follow. She gazed at the posed photograph. Angel looked so serious and so damned intelligent.

That was when her stomach first felt a chill. Then she found the Web site for the Human Genome Project. It was a modest undertaking — an international team of researchers were just trying to create a map of the three billion genetic pieces that made up the human body. Angel had done a stint there and Rett was now reading a paper she'd written during that experience.

When Rett looked at skin she saw color and

texture. What must Angel see? Pairs of banded chromosomes, DNA coiled in double helix strands? What was it Angel had said that first night? That everything a person could be was already written on her genes. Thirty billion gene markers made up one human body. Thirty billion pieces of information to understand a single human being. The scope daunted Rett, but apparently Angel thrived on the challenge of mapping the essence of humanity. Angel was trying to understand the blueprint of human existence, what some people might call the mind of God.

Endonuclease proteins ...

Rett swallowed hard and fought down a feeling of panic. The fragile woman's body she had held in her arms, with thighs of silk and fingers of pure magic — that small, passionate creature had a mind that could understand the universe's most secret workings.

Recombinant DNA ... genomic sequence ... autonomously replicating, extrachromosomal circular DNA molecules ...

It was terrifying. What would they talk about on long winter nights that Rett could possibly comprehend? Every science class had been a struggle for her. She'd never taken math beyond simple geometry. Angel was a medical doctor, too. She probably understood how vocal cords worked better than Rett did.

How does anyone compete with the universe?

The sequence-tagged sites were compared to the full genome duplication in the daughter cells ... Rapid and highly specific amplification was achieved by successive rounds of primer annealing, strand elongation and dissociation.

She closed the document window, packed up her things and bolted for the car.

She had no energy for anything as adventurous as a walk. Her thoughts turned in circles as she wound aimlessly through the area surrounding the motel several times. She walked until her sandals rubbed a blister on one ankle. She hadn't thought to change to walking shoes. She limped back to the motel and found it mostly deserted — it was already eleven, checkout time for most people.

She would forget all about Angel for a while if she practiced. Of course she would. She plugged in the Casio keyboard, played her Mozart fanfare and concentrated.

Feel your feet on the carpet. Feel the carpet on the floor. Feel the blister you shouldn't have gotten —

Damn.

Breathe in, breathe out. Her lungs obeyed and she vocalized middle C, holding it. Full voice, half voice, a whisper. There. She hadn't thought once about Ang —

Damn, damn, damn!

Screw note practice, then. She played the opening chord for "She Believed in Me" and found herself humming "Angel of the Morning" instead.

She wanted to heave the keyboard against the nearest wall.

She threw herself on the bed instead and stared at the ceiling. Just deal with it, she told herself. Okay, the woman is a certified genius. But she's a woman, just like you. She obviously finds you physically attractive — yeah, but there has to be more than that.

Good God, she thought, her friends will think I'm the empty-headed bimbo Angel keeps around for relaxation.

She rolled on her side. Don't do this to yourself, she scolded. That's just your mother talking. You are not a bimbo. You are not a lightweight. So you don't know a genome from a gerbil — what the hell difference does that make? It's probably a fact that not one of Angel's friends knows every word to "American Pie" and can sing the entire song on pitch *a capella*. Maybe they have stared the mysteries of the universe in the face, but they have probably never cradled a couple of hundred people in the warmth of their voice and felt that warmth come back as applause and cheers.

Maybe they would find a way to help millions of people live longer, pain-free lives. Give me a little more time, she thought, and I'll make millions pause in their daily grind and I'll give them a reason to smile, to let music lift them up for a minute or two.

There's nothing lightweight about that, she repeated. *Just let go of your inferiority complex and let go of it now.* Art is not more pure than science and science is not more worthy than art. Art is why people want to live and the desire to live is why Angel is trying to cure cancer.

You need each other. So there.

She sang the crap out of "American Pie" just for good measure.

* * * * *

Denton's Diner had always served awesome sandwiches. Walked and sung out, she tossed a swimsuit and towel into the car and headed for Woton for a late lunch. After that, any beach was on her menu. A little time in the sun wouldn't hurt her. This was a vacation, after all.

It was going to be a long time until Thursday night.

She found a shady place to park and wandered up Main Street. There were some elegant dried flower arrangements in one shop. Mrs. Bernstein would like something like that — not too big, rich but not gaudy colors. She made a mental note to stop back before she left. Her stomach growled and she turned toward Denton's.

She stood at the door to the diner and grinned at her luck. *Thank you, universe. We might almost be even now.* She went inside and slid into the booth to face Angel.

"Hi." Angel was obviously startled, but Rett didn't detect any displeasure.

"Hi. I was just coming in for a sandwich."

Angel indicated her half-empty plate. "They're still great. Pickles, too."

"I've decided you're right."

"About what?"

The waitress arrived to bring Angel a tall, frosty lemonade and to take Rett's order. "We had to make a new batch. Sorry it took so long."

"I'll have one of those, too," Rett said. "And a Reuben."

Angel waited until the waitress was out of earshot before asking, "What am I right about?"

"Slowing down." Time was what they needed. Time for Rett to get over feeling like a mental pygmy next to Angel.

"Oh. I'm right, am I? Which kind of slowing down did you mean?"

"The one you were talking about. About getting to know each other."

Angel was blushing. Rett felt the knot in her stomach uncoil. Okay, she might be a genius, but she could still blush. "You mean when we were walking in the water or . . . later?"

The waitress set down a lemonade for Rett and bustled away.

Rett knew her smile was devilish. "Which one are you talking about now?"

"Heya, Angel, Rett. Great to see you back in town." Keith Jolafson passed the time of day and chatted about the weather in what Rett thought of as a peculiarly Minnesotan ritual of greeting. He left with his takeout when the waitress delivered Rett's sandwich.

"It's not possible to have a serious discussion here," Angel muttered.

Rett bit the end off the huge dill pickle wedge. It was so sour — yum — the glands in her throat went gonzo. "Were you being serious? About in the water or later? You know, when we got to the trees."

"Wipe that grin off your face, young lady." Angel tried and failed to be stern. "We can't very well talk about whether we're going to —" She dropped her voice so low Rett almost couldn't hear her. "Well, you know what. Not while you're eating a pickle."

Rett could not help herself. "What would you rather I was eating?"

Angel's fingers clenched on her lemonade, and Rett had the feeling she'd barely escaped having the contents dumped on her head. "We'll go for a walk, okay? Nothing serious until then."

Rett enjoyed a huge bite of the corned beef and sauerkraut. It was slathered with Thousand Island dressing and a dash of spicy mustard. It was as close to Kosher as food got in these parts, which was not very. "It sure is hot, but I think there's been enough rain for a good harvest this year."

Angel said nothing.

"I was at the store the other day and I just couldn't believe the price of eggs. They've just gone up and up. I think I'll have to give up custard at this rate."

Angel glowered at her. She was very good at glowering. That expression must stop college freshmen in their tracks.

"Have you ever noticed that they can pass a law to make people pick up after their dogs but they won't make people pick up after themselves? What's this world coming to?"

Angel had a white-knuckled grip on her knife when she said, "If you don't stop talking I'm going to kill you."

"That knife isn't sharp enough."

"It is when you know precisely where to insert it."

Rett grinned at her and ate in cheerful silence. The more she smiled at Angel the more Angel frowned. The waitress dropped off the check and Rett snapped it up. "I remember owing you for the, uh, you know."

Angel looked confused.

"Accommodations?"

"Oh. Don't worry about that."

As Angel passed her on the way to the front door, Rett murmured, "You're adorable when you blush."

Outside on the sidewalk, Angel burst out, "Would you stop being so goddamned charming!" She set off toward the back road to town at a pace that made Rett breathless, and Angel had much shorter legs. Rett was glad she had switched to walking shoes.

She watched Angel's hinder — her shorts fit so nicely, who wouldn't? — as she hurried up the sidewalk. Her tank top left her shoulders nearly bare. Lovely shoulders. Now Rett, she admonished herself, remember that you agreed it was time to slow down.

They had left the wooden sidewalks of town behind them when Angel finally slowed. "You're agreeing that we should maybe wait to go to bed again until we spend some more time together."

"That's what I'm agreeing to, yes."

They walked in silence for several minutes, their footsteps crunching on the gravel shoulder. Angel turned onto one of the dirt roads. The afternoon air was much cooler in the deep shade, but Rett had walked as much as she wanted to. The blister was hollering at her to stop. "Can we sit — over here?"

They settled on the end of a log farthest from the buzzing activity of termites.

Angel rubbed her face with both hands, then swept her fingers through her hair. The short black curls were now in the same tumbled disarray they had been in when Rett had seen her at UCLA. "That first night with you I was so focused. All I could think about was how much I had wanted to be with you all those years ago. It was as good as I had ever fantasized. And then we didn't see each other and I know you lost my number and you didn't know my last name, but all the while I was imagining that you'd just gone on to your next conquest."

"That's not me."

"I couldn't know that. Half the news produced in L.A. is the sexual exploits of show business people. You could be the type of person who sees someone she wants, has sex and gets the desire out of her system in a single night."

"Were you trying to get me out of your system that night?" Rett touched the back of the hand nearest her with one fingertip.

Angel made a twisty-frowny face that made Rett want to smile, but she controlled herself. It was hard. "Yeah. It didn't work. All those years, you never thought about me, did you?"

Rett took a deep breath and kept her voice gentle. "I think if we're ever going to go forward, that should be the last time you bring that up. I never thought about you. I never thought about anybody else. High school was made up of her and not her. You were not her. Everybody else was not her. I was so miserable that, to tell you the truth, I have never consciously tried to think about high school at all. A photographic memory is near-perfect, but not flawless. As I'm sure you know."

Angel kicked at a hummock, then shook the dirt off her sandal. "I'm sorry. I keep telling myself to move on. I will not bring it up again."

"For the record, for now and all time, I will think of the first time I met you as the night I did karaoke — the night you seduced me."

Angel's chin lifted in outrage. "I did not — it was *extremely* mutual, remember?"

181

"If you say so. I just remember who was on top of who first."

"Stop it." Angel's plea was half-hearted. Her voice quavered slightly.

"Okay."

"So we're agreed. Let's get to know each other."

"Right. No sex for a while."

"Right."

"It'll be good for us."

"Absolutely."

Rett watched Angel get to her feet to ostensibly study one of the nearby pine branches. "So what shall we do to get to know each other better?"

Angel was sighing. "I hadn't thought that far ahead. I'm taking my folks out to dinner later. Even though most of the family is staying at Honey Lake in cabins, my mom has been cooking nonstop for a week."

"So we have an hour or two to do something to get to know each other. We could go shopping." Rett stood up.

Angel turned to gaze at her. In a low voice she said, "We're agreed, right?"

A wave of desire made Rett close her eyes for a moment. "Yes." When she opened her eyes all she could see was Angel's lips. Her breath was coming in short gasps. "I love shopping."

Angel swallowed so hard Rett heard it. "My desire to have life follow a logical path can be utterly irrational sometimes."

"I'm not going to argue with that." Rett was hardly breathing now. She had to keep her arms at her sides with a conscious effort, but nothing would stop her fingers from curling as if to cup Angel's face.

Angel made a face and turned away. "I'm in no mood to argue."

Rett staggered once Angel's gaze left her. She had felt frozen by the burning desire in Angel's eyes.

"Shopping," Angel said weakly. She looked skyward for a moment then spun around to face Rett. "Shopping. Fuck shopping."

In less than a heartbeat Angel was in her arms. Even as their lips met, Rett pulled Angel down to straddle her lap. She had not forgotten the way Angel tasted or the smell of her hair. Sensation evoked and reinforced memory as Angel returned her kiss.

Shoulders . . . the hollow at her throat. Rett bent Angel back in her arms to relearn the texture of the soft skin with her teeth and tongue. She slipped the straps of the tank top out of the way. Beautiful olive skin pulsed with the beat of Angel's heart. Angel yanked the tank top down with an earthy groan of desire. Rett filled her mouth with Angel's breasts and trembled with an ache between her legs that could take a lifetime to ease.

"Not here . . . oh . . ."

Rett's fingers slipped past the hem of Angel's shorts, remembering the way to welcoming heat and wetness. She put her other arm around Angel's waist to pull her closer.

Angel groaned out her name as Rett's fingers slipped inside her, then she burst into tears. Rett murmured, "Hold on to me, it's okay."

"I didn't want to love you again." Her hips moved convulsively. "Don't stop." Angel put both arms around Rett's neck and hid her tears in Rett's hair. "Don't stop."

Rett could feel the rapid beat of Angel's heart

against her cheek. She let Angel set the pace, listened for the cues she remembered so vividly. Slower, deeper, right . . . there.

Rett was hypnotized by the thumping of Angel's heart. She jumped slightly when Angel tipped her head back for a languid, satisfied kiss. She slipped her hand free and Angel made a little moan.

"We're not done," Rett whispered.

"Oh, I know." Angel brought Rett's wet hand to her breasts and sighed as Rett caressed her. "I'm only just beginning."

"Not here," Rett said hoarsely. "We can't possibly do what I want here."

"Slow down? I was insane. Promise me you won't slow down." Angel bit Rett's lower lip, then gave her a hard, thorough kiss. "And tell me your motel is close."

Rett didn't want to stop kissing. She murmured between their pressed lips, "It's most of the way to Litchfield."

Angel groaned in disappointment. "You mean I'm going to have to wait a half an hour to strip you naked and have my way with you?"

"I'll speed." From Angel's lips to her shoulders to her breasts — Rett's mouth explored the landscape of Angel's body again. "In the car, that is. After that I'm taking my time."

Angel shivered. "It's been a long time since I've — I've felt quite like this. If I ever have before."

"Like what?" Rett tipped her head back so she could gaze into Angel's eyes. Fiery flecks of yellow circled her brown irises.

"When we were together the first time all I wanted to do was . . ."

"Was?"

"All I wanted to do was fuck," she said all in a rush. Her ears turned red.

"That's what we did."

"Stop smiling."

"I can't help it."

"You're making me feel like a small-town virgin."

"Sorry."

"Well, it wasn't like me. I don't usually let myself go like that."

"Me neither."

"It feels different now."

"To me, too." Rett kissed the side of Angel's mouth. "Are we convinced now that neither of us is looking for a quickie?"

"I just wanted you to know how I felt. I want more than this." Angel opened her mouth to Rett.

"How greedy . . ." Rett felt as if she was falling. There was no blood left in her brain. It was all pounding through the rest of her body, every inch of which clamored to be touched.

The next thing she knew the ground slammed the breath out of her and Angel's elbow drove hard into her solar plexus. They'd gone over backwards onto a not very thick layer of pine needles and oak leaves.

"Jesus, are you okay?"

Rett couldn't inhale. Angel put a hand on Rett's stomach. "Did I get you here?"

Rett nodded.

"Just relax. Don't fight it." Angel's hand lightly

massaged the area just below Rett's sternum. "The muscles will all unlock when you need the air the most. Don't panic, it'll take longer."

Suddenly Rett could breathe again. "Shit, oh that hurts."

"I'm so sorry."

"Not your fault." Rett found she could inhale more and more deeply. The pain was receding quickly. "I lost my balance."

"Does that happen often?"

"Don't go doctor on me. I just had other things on my mind."

Angel's hand was still on Rett's stomach. "I could play doctor. Give you a thorough examination." Her hand slid higher under Rett's shirt. Fingers explored her ribs, then lightly brushed over her bra.

"I think we should head for the motel," Rett said shakily. "I'm not hurt."

Angel kissed her way from Rett's navel to her shoulders, pulling Rett's shirt up as she went. "In a minute." She bared Rett's breasts and caressed each with the tip of her tongue. "Just one more minute."

Rett had nothing to hold on to. Angel was making her body float. There was nothing to keep her on the ground. She no longer smelled the pine needles all around her, or saw the lace of leaves and branches against the summer sky. She felt as light as a balloon, tethered to reality by Angel's hands on her breasts, now at her waistband. One of her hands helped Angel unbutton her shorts while the other clung to Angel's shoulder to keep from floating away.

"There, there, please." Her shorts were around her knees. Angel was pausing — she put her head on Rett's stomach.

A car passed on the road, and as the engine's drone faded Angel's fingers slid hard inside of her. Music filled her ears — it was as if cellos played in her blood. Angel's moans against her stomach and breasts were the harmony to the pounding of her heart. It felt so good, so unbelievably good, and knowing that it was Angel holding her brought more tears to Rett's eyes. It seemed as if the ground under her rumbled for a moment as two fields of energy that had long resisted merging gave up the fight.

Rett wanted to doze longer, but the ground was too hard. Angel lifted her head from Rett's stomach. "Hello, sleepyhead."

"I'm only dozing," Rett mumbled.

Angel cleared her throat meaningfully and held out the wrist with her watch on it.

"It's nearly four?"

"I think I wore you out."

Once had not been enough and it had taken deliciously longer the second time. Rett felt her neck and cheeks stain with red.

"I didn't sleep well last night," she lied. She tidied her clothes without looking directly at Angel.

They sat with their backs against the log.

"I'll have to go home in a little while to get dressed for dinner."

Rett kissed Angel's fingers. "I am not going to wait until Thursday night to see you again."

"I have to go up to Rochester tomorrow for a meeting."

"After that?"

"No plans until the following morning."

"Spend the night with me, then."

Angel made a low sound that couldn't be mistaken for anything but anticipation. "I'd love to. But I will have to be up bright and early Wednesday morning for breakfast with the old Science Club."

"I've got practice with the Wiffenpoofs Wednesday lunch."

"My lecture is that night. I wish I'd never agreed. I've almost gotten work completely out of my mind and I really needed the break."

"How come you said yes?"

"Cinny asked so nicely."

The mention of Cinny's name didn't chill the air the way Rett had thought it might. "So, Wednesday night?"

"The lecture won't end until at least nine and I agreed to watch a documentary with my scientifically minded niece afterward. I want to encourage her all I can."

Rett chewed on her lower lip for a moment. "Thursday?"

"Rochester again." Angel peered into her face. "I'm sorry — it's a busy week, actually. Then we've got the family dinner on Thursday, but Friday is open. At least during the day. We're doing a slumber party at Bunny's that night, remember?"

"Don't remind me. What were we thinking?"

"That it would be fun."

"Oh yeah." Tomorrow night and then not alone again until Friday? It was an *eternity*.

"I really should be going. I need a shower before dinner."

"You're back is covered with pine needles." Rett

could still smell Angel on her lips. There was certainly something to be said for making love outdoors.

"Your back is worse," Angel said. "And if I were interested in such things, I might point out who was on her back first again. But I won't."

Rett tickled Angel furiously. "Tomorrow night we'll do things a little differently then."

"Tomorrow night seems like a long way away." Angel pulled Rett down for a kiss. "I'm so glad you saw things my way, though. Slowing down and all."

Rett helped Angel to her feet, then had to sit down on the log for a moment. She felt as if her legs were going to fold up. "You're sure you can't slip away tonight? After everyone is in bed?"

"My father is a night owl. He loves to watch old movies after Mama goes to bed. I want to spend as much time with him as possible. He's not as well as he looks."

Rett squeezed Angel's fingers. "I'm sorry."

"I am, too." Angel's tone was unsuccessfully nonchalant. "Knowing as much as I do about certain diseases, I have no illusions about what the next year will bring."

"Then don't let me take time away. Not too much, anyway." Her libido told her she was a fool, but for once in the last week her common sense won. Angel's time was precious to her father and taking too much would put being together at too high a price.

"It'll be okay." Angel untangled their fingers. "It's just that even in the middle of . . . this, there's life to deal with."

The middle of . . . this, Rett thought, the middle of falling in love. Was that what this was? She should be babbling with fear. She had thought their bodies were way ahead of their hearts, but now she wasn't sure that their hearts hadn't been leading them all along.

She missed Angel the moment she drove off, missed her with an ache that was too physical. She went back to her motel to shower and change. Her mood then took her to just south of Minneapolis to the Mall of America for a hedonistic shopping excursion. She found topaz earrings that would look beautiful with Angel's eyes, and a chili-pepper-shaped bowl for Naomi, who collected unique dinnerware. She dug through piles of clothing at Filene's Basement to find a single pair of slacks and treated herself to popcorn in the amusement park. She usually avoided popcorn because an inhaled kernel and the resulting coughing fit could add a rasp to her voice for as long as twenty-four hours. But she wasn't singing until Wednesday, and that was just a practice. She licked her buttery, salty fingers, which reminded her of Angel. She glimpsed her goofy expression in a window and hummed "Chances Are" off and on for the rest of the evening.

After walking only a fraction of the gigantic mall she ached all over and the blister on her ankle protested with every step. Soreness in some parts of her body had far more to do with how she'd spent the afternoon with Angel than any excessive exercise. Back at the motel she plopped herself into a bathtub full of steaming water and soaked for an hour.

She awoke Tuesday morning to the chirping of her cell phone. Work had seemed so far away that she hadn't even checked her voice mail in the last few days. Tamla reported that Rett was booked at the Top Hat for the weekend after next. That was very welcome news. In just a few days she'd gone from regretting agreeing to stay another week to euphoria at the idea. Getting paid to stay an extra week that she could spend with Angel was just plain wonderful. After that she had to return to some semblance of working for a living and she was certain Angel would as well. Naomi had a background vocal for a commercial scheduled right after Labor Day.

She just didn't feel like working. Not today. Today she felt like singing for the pure joy of it and not caring about how it sounded to anyone else. "Top of the World" suited her mood exactly. This kind of feeling, where everything was perfect and her body felt as if it had been reborn and rediscovered, was something to be reveled in for as long as it lasted. If she'd learned one thing in the last forty years it was that this feeling didn't come along often enough to be taken for granted.

She wasn't going to ruin it by seeing her mother today.

"It's a chore, you have to do it," she told her reflection. She tweezed a hair out of her left eyebrow and she sneezed suddenly. "You're ducking it. It's childish. It's really the only thing you have to do now. Everything else is just frosting."

She had that dopey grin on her face again because she was thinking of Angel as an angel food cake.

She made a stern face at herself. Adult voice talking: "You have the whole day ahead of you. Take care of business. Get it over with. You know you should. Grow up. Just do it." She stuck her fingers in her ears and sang, "La la la, I can't hear you" like a child.

She visited the Institute of Arts in Minneapolis instead, finding all the favorites she'd liked when she was a college student. The still coolness of the rooms slowed her rapid pulse. She felt as if her heart had still not slowed down from Angel's final kiss. She gazed at a Thomas Cole original and tried to think herself into the painting the way she had when she was younger. She could be just behind that tree, looking down into the river. Angel could be just behind the tree, too, and they could be —

She had to change to modern art with no trees or fallen logs to distract her.

The more she thought about the night ahead with Angel the slower time moved.

"I just won't think about her," she told herself. "Time will fly by."

It was the longest day of her life.

9

"You're so much nicer than an alarm clock." Rett drew Angel's arms around her, enjoying the warmth of her body at her back. She'd been awakened by persistent kisses on her shoulders and back and a pleasing series of events had then ensued.

"I'm starving," Angel said. "And I'm going to be late to the science club breakfast." It was just past eight.

"Stupid science club," Rett said.

"I could say stupid Wiffenpoofs, which is where you'll be at lunchtime."

"True." Rett rolled over with a grin. "Let's both play hookey." She didn't expect Angel to agree and wasn't disappointed when Angel's look said that was out of the question. "Did I tell you I'm doing another Friday and Saturday at the Top Hat weekend after next? So I have to stay another week?"

Angel kissed her jaw and tickled her earlobe with her tongue. "That is positively wonderful. We'll have lots of time — no reunion stuff going on. I'm not heading home until just before Labor Day. We can just, well, get to know each other."

"Ah yes, the Getting To Know Each Other. We'll have to draw up an outline."

"Ugh," Angel said. "Don't mention outlines, theses or papers. I'm on vacation."

"You've got that lecture tonight. I hope I can still get a ticket."

"I've got extras — had to pass them around the family. I don't know why they're all so insistent on coming. It's not like you're going to sing. I'm not entertaining the way you are." Angel scratched her stomach, then pushed Rett's hand away when she began scratching, too. "That tickles."

"Maybe they love you and are interested in what you do with your life." So Angel was ticklish. Rett walked her fingers back across Angel's stomach.

"Maybe. What's your reason for wanting to be there?"

Rett knew instantly the question was far more serious than Angel's light tone indicated. She had to clear her throat. "I think I may have the same reasons. I find Dr. Martinetta a fascinating woman

194

and I'd like to really meet her." The icy feeling in her stomach came back, but she couldn't feel intimidated by Angel when she was naked.

Angel's eyes were shining but she said nothing more. After a moment she asked softly, "What are you staring at?"

"You. I'm committing you to memory."

"Good. I have to get up now."

"I'll let you get up if I can shower with you."

"No hanky-panky. I'm going to be late as it is."

"No hanky-panky."

"You're lying."

"Yeah," Rett admitted. She learned in the shower, though, that Angel on a mission could not be swayed from her purpose. She got a kiss and a shampoo for her trouble, though, and had to be content with that. Angel hurried out the door with her hair still wet.

Rett sat down on the bed and felt a little deflated, but an appointment was an appointment. She had her practice, after all. Fair was fair. Still, she felt lonely.

A sudden pounding on the door made her jump.

"It's me," Angel called.

"What did you forget?" Rett opened the door while hiding her naked self behind it.

"This." Angel pushed Rett against the wall and kissed her so thoroughly that Rett was left gasping as a delicious tingling shot up her legs and down her arms. "See you tonight."

Oh my, was all Rett could think. She peeked out the window and watched Angel's rental car leave the parking lot. *Oh my.*

* * * * *

She did her warmups in the car as she followed the directions to Wayne Igorson's house. His single-story farmhouse was typically Minnesotan, but a large studio sat behind the house with enough room and soundproofing for a band to practice without waking any neighbors.

Wayne had indeed continued his guitar work, and he played exceptionally well in the classical style. Everyone quickly agreed on an old favorite, "Scarborough Fair" as done by Simon and Garfunkel, to showcase Wayne's finesse and the harmonies they'd devised so many years ago. They sounded as good to Rett now as they had then.

Tom Stoddard's sharp falsetto was still sharp, so they worked out a song to have fun with that, and then two more numbers featuring all the girls with boys on backup, and then vice versa.

Lisa Goodings plinked her ukulele and tried to get it back in tune. "You'd think that at some point I would have bought a decent one — I got this one with Blue Chip Stamps."

Jeanette Carlson put down her accordion with a sigh. "It gets heavier every year."

"I want to hear Rett do a solo." Lisa twisted a tuning knob and grimaced at the result. "She and Wayne are the only ones who actually get paid for this."

"Then let me sing something with Wayne accompanying," Rett suggested. She had a song in mind and she hoped Angel would like it.

Everyone agreed and they settled in to practice. Rett couldn't remember the last time she'd laughed so much. It brought back what had been really good times. High school had not been one bleak day after another, she reminded herself. Unfortunately, these good times had always ended with going home to brutal reminders that practice was a waste of time because she would never get out of Woton. At her mother's relentless insistence she'd gotten a part-time job at sixteen doing dishes at a diner she could bike to over in Green Mill. It was a useful skill, her mother said, far more useful than sitting around dreaming about being a star.

You don't have to go back to that today, she reminded herself. You are your own woman now. But that sensible adult voice would not let her forget that she wouldn't be her own woman if she couldn't at least walk into her old home. Until she did that, she'd still be frightened of turning into what her mother predicted she would become: a nobody.

Tomorrow, she promised herself. Tomorrow and no excuses.

She ended up being very glad she had bought the new slacks. She'd brought apparel for performing, a dance, a picnic and Minnesota's muggy summer weather, but nothing quite suitable for a serious medical lecture. She was hypersensitive to what Angel's family would think of her now, and she didn't want to appear in any way disrespectful of Angel. Slacks and the only button-up blouse she'd brought with her with a simple necklace would have to suffice.

"You look like a nun," she told her reflection.

She found her way to the campus courtesy of the directions in the reunion materials, but it took longer than she expected. She slid into a seat in the back of the auditorium just as the speakers were beginning. She recognized a number of people from the picnic, but students with notebooks occupied the majority of the seats.

The Vice President of the University of Minnesota introduced Dr. Martinetta. After a long recital of her published papers and research team projects, he concluded with a brief summary of the project that had resulted in her being given the National Science Award. It was odd to hear her referred to as "Doctor." Rett took a deep breath. She was about to see an Angel she absolutely did not know.

Angel stepped up behind the lectern to welcoming applause, and then hushed expectation fell over the room. She's nervous, Rett suddenly thought. It was in the tiny flutter of her hands as she smoothed the papers in front of her. That she could be nervous caught Rett off guard. Angel wasn't a master-scientist-sex-goddess-supreme-being. She was human, she was a woman, and she was perfectly imperfect. Rett's heart flooded with a nameless emotion that left her palms sweating.

"I recognize that a number of you are science and medical students, but you won't need notes tonight. I won't get that technical," she began. Her voice was a little husky, which Rett liked. "In fact, I'm going to go out of my way not to be technical. I think part of the battle in our fight against disease is overcoming the chronic misinterpretation of technical data."

Once Angel's voice steadied and found a rhythm, Rett relaxed. She had been so afraid that she would not be able to see beyond the dispassionate scientist, but she did. But not so much that she wasn't repeatedly awed by Angel's ability to converse in the language of the universe.

"When my colleagues and I published our results on the genetic predisposition for ovarian cancer, we were largely misquoted. The vaunted *New York Times*, for example, said we had found a way to identify those women who would develop the disease. It isn't true. That's not what we did."

Angel touched a switch on the lectern and the projection screen behind her lit up with what Rett recognized as the symbols for genetic code.

"What we found was that this sequence right here was present in over eighty-five percent of women who had developed ovarian cancer." She used a laser pointer to highlight the sequence. "That means that fifteen percent of women who have ovarian cancer do not have this genetic sequence. Importantly, we found the sequence in older women who had no signs of ovarian cancer."

Angel stopped to sip from her water glass. "The difference is not a matter of semantics. It means that while we can tell a woman she has a higher risk of developing the disease if she carries this genetic code, we can't tell any woman whether she will in fact develop it or that she is immune because she does not have this code. That means that all women need to be aware of the risk factors for ovarian, cervical and uterine cancers, and all women must do their best to mitigate those factors if they wish to improve their personal odds of avoiding these diseases."

Any nervousness Angel might have had was gone. Her voice crackled with authority. She covered the relevant statistical data with absolute conviction in her conclusions and rattled off eight- and nine-syllable scientific terms as easily as if they were children's rhymes. If this was the nontechnical version, Rett couldn't comprehend what the technical version might be. The story that Angel wove with her statistics and anecdotes was fascinating, though. She hadn't thought of Angel as a genetic detective. It was obvious that mysteries fascinated Angel and she had the confidence to believe she could solve them.

Angel concluded the data presentation and momentarily switched off the slide projector. "What I want to avoid is giving any woman the impression that she can have a genetic sample taken and then be told whether or not she will develop a given disease. If genetics were all that mattered, then first-time cases of breast cancer would not be occurring in many family clusters today. It's frustrating. I read in the media almost daily that Vitamin This or Herbal That hinders the development of one disease — only to read the next day that Vitamin This or Herbal That increases the risks of another. How is anyone to know what to eat and what not to eat? What to be tested for and whom to believe? That's really the question I've come to answer tonight. What are the most important things a woman can do to reduce her risks of cancer and other diseases?"

Angel switched the slide projector back on. "First and foremost, educate yourself. Don't be at the mercy of advertisements and anecdotes. One of the best ways to educate yourself is my second point. Talk to your doctor about what concerns you in your family's history and your own lifestyle. Your doctor will help you identify your risks and discuss what you can do to lessen them. Your doctor can tell you what you should do in the way of regular health screenings, which is my third point. For God's sakes, get an annual pap smear. If you're over forty, get an annual mammogram. It will save your life."

Rett realized guiltily that she had not visited a gynecologist for a couple of years. She was officially over forty, too. Angel made her want to make an appointment right away.

"Last but not least, I speak empowered with the voice of mothers everywhere. It's a sad, sad message." Angel's smile was at odds with her words. She leaned into the microphone. "Eat your fruits and vegetables."

The audience laughed and Angel took advantage of it to drink more water. Rett knew how her throat must feel.

"Leaving the specifics of my own research behind, what we know from numerous clinical research studies is that nutrition matters. But as I said before, what isn't clear is what foods increase or decrease our risks of disease. In one study, red meats have a causal link with cancer; in another, red meat might reduce the risk of one specific type of cancer. Caffeine is linked to high blood pressure and, on the other hand, reduced incidence of gallstones. One study might suggest that a very high fiber diet reduces colon and rectal cancer while another might suggest that there's no link at all. But one fact is consistent among all studies."

She paused for emphasis. "All studies. Low incidences of not only cancer, but diabetes and heart disease and many other diseases, is always accompanied by a diet rich in fruits and vegetables. That means that in clinically controlled research studies, people who ate lots of fruits and vegetables tended to have less incidence of all types of cancer and many other diseases. That doesn't mean that they won't necessarily develop those diseases because of other factors, like genetics, but it does mean that if you want to use your diet to bolster your resistance to disease, then fruits and vegetables — not supplements and pills — are the only sure thing. They will never let you down."

She held up a hand to emphasize her words. "Fruits and vegetables, washed properly to be pesticide-free, will never let you down. For people like me who do not care for leafy greens and broccoli, it's just about the saddest message I can give. I personally think that's why we don't hear this message often enough in the media today. No one wants to be the bearer of bad news. It's also not really possible to make a fortune selling fruits and vegetables — not the same way it's possible to make a fortune selling pills and supplements, which are rarely shown to have preventative value."

Even from the back of the room Rett could see the blaze in Angel's eyes. This was the passionate woman that Rett knew. "As a doctor, it frightens me that in this day and age people are afraid of a doctor's message based on millions of dollars and years of research, but they'll believe someone they've never met who has been paid to sell them a product. So women don't get annual pap smears but will drink a soft drink that's been laced with an unspecified amount of an herb that has never been clinically proven to reduce any cancer risk. It frightens me."

Angel moved on to explain the difference between clinical, retrospective and prospective research studies and how to evaluate news reports about research, then took some questions from the students. Afterwards,

Rett milled about with the rest of the crowd, but she kept an eye out for Angel's family. She wanted them to know she had taken the effort to be there, that she knew Angel was more than just a beautiful body. She fought a blush — she'd known there was more to Angel than that, she just hadn't seen it for real. Dr. Angelica Martinetta completely unnerved her and probably always would.

She quickly spotted the gathering clan. She would have been content just to agree with everyone that Angel was an amazing woman and a terrific scientist, but Mrs. Martinetta stopped her from a quick exit.

"Angel said you would be here. Wasn't she wonderful?"

"Yes, she was. She's hardly mentioned her work, though I've asked about it, but now I know more about what she's interested in." She felt as if she had to get to know Angel all over again.

"You would never know she had stage fright, would you?"

"She seemed only the tiniest bit nervous, and that was right at the beginning."

Tony Junior leaned toward his mother. "Did she puke beforehand?"

"Oh hush," his mother answered. "She gives so many presentations that I'm sure she's no longer troubled that way."

"If I was, it would only be because all of you were here." Angel's arrival elicited a round of hugs.

Angel smacked her brother on the arm. "I didn't puke. How old are you, anyway?"

"Old enough to be the older brother who's going to take everyone out for hot fudge sundaes at Zeb's Creamery." There was a collective *ooh* of approval. The

St. Cloud creamery was legendary for its homemade ice cream. "I figure we all stuck our mates with the kids, so let's party. I called ahead so they could put broccoli in yours, fry."

"Shut up," Angel said fondly.

"You'll come with us, Rett?" If Rett had ever wondered where Angel got her evocative eyes, she would have only had to look at Angel's father to know the source.

"I don't want to intrude, really." They would have none of it, so Rett found herself included. Angel ducked back into the hall to thank various people. Rett saw her pause a moment with Cinny, smile and then hug her.

All Rett could think was that life was strange.

As they left the creamery, she and Angel out-distanced the rest of the family. Angel said quickly, "My meeting in Rochester tomorrow was moved back a half an hour. I'll be back in time for dinner. I don't have to leave until eleven. Judy Longworth roped me into breakfast with one of her clubs, though. I don't know what I was thinking when I said yes, but that should be over by nine-thirty at the latest." She bit her lower lip.

Rett did some time computation. "So if I want to see you alone tomorrow, it's between nine-thirty and eleven." It was barely long enough for what Rett wanted to do.

"Give me fifteen minutes to shower."

"Nine-thirty and ten forty-five." It would have to suffice.

Angel nodded. "I'm sorry."

"I'll just stay in bed then." She could tell that Angel

wanted to kiss her, but her entire family, which included siblings who seemed to love to tease her, were bearing down on them. "I don't suppose I can check your wisdom teeth with my tongue at this moment."

Angel smiled coolly as her brothers came within earshot. "Thank you for sharing that idea. Say good night, Rett."

"Good-night, Rett."

"Just go, will you!" Angel's eyes flashed with warning.

"Good-night, everyone," she called. "I'll see you tomorrow at dinner."

"Angel is going to pick you up so you have no trouble finding the place," Mrs. Martinetta pronounced.

"I have to come back from Rochester, Mama. I wouldn't be able to pick Rett up much before six."

"We won't start until you and Rett arrive."

"I guess I'm picking you up," Angel muttered.

"See you then," Rett said sweetly. Mrs. Martinetta was proving a valuable ally indeed. She sensed that Angel's reluctance to encourage her mother's pro-Rett stance was a mother-daughter thing, but that was no reason she shouldn't take advantage of it for her own purely altruistic reasons. She only wanted what was best for Angel, just as her mother did. And they both seemed to agree that Rett was best for Angel. Between them they would get Angel to agree.

Rett was up early Thursday morning and wished for something more than morning television to pass the time until Angel arrived. There was such a thing as books, she thought. If Angel stayed this busy, she might have to find a bookstore.

Angel arrived in a whirlwind, fifteen minutes ahead of schedule. She undressed while she kissed Rett and they rolled into bed with happy sighs that turned to kisses.

"You were terrific last night," Rett said into Angel's ear. She kissed the back of Angel's neck right where her hair was tickling Rett's nose and savored the heat of Angel's back against her breasts.

"Thanks."

"I felt like I didn't know you."

"Why?"

"I haven't yet been introduced to Dr. Martinetta."

Angel caught Rett's teasing hand and placed it firmly on her breast. "I tried to leave her in Los Angeles. She's very tedious and doesn't like sex as much as I do."

"Why do you do that?" Did Angel think she wasn't smart enough to understand her work? The insecure icicles were dangling in her stomach again.

"What?"

"If I was a paranoid person, I might think you didn't want to talk about your career with me. I blab your ear off about concerts and contracts and every little thing."

"I didn't realize I was doing that." Angel had tensed.

"If you say so." Rett rolled onto her back.

"I'm sorry." Angel twisted around so she could look at Rett. "I wasn't really sure you were interested."

Rett knew an evasion when she heard one. "Or maybe it's that I don't have the brain power to be interested."

"What?"

Rett gazed at the ceiling. "I barely scraped through geometry."

"What's that got to do with anything?"

"Nothing, I guess." Tears abruptly clouded Rett's vision.

"Tell me what you're thinking, please. Don't hold it back."

Rett took a deep breath. She didn't want to look at Angel. "I'm not — I'm not just eye candy, am I?"

"What?" Angel sat up. "Eye candy? Whatever gave you that idea?"

"Well, I've asked about your work and you keep evading like you don't think I'll get it. Like you're glad you don't have to think heavy thoughts when you're around me." To her mortification her voice broke and she sniffed.

"That's not why. Look at us." She gestured at their naked bodies. "We've spent more time in bed than out of it. I thought I was being who you wanted me to be."

"I want all of you. I may not understand your work in its entirety, but it doesn't mean I'm not interested. It's part of you."

"I'm not explaining very well. It's like we're out of our own time, on vacation. I just wanted to show you the part of me that won't ever change, that wants you. I wanted you to know the woman, not the scientist, before anything else. It doesn't mean I think you're too stupid to know the scientist, I — I just hate it when that's all I am to people. To friends and lovers."

Rett wanted to give in to the electric tingling that ran up and down her spine as Angel trailed her fingers down her stomach. She tried to lighten the atmosphere. "So you're admitting there have been other lovers before me?"

Angel's hand stilled. She said seriously, "Of course there have been."

"I was teasing. But now that you mention it, we haven't yet swapped ex-lover stories." Rett remembered Angel's oblique reference that first night at the bar to a painful breakup.

"We only have an hour and I really —" Angel leaned down to gently bite Rett's lower lip. "I really would like to make good use of it."

"Give me the abstract, professor, and we'll go over the whole paper later."

Angel laughed. "She was a lot younger than I was. We met while she was finishing her master's — friends introduced us. She went into a Ph.D. program that was grueling, and I tried every way I knew to be supportive, to encourage her. I fucked it up. She took my encouragement as patronizing and felt that I still saw her as an inexperienced grad student while I was the big kahuna with the National Science Award. I knew we had problems. She'd stopped talking to me. When I suggested therapy she fell apart. I never realized she felt that way until she was screaming it at me. The more successful I was the more she felt she could never catch up. I would always have more degrees, more awards, more published papers, more money. I didn't mean to make her feel that way. I know a lot of it was her problem to work on. When I met you that night you were so fabulous on stage. It was so obvious you knew what your talents were and had confidence in them. There was no competitive subtext —"

"What subtext? We screwed our brains out."

Angel's smile finally reached her eyes. "It was so easy to be with you. It still is. I wanted to keep it that way for as long as possible."

"We have a lot to talk about," Rett said softly. "You intimidate me sometimes —"

"I intimidate *you*?"

Rett used her near-perfect recall. " 'Meiotic recombination can result in the separation of two markers originally on the same chromosome.' " Angel blinked. "I read it but I don't understand a word of it. Wait, that's wrong. I understand all the words with three letters or less."

Angel put a finger on Rett's lips. "Don't sell yourself short."

"I'm trying hard these days not to. But it's intimidating."

Angel looked caught between laughter and tears. "Are you crazy?" Her lips trembled and Rett wanted very badly to kiss her.

"I try not to be —"

"Listen." Angel took a deep breath and sang a note. It started at D-flat and ended somewhere around C, but it had no intrinsic musicality. Rett did her best to hide her inner cringing. "Voila!" Angel ran her hands through her hair. "There you have every bit of my musical talent. I come from a family of musical people and I can't sing or play a note. And there you are — every word you say sounds like music to me. I hear music and it sounds pleasant, but that fabulous mind of yours hears music as a language. I can't even conceive of what that must be like. And when you sing, it just melts my bones. And I intimidate *you*?"

Rett was trembling with emotion — it was pleasure and amazement churning with desire and that pounding in her heart that had started last night and she couldn't name. Not yet. "Is that something that is written on your genes? Bone-melting?"

"I'll give you my diagnosis later. We have fifty-three minutes left and if you don't kiss me right now —"

Rett sat in bed after the door closed behind a freshly showered and redressed Angel.

I intimidate her, Rett thought. Who would have thought it? Who would have guessed that mutual intimidation would transform into mutual respect? She hugged herself, feeling complete for one perfect moment.

She glanced at herself in the mirror, then was sorry she had. Adult voice reminded her she'd made a promise to herself. *You have to do it today or face the fact that part of you is still a frightened teenager.*

"You're not a frightened teenager," she said to her reflection. "She has no power over you anymore. So why not get it over with? What could be so bad?"

She knew that a day had not passed without a severe judgment or screaming demand from her mother for Rett to do something right for once in her life. Her memory was perfectly clear. Her mother had never stirred herself to come to any of Rett's school performances, citing endless weariness from waiting tables in bars. She had never heard Rett sing in public. When Rett had had the temerity to ask if she would come to the school play, her mother had taken a long drag on her always lit cigarette and shrugged.

"Why bother? The radio's better and I can put my feet up."

At the time she'd been furious and crushed, and after all these years the hurt was still there. It was incomprehensible and that, she told herself, is why you have to go. As an adult, you just might understand it.

She took a shower and blinked back tears the whole while. *I will not cry.* She'd quit crying twenty-three years ago. *I'm a grown woman now.* One way or another, it was time to let it go.

As she rinsed shampoo out of her hair she found she could not hold her breath under the stream of water. She gasped for air and eased herself to her knees, recognizing the signs of hyperventilation. She'd done it once on stage and the lack of control was frightening. She put her head down and triggered her breathing exercises, but they didn't help. She couldn't calm herself.

Disoriented and dizzy, she knelt in the tub and tried to conquer her breathing. Was it fear? Did the idea of facing her mother frighten her this much?

Her hands were clenched into fists and she realized she was beating them on the wall of the tub. Anger . . . she shuddered all over. Yes, anger, she was so angry that it frightened her.

Let it go, she told herself. It's a waste of energy. *Breathe in . . breathe out . . .*

The water had long since turned cold when she

211

felt she could sit up. She had to consciously unclench her fists. She finally made it to the bed with a towel wrapped around herself and huddled under the covers until the shivering subsided.

There had been a time when she'd thought about therapy, but by the time she could afford it she had felt she no longer needed it. Her mother had been far away and buried under a fog of time. Now that she was back in Woton, however, the fog had lifted. All the rage and hurt was still there. Carrying it around was exhausting.

There had to be an end and the end was today.

As she knew from her drive-by on Sunday, the house was unchanged. She couldn't be certain her mother was home, but the chances were good. Unless she'd changed careers, her mother had always worked in one bar or another until two A.M. and slept in until noon. Rett always remembered arriving home from school to find her mother watching television and working on her third or fourth beer. An hour or so later her mother was off to work again. On school days when Rett stayed after for rehearsals they didn't even see each other.

She got out of the car at the bottom of the oil-slicked, weed-choked driveway and noted that the mailbox bore only the name "Lorena Jamison." Whenever some guy had moved in her mother had always gone to great pains to add his name to the mailbox. So she was living alone then. Rett didn't know if she should be relieved. She pressed the doorbell before she remembered that only salespeople used doorbells in these parts.

The front door was snatched open. "I don't want any — well, well, it's you."

For a moment Rett thought she was looking in a mirror. The similarity between their faces stunned her. Same cheekbones, same nose, same eyes. The biggest difference was that her mother's face was covered with a network of fine wrinkles — smoking had made her look older than sixty-two.

"I wondered if you'd find the time. I read about the reunion in the *Weekly*." Her mother stepped back and held the screen open for Rett to come in.

The stench of stale cigarette smoke made her suddenly nauseous. God — she'd forgotten that she'd always felt sick when she was at home. It was the smell. Stale air and unrinsed empty bottles of beer. Her stomach threatened to heave.

"Have a seat if you're going to stay." Her mother settled into what had to be the same deeply indented recliner she'd always favored and lit a cigarette.

Canned applause blared from a game show and Rett crossed the room to turn the set off. She stood between her mother and the TV and could not think of a thing to say.

"I was watching that."

Her mother's indifference stung her into words. "There's always reruns. It has been twenty-three years, after all."

"You've always known where to find me."

"I know. I've avoided the entire state like the plague to put off this moment."

Her mother blew smoke into the air. "I'm not sure why you bothered. I think the last thing you said to me was that you were never coming back."

"Twenty-three years is close to never."

Her mother shrugged. Silence stretched for several minutes as she finished her cigarette. Finally, she said,

"You want to say something to me or you wouldn't be here — go ahead."

What do you want, Rett? Why did you come here? She hasn't changed, but you have. She swallowed back another wave of nausea. "I'm trying to understand you. I'm trying to figure out why you treated me the way you did."

Her mother studied her through the smoke that curled from the tip of another cigarette. "What did I do that was so bad? From the look of you, I'd say you turned out pretty good."

"No thanks to you, Mama."

"I never knew where you got your ideas about life being a bed of roses. It never was for me and you weren't going to turn out any different."

"How did you know that for sure? I feel like I was raised in a dark room and you never once told me to look for the light."

"I was busy putting food on the table. I taught you to stay on your feet when life kicked you."

"Slapping me down every day was just preparing me for life? That's a classic excuse for abuse."

Her mother coughed into a tissue, then said raspily, "Don't tell me I was abusive. You never had any idea what I gave up for you."

"It seemed like very little. I don't recall you ever going without what you wanted." Rett took tiny breaths to avoid inhaling the stale air and felt the prickling of hyperventilation again. She could never breathe in this house.

"You never thought I might have had dreams."

"Then why did you even have me?" There, she thought. That was the question she wanted answered. The answer was why she was here.

"I got pregnant and had no idea how to find a back-alley abortion. Couldn't have paid for it either."

That was the answer she had expected, but still Rett had to sit down. She sank gingerly onto the sofa. "Why didn't you give me up for adoption?" Her memories were accurate and she realized she had hoped they weren't. She hadn't imagined the antipathy. Her mother didn't just not love her, she resented and blamed her as if Rett had had a choice about being born.

"I should have, for all the trouble you were."

Rett rested her head on her knees. *Why did you come here?* "Are you trying to make me hate you?"

"You think I was a rotten mother. You always were judging me. I think you turned out okay anyway."

It was praise. Meager and backhanded, yes, but still praise. "But what might I have been, Mama? It took me all these years to realize that not only could I succeed, but that I wanted to be more than mediocre. I have finally made a success of myself. One word of encouragement from you might have made it happen for me much sooner."

"My mother told me I could be a star. I ended up here."

"You've never mentioned your mother before." She had asked about her grandparents, but her mother had refused to answer any questions. The past just didn't matter, she'd said. Until she'd come back to Woton, Rett had believed that.

"I don't need pity from you. I never needed anything from you. She and Daddy up and died one year from a flu epidemic. I was fourteen. I hated the relatives who took me in and I ran away finally, lived from place to place until I knew that that whole lie about dreaming big was nothing but smoke." As if to illustrate, she blew a long stream of smoke into the air. "You might have wanted me to, but at least I didn't die on you. You had a roof over your head. You could have had it worse."

Rett felt an unwanted flicker of pity. Her mother had felt abandoned by her own mother and had passed on the pain to Rett. It didn't make the pain any less, but at least Rett could begin to understand.

She had her breathing under control again, so she straightened up and steeled herself to look at the face that was unnervingly too like her own. "What kind of star were you going to be?"

"I was going to be a big singer, just like you. I hung out with beatniks, sang in a few clubs. Then I got pregnant, small wonder. Sex was like breathing in those days." Her mother glanced at her then went back to studying the tip of her cigarette. "You can take that look off your face."

"What look?" Rett felt so numb she would have thought her face devoid of expression.

"You're no better than I am, I'll bet. You like it as much as I ever did, I'm sure. You just don't think your mama has a right to like sex."

"You were always honest about that, I'll give you that. I know you don't have any idea who my father is." Rett shrugged. It was a fact of life she had come to accept a long time ago. "I only objected to the men you brought into this house to knock the both of us around."

Her mother angrily stubbed out the cigarette. "You know if any of them laid a hand on you I kicked them out."

"When they hit you it was like they hit me."

"I never put up with it for long. Don't tell me no one has ever popped you — you were always too lippy."

Her mother's unquestioning acceptance that relationships always included violence chilled Rett to the bone. "I shoved her face into the wall. I'll admit I learned one thing from watching you — that no matter what I'd be nobody's victim."

"Her? Still muff-diving?"

The crudity of the remark made Rett's stomach threaten to heave again. She could tell her mother from now to doomsday that the relationships she had with women had all been healthier and more supportive than any her mother had ever survived, and that included Trish. But what would be the point? *Why did I come here? For validation from this bitter, hateful woman? So she had a rotten time — she didn't have to dump it all on me.* "What I do with my body doesn't affect you at all. You don't like my judging you, so why not let me off the hook, too?"

"Sure. Whatever you want. Are we done now? *Wheel of Fortune* is coming on and then I've got an early shift at the Glass Turtle."

Rett stood up, then regretted it when her vision swam for a moment. "I guess we're done. I have one last question."

"Jesus. Haven't you bothered me enough?"

I left you alone for twenty-three years! Rett wanted to scream. She shoved the anger down and put her shaking hands behind her. "Did you ever in any part of your soul have one glimmer of affection for me?"

Her mother lit a fresh cigarette from the one she was smoking and studied Rett through the smoke again. "I never had the time for that. You wouldn't drink formula. I had to breastfeed you and my tits were never the same. You screamed for hours, sometimes all afternoon. You woke up all night. I didn't step foot outside this house by myself for nearly a year. It was like you drained me dry — there was no time for liking you. The older you got the harder it was to control you."

Her mother should have never had a child. She'd been too young, too unprepared, too alone. "Even when I was older, every day you told me something I'd done wrong. You never told me I did anything right, not one thing."

"You never did. You dropped plates and ground up silverware in the disposal. You always burned dinner. You never did learn how to do the laundry properly. And the noise was endless. You running around pretending you were one stupid thing after another, and singing at the top of your lungs. You drove me crazy. I couldn't think."

Rejection, rejection, rejection. God, she thought — did I put up with Cinny's teasing because I thought rejection was all I was worth, all I could expect? I didn't take it because I was a lesbian, I took it because that woman taught me to believe that rejection was all a miserable human failure like me deserved. Rett was trembling with anger. Through a haze of red she saw her mother's mouth moving, but she no longer heard the words.

"I was a bad household servant, is that it?" Rett stood over her mother, nearly choking on the smoke and bile in her own throat.

"You never did earn your keep around here. You were like a damn puppy, making messes and always wanting more food. Always wanting a pat on the head for every damn thing. 'Look what I did,' you'd say, and you'd expect me to love you for whatever the hell it was. I'm not built that way and I'm damned sure not gonna apologize for it now."

I am not my mother and I will not make her mistakes. The flash of clarity pierced her rage. Rett realized she was on the brink of being her mother long enough to dump all her rage and frustration with words of pure poison, words she could never recall. *I am not her and I will not dump my emotional trash on her, because that's what she does.* They might not have any love for each other, but that didn't mean they had to hate each other instead.

She backed away and took a steadying breath even though it made her lungs ache. "I didn't used to feel sorry for you. But now I do. Maybe I was asking to be loved all the time, but don't you know that I wanted to love you? I tried to love you and you never wanted it." Don't cry, she told herself. It's too late for that. "I'm sorry that my coming here hasn't made anything better between us. I had to try one last time."

"Am I supposed to applaud?"

"Don't bother." Rett turned the TV back on.

"You were always selfish. You don't know what it cost me to have you."

This is where I came in, Rett thought. "All I know, Mama, is that I paid and paid and I'm done now."

Outside, she leaned on the car and filled her lungs with fresh air. It was as bad as she remembered — even worse. She'd gained nothing but a measure of self-respect for facing her worst demon and managing to survive it without an emotional break- down. She'd wanted to smash the ashtray and scream that she'd gone without dinner when all there was in the grocery bag was cigarettes and beer. That it had been agony to wear garage-sale clothes the other kids recognized as theirs to school while her mother had always worn the latest in man-trawling skirts and heels. They got bigger tips, her mother had always claimed. Now all her mother could say was that it could have been worse. Maybe there were six degrees of hell and she'd only been in the first — but it had still been hell.

Her shaking hands made it difficult to get the key in the ignition. She looked back at the house. Her mother had made the effort to come to the window and they stared at each other through the separating panes of glass. Rett could not interpret the expression on her mother's face. Could it be regret? Or was it just annoyance? Her mother let the curtain fall back into place after a minute and Rett started the car.

"It's over," Rett repeated, stunned by the emptiness she'd felt in that house. It had sapped her completely. She was beyond tears — there wasn't any emotion left in her.

She stopped at Denton's Diner for a lemonade and a chance to breathe in nothing but cool air. She was waiting numbly at the counter when she heard her name.

One of the men at a nearby booth was looking at her. "I thought that was you."

Thor Gustafson, Bunny's brother, and from the looks of it, Jerry Knudsen and Dwayne Cook. The gang of three whose chosen mission in high school was making sure everyone else, including Rett, felt like a loser. She'd avoided them at the picnic and didn't have the strength for banter right now. She just wanted to sit and stare at the sky until it filled her up again. "It's me. How have you been?"

"Just great." Thor looked like he could still play football. The forearms that bulged out of his canning plant uniform seemed larger than her thighs. "Bunny says you're a big star now."

"I don't know about that," Rett said. She wished the waitress would bring her lemonade so she could go.

"A big something," Jerry muttered. Rett remembered now that Jerry had been the mentally impaired member of the gang. "Or is that a lot of *bull*?"

Christ. His pea brain was trying to find a way to use the word *dagger* in a sentence. She didn't have any patience for his stupidity. She put her back to the counter. "Did you have something you wanted to say to me, Jerry?"

"Knock it off, Jerry," Dwayne said. "It wasn't that funny twenty years ago."

Jerry smirked. "I was watching one of those home shopping shows. Had all kinds of knives. Fancy swords. Lots of *daggers*."

The waitress brought her lemonade. Rett quickly paid. She wanted to just walk out the door, but something made her head the other direction, toward their table. She wasn't going to tuck tail and run from a moron like Jerry. She'd driven his nuts into his pelvis once and she would do it again. Jerry was staring at her boobs — typical. She kept her tone conversational. "The word is *lesbian*, Jerry. *Bulldagger* is something ten-year-olds say when they have no idea what it means."

Jerry's jaw dropped. "Are you really one of them?"

Oh, Christ, Rett thought. They'd only called me that to hurt me because I was too weird for them. They never knew. "It was one of the few things you ever got right, Jerry."

"You don't need to flaunt it, Rett."

"Tell me how buying lemonade is flaunting anything but thirst, Thor."

"You don't have to talk about it." Thor sipped his coffee with an air of having had the last word.

"Jerry brought it up. I could have said I had an erotic dream about him and woke up a lesbian the next day, but the truth is it has nothing to do with any of you. I was just trying to improve his vocabulary."

Dwayne said, "Jerry's an idiot. Always has been, always will be."

"Shut the hell up, Dwayne." Jerry cracked his knuckles. The sound had the same effect on Rett as an out-of-tune violin.

"See you at the dance," Rett said. "I'll be in my lesbian dress, with lesbian shoes and lesbian earrings. It's got lesbian sequins on lesbian silk in a lovely shade of lesbian green."

"Christ, Rett." Thor looked like he'd found spit-up in his coffee.

She winked at him and walked out. She was in the rental car before she started to laugh, and she let herself go — it was better than crying. Those idiots hadn't even known she was a lesbian; they'd just called her one because she was different. Her mother hadn't loved her not because she was unlovable, but because her capacity for love had been exhausted long before Rett had been born. She hadn't been in love with Cinny all those years ago and she'd missed the love that was there — not just the love Angel had offered, but the affection and caring of friends. High school hadn't been one hellish day after another, it had only seemed that way because she'd been hopelessly infatuated with someone who would never love her, and she'd been trained not to expect anything better. Forty years old and she had just figured it out.

Therapy probably would have been a good idea. *Oh yah.*

She showered again when she got back to the motel, fancying that she reeked of cigarette smoke and stale beer.

It was never your fault. Rett brushed out her hair and studied her face in the mirror. Her mother's face.

I am not my mother, and I will not make her mistakes. Now more than ever she understood how important her mantra was. Was she supposed to be grateful her mother had shown her how miserable and empty a person could be so she could try to be different? Gratitude, like forgiveness, had a rat's chance in hell of ever crossing her mind.

"Maybe someday I'll be that evolved," she said to her reflection. "But not today."

She dressed with care. Although it was warm, she put on her newest pair of jeans, suspecting that Mrs. Martinetta would appreciate some effort for a family dinner. She'd have worn the slacks, but they were dirty. So she dressed up the jeans with a sleeveless blouse stitched with rhinestones that she'd bought at Pike Place Market in Seattle. She slipped hammered silver earrings on and surveyed the result. She rebrushed her hair. Dressy casual. She hoped she passed muster. Mrs. Martinetta's good opinion was worth courting.

Angel arrived at five-thirty. "Traffic was easy," she said. Rett returned her kiss with pleasure. Angel still had her business regalia on, but she looked relaxed and happy.

"Do you have any ice? I'm parched. I kept meaning to stop for a soda, but I never did."

Rett put some ice in a glass and caught Angel staring at her in the mirror.

"What's wrong?" Angel came to take the glass away.

"Nothing," Rett said.

"Not nothing. You look — different."

Rett took the glass back and went to fill it with water. "I'm fine."

Angel drank thirstily. When she was finished, she gave Rett one of her laser-beam looks. "You look like you've had a shock."

"Can I tell you about it later?" She put her arms around Angel and looked down into the face she would now never forget. "It's nothing to do with us. Something I did today that didn't go as well as I had hoped." *I thought I had no hope, but I must have or I wouldn't feel so sad.*

"You went to see your mother."

Surprised at Angel's perceptive conclusion, Rett let go and tried to change the subject. "Should I wear these shoes?"

"Rett."

She sat down on the bed. "I can't talk about it right now."

"Okay. I'm ready to listen when you want to talk."

Angel ran one finger over the tip of Rett's ear. "Is there anything I can do?"

Rett put her arms around Angel's waist and rested her head for a moment. "You've done it."

"Mama's not expecting us for another twenty minutes. You don't suppose . . ."

"I just got dressed, you wench."

Angel kissed her thoroughly. "That will have to do, then. It occurs to me that if I'm picking you up, I'll have to bring you back. It's *such* a long drive, and it'll be *so* late, and I've been on the road so *much* today that it would be so much *safer* if I just stayed here tonight."

Rett hugged her until she protested. "That may be what your mother had in mind all along."

"What a cruel thing to say," Angel said tartly. "I'm still not old enough to want to give in to my mother's machinations, you know. Even if she's right. The fact that she's right only makes it worse."

"I think your mother approves of me."

"I'll be forty next year. At this point, my mother would approve of an orangutan."

"Gee, thanks."

Angel grinned. "Okay, let's be early. She'll love you even more."

10

"Is this the way to Manderley?" Rett asked. Angel
had turned off the main road into Woton onto a
tree-lined gravel drive that wound between two modest
hills.

"I've always loved our driveway. Hey, what gives?"

The drive had given way to a large cement and
brick area that reminded Rett of an Italian piazza. To
one side was an expanse of neatly mown grass with
green and white striped umbrellas shading tables and
chairs. A hammock promised rest beneath a cluster of
pines. Scarlet geraniums and petunias lined the walk

to the front door. The colors were dazzling, the antithesis of the dying plants and grass in her mother's yard.

There were already several cars parked in front of the house. Three ladders were propped against the house, and sweaty male family members swarmed about.

Big Tony waved from the top of one ladder. Angel's two brothers-in-law occupied the other ladders. "We decided this morning on a painting party. This is the last bit."

Little Tony, Big Tony's oldest son, not to be confused with Tony Junior, handed up another tray of paint. Little Tony was taller than either his father or uncle. "This is hard work for a vacation, but it's worth it. Nana's making *timpano*!"

"*Timpano*," Angel breathed.

The word was repeated like a prayer by everyone in earshot. Rett had no idea what *timpano* was but she had a feeling she was not going to regret finding out.

Angel's father came around the side of the house with a heavy bucket of water. Rett saw T.J.'s son, Carmine, start forward to help, then stop at a gesture from his father. Rett was touched by the love and respect shown by son and grandson.

Stop that, she told herself, but the comparison was inevitable. This is what it looks like when children love their parents, she thought. Once upon a time when she'd felt that way, she must have. The affection she might have felt had died from lack of care.

"Use this to rinse up your brushes." Mr. Martinetta wiped his brow. "Angel! You're early. I'm sorry I'm such a mess to greet you, Rett."

227

"Don't worry about it," Rett said. She shaded her eyes to survey the house. They'd painted over with the existing colors. It was a lovely two-story house — a soft ivory with brick-red trim and gardenias in the upper window boxes. "You had some competent help."

"The boys did all right," Mr. Martinetta allowed. "I was going to do it last month, had the paint all ready in the garage, but then we had that heat wave and the paint will crack when it's that hot. I'm hardly done with my breakfast when I hear them out here clattering about. Went and borrowed ladders from the neighbors." He was clearly pleased, and his sons had handled the matter with enough diplomacy to avoid bruising their father's independence.

"Angel," Mrs. Martinetta called. "Bring Rett in out of the sun."

"Yes, Mama." They stopped on the way for Angel to say to T.J. in a low voice, "This was great."

"I didn't want him up on a ladder, did you? Maybe you can get Mama to sit down for two minutes."

"I'll try," Angel said. "But *timpano*"

"*Timpano*," T.J. echoed.

The aroma of too many good things to identify assailed Rett's senses. Tomatoes and garlic and onions — something bacony and a smell like fresh bread. The last remnants of cigarette and beer stench were vanquished.

"Rett, *cara mia*, welcome to our home." Mrs. Martinetta's hug was heartwarming. "Please come in and be one of the family."

"These are for you." Rett proffered a lavish bouquet of daylilies, iris and gladioli.

228

"You shouldn't have." Mrs. Martinetta inhaled the heavy scent of the lilies. "These are one of my favorite flowers. How thoughtful."

Angel's sisters, Tia and Carmella, were tearing greens and chopping vegetables at the farm-style table in the kitchen. Rett accepted a glass of red wine from Angel, who then excused herself to change into something more comfortable than her crumpled suit.

"Is there anything I can do to help?"

"You're our guest. Just relax," Mrs. Martinetta said. She was stirring a pot of something that smelled divine.

"You told me to be one of the family," Rett reminded her.

Tia grinned. "Good one — but it's no use. We had to beg for this job."

"Mama let me grind the meat for the *timpano*," Carmella added. "That was the limit of her tolerance for anyone else in her kitchen."

"Nana, where do these go?" If Rett remembered right, the teenager with Angel's eyes and nose was Carmella's oldest daughter, another Angelica, but everybody called her Angie. She had a handful of relish forks.

"I'll show her," Tia said.

Carmella's other daughter, Margie from Margaretta, banged in the front door. "Mama, does paint come out?" She was spattered from head to toe with the same brick red the windowsills sported.

Carmella wasn't fazed. "With soap and water, so hit the shower or you'll miss the *timpana* No one in this family will save you a slice."

"Got it, Mom." She dashed off.

Carmella grinned at Rett. "I was so proud. You should have heard her this morning. She informed her uncles that their decision to have a gender-based work crew was a denial of her basic civil rights. She threatened to file an action under Title Nine."

Rett laughed. "She obviously got her way."

"She can be very persuasive. Angie of course wanted to watch Nana assemble the *timpano*, which took most of the day."

"Forgive my having to ask, but what is *timpano*?"

"A little of this, a little of that," Mrs. Martinetta said, as if the *timpano* practically made itself from leftovers in the icebox.

Tia said from the dining room, "It's a pastry drum filled with layers of meatballs and peas and angel hair pasta and sauce and pigeon breast —"

"I couldn't get fresh pigeon, so I had to use chicken," Mrs. Martinetta corrected.

"Chicken breast, then, and a sauce that simmers for hours — pancetta and sausage, onions and garlic."

"Wow," Rett said. "I'm honored."

Carmella's lips twitched. "You should be. Mama has a way of telling you how she feels about you with food. The first boy I brought home? Bottled sauce. When I brought home Michael it was two-day cacciatore."

Tia sat down at the table again and resumed chopping olives for the salad. "Remember what she made for Big Tony's first serious girl?"

"She was not a girl," Mrs. Martinetta interjected.

Carmella was giggling. "*Ragu di puttanesca.*" She and her sister went into peals of laughter.

Rett took note of Mrs. Martinetta's innocent smile. "I wish I knew more Italian."

Tia filled her in. "This woman was fifteen years older than Big Tony — who was what, eighteen? She'd already been married twice and she went around the house picking up things as if appraising their value." Tia was still giggling. "So Mama put the *ragu Neapolitan* — that's a traditional, homey marinara sauce — in the icebox and throws the ingredients for *ragu di puttanesca* in the frying pan. Whore's sauce. So named because it's fast enough to make between . . . appointments."

"She said she liked anchovies," Mrs. Martinetta observed. "My recollection is that she loved the meal." It was obvious Mrs. Martinetta was not above using any means to steer her children in what she felt was the right direction. No doubt the children at times resented her interference. Angel objected to it on principle even when she agreed with the end goal — being with Rett, for example. Rett wanted the time to get to know her and understand how a woman her age, who wore a crucifix, could throw herself with such energy into matchmaking for her lesbian daughter.

The men began tromping in for cold drinks and to get in line for showers. But when the timer on the oven dinged everyone froze.

"Do you need help lifting it out?" T.J.'s voice was hushed.

"Don't be silly," Mrs. Martinetta said. She opened the oven. A puff of fragrant steam drenched the kitchen with the most savory aroma Rett had ever smelled.

There was a collective *oh* and then an *ah* when

she pulled out the oven rack. The earthenware baking dish was shaped like a drum and about thirteen inches around.

Mrs. Martinetta gave the oven mitts to T.J. "I think I would like some help after all."

T.J. put on the mitts as if they were sacred vestments. Rett found herself holding her breath like everyone else as he lifted the heavy dish to the counter to set it gently on the cooling rack his mother pointed out.

There was a collective exhale, then Mrs. Martinetta picked up a tray of sliced bread drizzled with olive oil and spices and slid it into the oven. Only when the door was closed did normal talk resume.

Angel slid into the chair next to her. "How you doing?"

"I love your family." She blinked back sudden tears.

"They're not too bad," Angel said. "The Tonys have only come to blows twice and even though Tia took my favorite blouse when I was fifteen, I haven't mentioned it." An olive bounced off Angel's chin. She started to throw it back at her sister, but grinned and ate it instead. "Do you want some more wine?"

"I'll do impulsive things," Rett said. She tried to say with her eyes that she'd found the name for what her heart ached to say.

"Like what?" Angel's lips curved in a just-between-us smile.

"Propose to your mother."

Angel laughed and Rett didn't miss the significant look that Tia gave Carmella. Their affection for their sister was as tangible to Rett as the aroma of the *timpano*. They were Catholic — Angel had said so —

but their love made whatever qualms they had for the fate of their sister's soul remain neither spoken nor implied. Love and family came first. Free your heart and the rest will follow, Rett thought.

After a short but heartfelt grace of thanks from Mr. Martinetta, Rett was presented with the first slice of *timpano*. She savored a delectable mouthful, looked around the long table gleaming with china, crystal and silverware and saw the expectant expressions of Angel's family — faces she hoped would fill her future. She told them the truth. "In my life, I have never tasted anything so delicious."

There was a collective sigh and plates were passed while Mr. Martinetta sliced the drum into wedge after wedge of layered pasta, meatballs, chicken and a thick pancetta and tomato sauce. The two salad bowls made it around the table, then passed back to the table in the kitchen where all the teenagers were devouring the *timpano* with an obvious eye to seconds.

"That was just an appetizer?" Rett's voice was squeaky when she saw the giant bowls of penne and sauce arrive at the table. Strips of garlic-rubbed steak that had been holding in the warming oven appeared on platters — it was like something out of a food fantasy.

"We're Italian," Mr. Martinetta said. "Food feeds the soul."

After the meal the younger crowd was offered use of family cars to go to the movies in St. Cloud, but only if the kitchen was cleaned up first. The older group settled with groans of full stomachs in a large greatroom that Rett loved for its homey informality.

"I love this room," Rett told Mrs. Martinetta. "Was it part of the original house?"

"Oh, no. We bought this house when it was just the two of us. Even on an accountant's salary we would never have managed without a veteran's loan. We didn't know God would bless us with five children. My Tony added this entire section on when the kids were still in grade school. It took an entire summer, but we needed the space. That's when I got my large kitchen and we managed to squeeze in a bathroom for the boys and one for the girls." She chuckled. "Otherwise, the girls were going to kill their brothers for leaving the seat up."

Rett found herself telling Mrs. Martinetta about her travels and future singing engagements. As the light lengthened and Rett could actually have contemplated eating the tiramisu Mrs. Martinetta had chilling in the icebox, Mr. Martinetta took an ancient but obviously well-loved concertina from a case near the upright piano.

He settled back into his chair and his fingers played over the keys and buttons.

" 'O Sole Mio,' Papa." Tia put her head on her husband's shoulder.

The song flowed out of the little instrument with clarity and feeling. Angel took her hand and they sat in the dim light until the final notes became memory. "That was beautiful, Papa."

"Play something for us, Carmella."

Rett was fairly certain the piano piece was from an opera, but she was going to have to bone up if she wanted to understand why everyone smiled as Carmella played.

Mrs. Martinetta turned on a light or two and everyone became livelier after consuming the tiramisu. The coffee was as rich and satisfying as Mrs.

Bernstein's Viennese roast. It made Rett feel like she'd been reborn into a perfect world. The afternoon's trauma seemed utterly irrelevant to the future.

"I don't want to impose," Mrs. Martinetta said, "but I would be honored if you would sing for us, Rett."

"It would be my pleasure. I would gladly sing for my supper anytime."

She knew her way around a piano just enough to accompany herself to "So in Love." At the song's bridge her poor playing was bolstered by Mr. Martinetta's more expert performance on the concertina. By the time she got to "in love with my joy delirious," her hands were in her lap and Mr. Martinetta followed her mood to a closing that was almost a bossa nova. T.J. and his wife were swaying together at the far end of the room and Angel gave her a look that made Rett's stomach flipflop. Angel's look said she had melted bones.

"That was lovely, thank you," she said to Mr. Martinetta. "I should have paid more attention to instruments."

"Your voice is your instrument," he said. He began to play "And the Band Played On," and Rett was joined by the rest of the family.

She went back to her seat by Angel after that.

Angel whispered, "I've just made a decision and I want to tell everybody. I was going to think it over for a few days and . . . and . . . and talk to you, but I want to tell them now. I know it doesn't make sense. I'm sorry I didn't tell you first — don't be upset. We can work it out, I know we can. Oh, I should have told you. Say we'll work it out later."

Rett was puzzled, but Angel was looking at her

with such a plea for understanding. "We'll work it out later."

"I want to tell everybody something," Angel said immediately.

Mrs. Martinetta looked hopefully at Rett. "You have some news?"

"Yes, Mama. I just made up my mind and I think you'll be happiest of all. As you know I've been up to the Mayo Clinic twice to do the usual talk-talk that scientists do."

Of course, Rett thought. Her brain went *click*. The Mayo Clinic had put Rochester, Minnesota, on the map. She should have connected that dot earlier.

"This afternoon they offered me the lead of a two-year research project into ovarian cancer, population clusters and nutrition, herbal supplements, et cetera. I've decided to take it. So I won't be going back to UCLA after all except to pack up."

She turned to look at Rett, who was numbly aware that the eyes of the family were on her. So much for her idea that they would be together, share a home. The evening had been too perfect. She'd forgotten to look for the other shoe and she felt as if she'd been thumped on the head. She didn't know what her expression was, but she managed to say, "You'd be a fool not to."

"Oh, Angel," Tia said. "That's wonderful, wonderful news. To be so near home . . ." Her voice trailed away and Rett realized they were all thinking of their father's health. Of course — she would want to be here. She'd been listening to her father play and realizing the times she would hear it were definitely limited.

I can't hold her back from being with her family,

Rett thought. If we have any chance at all it can't have a price tag that high. What were they going to do? Two years was a long time, her body said. Her heart said it was nothing. Her mind was in turmoil.

They were in Angel's rental car heading toward Rett's motel when Angel broke the heavy silence. "I'm sorry."

"I understand." She did understand. It didn't make her hurt any less, but she understood.

"I was going to tell you when I picked you up, but when I saw you all I wanted was to go back to L.A. with you and be together. I want to spend every night with you."

"You have to take it. You need to be here."

"He looks so healthy, but I saw the test results myself. We're strong — I didn't sugar-coat it when I told Papa and Mama first, then everyone else, that his doctor was right. A year, maybe two. He's had symptoms of ALS for two years now and didn't tell anyone that his doctor had diagnosed it."

"ALS?"

"Amyotrophic lateral sclerosis. Lou Gehrig's Disease. It's incurable."

"I'm so sorry, Angel." Her worries about how they would maintain a relationship over a long distance seemed petty.

Angel swallowed convulsively, then cleared her throat. "Not to go to perhaps an even less cheery subject for you, you were going to tell me about seeing your mother."

Rett felt pummeled. "There's actually nothing to tell. I feel much better about that than I did this afternoon." I just suddenly feel a whole lot worse about us, she wanted to add. Not now. Angel's nerves

237

were too raw. "She has never felt anything but annoyance for me and she never will. I accept it."

"Under it all, she must —"

"You don't have to comfort me." Rett said it more sharply than she intended. "Really," she said more gently. "I think I went because I thought that way. I thought I might see a glimmer under her bitter exterior. But there really isn't anything there."

"I can't even conceive of it." Angel was pulling off the road.

"What's wrong?"

"I just want to hold you." She turned off the engine and pulled Rett into her arms. "Or you can hold me. Just hold me."

They sat in silence with Angel's head on Rett's chest. Rett was burning with what she wanted to say. The words were in her mouth. They wanted out. Her heart was pounding so loudly she thought Angel would wonder at the cause. She had never felt this pressure in her heart to put a name to the feeling. She'd said the words before and thought she'd meant them. This time was different. This time she felt like a child diving into the deep end of the pool for the very first time.

"I love you." Tears spilled down her cheeks. She'd gone so many years not letting herself completely love anyone because she'd felt her love wasn't of value. Thinking if she offered it to anyone they'd spit on it and throw it back in her face. She'd never loved Trish, she'd only loved the ego-stroking Trish gave her. She was filled with love for Angel, all of her, even the parts of Angel's mind that went to places she could never follow. Love crept into dark places she'd always known were there. In that instant, with the words she'd managed to say echoing in her head, all the dark places were suffused with light.

A barely audible sniff told her that Angel was crying. Muffled from her chest the words floated up. "I love you, too."

Is this happiness, Rett wondered? The euphoria was more powerful than the post-performance rush. The words were addictive — she wanted to say them over and over. "I love you."

"I've always loved you, you shit."

Rett grinned. "Now that's romantic. You think you can drive so we can go make up for some more lost time?" What did living two thousand miles apart have to mean, anyway? It was just a plane ride. They could work it out.

Angel found a tissue in the glovebox and blew her nose. "Say it again."

"I love you, Angelica Martinetta."

"Say it a lot."

"I love you, I love you, I love you."

"More." Angel pulled out onto the road again.

"I love you."

"Sing something romantic. Make my bones melt again."

" 'A-B-C, one-two-three, baby, you and me.' " Rett kept singing the boisterous little Jackson Five ditty until Angel's playful slapping made her stop.

"My sisters and nieces want to go to the Mall of America — are you up for that?" Angel pulled one of

Rett's tank tops over her head. It could have been a short dress on her. "I wish I'd remembered a change of clothes," she said for the fourth time.

"I'd love to go back." Rett toweled her hair a little longer, then reached for her brush.

"I want to find a different dress to wear tomorrow night. The dress I brought is very professorial. I don't feel professorial and it is a wonderful feeling."

"No, you're not in the least professorial. I'll sign an affidavit."

"I intend to dance with you, Rett Jamison."

"We'll start a riot." Woton High had not had many lesbians dancing in its gymnasium.

Angel kissed the end of her nose. "It's overdue."

"Find a dress to go with these." She handed Angel the little velvet box with the topaz earrings.

"Rett, these are beautiful."

"They reminded me of your eyes."

"I don't know what to say." She held the simply set stones up to her ears. "I don't have pierced ears."

"Shit."

"I'll get them pierced."

"It'll be less painful to take the earrings back and find clip-ons."

"You have a point."

The shopping trip was great fun. Rett hadn't been around teenagers very much. Angel's nieces were confident and friendly without being petulant, a quality she'd been told countless times was synonymous with "teenager."

Angel assured her, however, that all of her relatives

seemed to be on their best behavior. "Hang around long enough and you'll see us with our hair down," she had said.

Rett wanted to kiss her all over, but public kissing was akin to a strip show in Minnesota. "I'll hang around, then." She didn't know if Angel understood it was a promise.

When they got back to the motel Angel refused to show her the dress she'd bought, saying she'd been ably advised by her nieces and wanted to surprise Rett. Rett realized suddenly that the dance tomorrow night was sort of like a date. An official Date with Serious Clothing and Shaved Legs.

"If Bunny hadn't made such a point of it, I wouldn't go," Angel was saying. "I'd rather sleep with just you." She stuffed pajamas borrowed from one of her nieces into her small overnight bag. They'd stopped at Rett's motel for her things before coming to Angel's parents where she bunked with her nieces who had wanted to be closer to Nana and Nana's kitchen. The rest of the family was occupying several of the cabins at the nearby lake resort.

"I feel exactly the same way."

"A slumber party, at our age." They looked at each other and Rett knew a word from her would send them back to her motel for the night. "We have to go," Angel finally said. "It's the right thing to do. Bunny went to a lot of trouble."

Later in the evening Rett was glad Angel had prevailed when it became clear that more than half of the twenty or so women Bunny had invited weren't going to show. When they settled on sleeping bags arranged around the room there were eight of them. Bunny had already sampled heavily from her homemade rum punch, and Lisa, Mary and Kate were also in various stages of intoxication. Natalie was so butch in her Army-issue pajamas that Rett's gaydar would not stop going *ka-zing*.

After a walk around the acreage to see the small farm and enjoy the sunset, Angel and Rett had changed into their PJs and sat down with the others. Bunny had reached the stage where everything was funny. The only one who didn't seem to want to get in the mood was Cinny. A week ago the sight of Cinny in her orange silk pajamas would have put Rett in a fever, but now she found Angel in her niece's Batgirl nightie far more alluring.

"This is really good." Rett sipped from her punch again. "I don't usually go for hard liquor, but this is way excellent. "

"Almost better than sex," Kate said. "It *is* better than the sex I got in the last year of my marriage."

"Oh, don't start ragging on men again," Lisa said. "Rett and Angel will probably join in and then I won't be able to resist."

"I've got no reason to rag on men," Angel said. "I've never had a bad relationship with one."

"You always were the smart one," Kate said. "I wasted eighteen years trying to make Alan happy, and he trades me in for a bimbo with abs of steel."

"You have to tell me, Angel." Mary rolled onto her stomach and waved her feet in the air behind her like a child. "Is life without men really satisfying?"

Rett rolled her eyes. Typical preconceived notions.

"There are lots of men in my life," Angel protested.

Kate took another sip of her rum punch. "She means sex without men."

"Works for me," Angel said nonchalantly. "What about you, Rett?"

"What can I say? I can't speak to what I've never had, and that's a man in my bed, but I have no complaints and have heard none." She couldn't help the dopey grin she gave Angel.

Bunny choked on her drink. "Wait a minute — you two? No way!"

"Oh, man," Mary groaned. "You've probably had, like, oral sex more often in the last four days than I've had in the last four years."

Rett enjoyed the blush that ran up Angel's neck. "I'm not admitting to anything."

Mary nudged Lisa. "Just think about it — oral sex isn't just a birthday present. It's required. Like, every time."

Lisa giggled. "It's your problem if Mark is delinquent in that area. Lee may have been an asshole, but he was not reluctant when it came to that."

"I've got no complaints," Bunny said adamantly.

"Are we going to talk about sex all night?" Cinny was still sitting up, her drink untouched. She was pale.

"What's wrong with that?"

"There's more to life than sex," Natalie pronounced. "You go without for years at a time because if you don't you'll lose your career and pension and you'd be surprised how unimportant sex can be."

Rett thought that was a major hint from Natalie.

If she hadn't wanted to talk about it, she wouldn't have brought it up. "Don't ask, don't tell is a real bitch, isn't it?"

"Damn square. I spent a lot of time on the dance floor burning off excess energy." Natalie chuckled. "I'm bugging, you know. I thought I was the only lesbian to ever graduate from Woton High, and here are the three of us."

"That's a trip," Bunny said. "Something in the water, maybe?"

"As far as I know, there's been no research study into water and homosexuality." Angel was serious. That lightning quick change from laughter to reason fascinated Rett.

Bunny hiccuped. "Just kidding. Who wants some bagel bites?"

"If I don't eat something I'll get blotto," Rett said. "I don't like getting blotto."

Bunny turned her head sharply. "What the hell is that?"

Rett heard a long, persistent scratching noise. There was a tap at the window across the room, then the front door rattled. Mary squeaked in alarm.

"It's the boys!" Bunny sat up. "Tom and some friends. How high school are they?"

Natalie scrambled across the floor to turn off the lights. "I say we free our territory of desperadoes."

Lisa was laughing so hard she almost couldn't stand up. "Who do they think they're dealing with?"

Bunny stumbled to her feet. "We are not the girls we used to be." She came back from the garage with two AK-47-style water rifles. "I didn't want Tom to buy these for the boys, so I'll be glad to get even."

Natalie grabbed one. "Let's get ready to rumble!"

Mary took charge of the other water gun. "I'm in the mood for this."

After a few questions to Bunny, Natalie planned a course of attack. Two long hoses at the back of the house would provide the containment barrage, preventing the desperadoes from moving beyond the front yard. The water guns would attack from above while water brigades using buckets would provide refills for the air attack and take care of any downed enemy.

Natalie slipped out the back door and used the farm tractor parked behind the house to reach the rain gutter. She swung herself up with ease, then helped Mary and Lisa onto the roof. Bunny and Kate headed for the hose bibs at opposite ends of the house while Angel and Rett filled buckets in the mud sink to hand up to Cinny on the tractor, who handed them up to Lisa.

Rett heard the scuffling of feet on the roof, then from around the corner of the house the approach of whispering voices. There was a hiss as the hoses slowly filled.

All was quiet for just a moment. Even the crickets stopped chirping. Then the night was split with a Xena-like yell and very close by a man exclaimed, "What in hell was that?"

Bunny let out her own banshee yell and opened her spray nozzle full force while Natalie shouted positions and instructions from above. Rett kept passing buckets up to Cinny, who got drenched when one slipped out of Lisa's hands.

Lisa screamed with laughter and gasped out, "I'm gonna pee my pants," while Cinny swore and turned the next bucket upside down on Rett, who in turn dumped a bucket on Angel. Angel returned the favor, and then they all fell back as heavy footsteps pounded across the backyard toward them. Angel grabbed the next full bucket and flung the contents in that direction.

Curses faded into the night.

"The enemy is in retreat," Natalie hollered from the rooftop. She let out another Xena yell.

Mary screamed, "Loooooosers!"

Natalie stayed on the roof while Bunny went to turn on the front-yard lights. There was movement at the end of the driveway behind Rett's rental car.

Rett found her voice. " 'These boots were made for walkin'!' " The other women chimed in and they repeated the verse several times before something that looked like a white flag was waved over the rental car trunk.

"What are the terms of your surrender?" Natalie called out.

Tom's voice floated back. "I just want some dry clothes, Bunny."

"You wuss," another voice judged.

"I want some dry clothes," Tom repeated. "You'll have some when we get back to your place, but they won't fit me."

"Is that you, Mark?" Mary brandished her hose.

"We're going now, honey."

"Bunny? Sweetie? Can I at least have dry pants?" Tom risked raising his head above the car.

"You better git!" Natalie punctuated her orders with another squirt from her water gun. There was a satisfying curse in response and the desperadoes quit the field of battle.

They dragged the hoses and buckets back to the

246

rear of the house while Natalie shinnied off the roof and helped Kate and Lisa down. Rett went back to the front of the house to see if there were any more buckets. Finding none, she went around the side for a last look there.

"Rett."

She turned in the direction of the voice.

Cinny stood in the shadows. "I need to talk for just a minute. Alone."

"Okay." Rett joined her in the shadows.

"You and Angel — pretty serious, huh?"

"Yes," Rett said honestly. "Very serious."

"You're in love with her, aren't you?"

"Yes, very much so."

"That makes me the most pathetic person on this planet."

"Cinny, don't. You're not pathetic. You're just trying to figure it out as you go along, just like the rest of us."

"I don't want your pity." Cinny put her arms around Rett and hugged her tightly. Rett began to wonder how she could extricate herself without further hurting Cinny's feelings.

"I made my choices and I'll live with them." She let go and stepped back.

"Do what makes you happy, Cinny. That's what matters."

"What makes me happy . . . If only I knew what that was when I could actually grab hold of it."

"Oh, Cinny." Rett didn't know what to say.

"I know. I blew it." She turned on her heel and went into the house, leaving Rett to fight demon guilt — there should have been something she could have said to help Cinny through this. Not every

247

lesbian sprung from Martina's forehead fully developed and clad in boxers.

She followed Cinny's path to the back door and kicked off her soaked shoes into the pile with the others. Her pajamas were plastered to her. She'd have to sleep in the T-shirt she'd brought for the morning.

Mary was pulling what looked like one of Ted's T-shirts over her head when Rett went into the kitchen. "Bunny will find you something." She gave Rett a puzzled look. "You're in pretty bad shape."

Rett went on to the living room where everyone had changed but Cinny. Bunny stopped in the middle of handing Cinny a T-shirt to stare at Rett.

"What happened to you?"

Rett looked down. The fabric over her breasts was highlighted with brilliant orange dye — the very same color as Cinny's silk pajamas. The stain continued less intensely to just below her crotch, where Cinny's short pajamas ended. She could feel everyone's gaze going back and forth between them, matching up the body parts that had obviously been in prolonged contact.

Think fast, Rett. As naturally as she could, she said, "Geez, Cinny, it never pays to get silk wet, does it? It must have happened when I helped you down from the tractor."

Kate was the one who didn't want to leave it alone. She looked Rett up and down from her seat on the floor atop her designated sleeping bag. "Uh-huh. That was some assistance."

"Drop it, Kate," Angel said. She did not meet Rett's gaze. "Nobody here owes anyone explanations about anything."

"There's nothing to explain," Rett said. Angel was making it worse. Why wasn't Cinny helping out?

Cinny just stood there, ghostlike.

"Hey, after all that talk of sex, I can't blame Cinny for trying. I'd try it if I thought it would float my boat." Kate chewed on the end of her straw and she listed to one side before pulling herself upright again.

What bullshit, Rett thought. "Is that what you think? I'll hop into bed with any woman who says she's willing to give it a try?"

"Maybe you're your mother's daughter."

Rett exhaled slowly. "You've had way too much to drink, Kate." Why wouldn't Angel look at her?

"This isn't productive." Bunny tried to ease the tension. "We're all half drunk—"

"I haven't had more than a couple of swallows," Cinny said. "I'm not drunk."

"Then you knew exactly what you were doing, didn't you?"

"You can be such a bitch sometimes, Kate." Cinny stripped off her wet pajamas heedless of modesty and yanked Tom's T-shirt over her head. "Rett said something nice to me and I hugged her. There's nothing more to it than that."

Angel said with utter conviction, "Of course there wasn't."

Rett's world went right again.

"Must have been something very nice."

Mary appeared from the kitchen. "Will you just shut up, Kate?"

Cinny was shivering and Rett knew it wasn't cold. "She told me I should do what makes me happy. The first person in my whole life to think I could make a decision about what makes me happy."

"It's okay, Cinny." Bunny tried to get Cinny to sit down, but Cinny shrugged her off.

"Everybody knows what makes you happy," Kate said. She drained the rest of her glass. "New clothes, a Caddy that zigs, nice husband with money, lots of compliments about how you never seem to get any older." She hiccuped and lost her battle with gravity. Sprawled across two sleeping bags she said, "I think you've been sacrificing virgins."

"I'd be happy if you'd shut up," Lisa said. "You've been a bitch since the divorce and Cinny's just the person handy."

This wasn't going to end well for anybody. A slumber party — it sounded so innocent. Rett tried to derail Kate with, "Is your divorce final?"

It might have worked if Cinny hadn't leaned over Kate and said slowly and clearly, "Do you really want to know what makes me happy, Kate? Really?"

"Tell me, Prom Queen, what makes you happy? Hugging Rett here, who has been doing the deed with Angel all week?"

Cinny went down on her knees and straddled Kate, lowering herself inch by inch as she spoke. "You know what makes me happy? A woman's tongue reaching places that you've never had touched, and a woman's body hot with sweat as I touch and lick places inside and out to make her scream with ecstasy. You've never screamed, have you, Kate?" Cinny's lips were inches from Kate's. "What makes me happy is the kind of screaming, scratching, wild jungle-fever sex that only another woman can possibly do for me and if I *never* have sex again for the rest of my life I'll die knowing I still had better sex in one minute with a woman than you'll ever have no matter how many men you ever find to take pity on your sorry, drunken ass."

"Jesus, Cinny." Kate made a feeble attempt to back out from under her.

"So don't you ever assume you know what makes me happy." Cinny got to her feet. "I need a drink."

The only sound in the room was Bunny's pouring a rum punch over ice. She handed the glass to Cinny without a word.

Lisa broke the silence. "Um, Cinny? Are you trying to tell us something?"

Cinny perched on the sofa with her legs curled under her. She shrugged. "It shut her up, didn't it?"

"Bravo," Natalie said. "She's also passed out."

"Thank God," Mary said. "I love her like a sister, but lately when she's had too much she gets mean. She always says sorry the next day, but the damage is done."

Angel said quietly, "She needs help if she does this all the time."

"The divorce just killed her. That bastard cleaned out their accounts and moved to St. Paul in a single weekend. Left her with the mortgage and the car that has a payment." Mary lifted Kate's head and slipped a pillow under it.

"Men are bastards," Lisa said.

"We're back to a safe topic," Bunny said. She indicated the glass in her hand. "Damn. I'm sorry I made these things."

"They're potent," Natalie said. "I've had my limit." She laughed. "I want to be sober if Cinny wants to go through that little speech with me."

Everyone laughed, but Rett saw the speculative glances that Bunny and Lisa shared. Cinny must have seen them, too.

"I lied," she said into the silence that fell after the laughter. She started to sip from her glass, then set it down with an expression of distaste. "Dutch courage."

"You are trying to tell us something, aren't you, Cin?" Lisa sat down next to her. "Maybe you should tell Sam first."

Cinny was looking right at Rett. "I already did. Yesterday. Pity I didn't wait until tomorrow." Her gaze flicked over Angel.

"I'm so sorry, Cinny." Good God, Rett thought. She did it for me. After all these years, she did it for me.

"I'm not," Cinny said carefully. "You know I'm not sorry at all. It's over."

Lisa put her arm around Cinny. "What are you trying to say? Just tell us."

Cinny's usually flawless skin was mottled with red patches and her eyes shimmered with tears. "I'm . . . I'm like Rett. And Angel. And Natalie." In a whisper she added, "A lesbian."

"Christ, Cinny, are you sure?"

"Of course I'm sure, Bunny." Cinny pushed Lisa away. "I spent twenty-three useless years trying not to be one. I've walked away from love and I've hurt Sam, who doesn't know what hit him. I've made a ruin of everything because I just couldn't admit it to myself, and because I was afraid you'd look at me just the way you're looking at me now."

"It'll take some getting used to." Bunny was looking everywhere but at Cinny. "You know as well as I do there's folks in this town who won't like it."

"Fuck them." Cinny picked up her drink and drained it. She lurched to her feet. "I've been what

252

everybody wanted me to be for way too long and now it's my turn." She stood in front of Rett. "I have lousy timing. If I'd found some courage a couple of days earlier it might have worked out."

"Don't torture yourself about it," Rett said. She wanted to make it better but knew her words could hurt too. "We might have had something together once upon a time, all those years ago. Who knows?" she said softly. "I'm hers, like I was meant to be all along. She's the only one who knew what she wanted from the beginning."

Rett looked at the faces around the room. Angel clearly had sympathy for Cinny, but her eyes shone when she met Rett's gaze. Mary was carefully non-committal, while Bunny seemed stunned into silence. Natalie, on the other hand, had the look of a woman who had just won the lottery.

Lisa hopped up from the sofa. "Well, I sure feel like going to sleep. Anyone else?" Six pairs of eyes looked at her as if she had lost her mind. "Please. Irony? Get it?"

Cinny wiped her eyes and turned away. "I think I'm going to go home. I'll see everyone tomorrow night. The pajamas are ruined, Bunny. Just toss them." She gathered up her things and went out into the night in her bare feet and Tom's T-shirt.

Angel darted after her. Rett watched them talk for a moment, then Cinny embraced Angel before going around to the passenger side of the car. Angel looked back toward the house and Rett held up one finger.

"Angel's going to drive her and I'll follow to bring Angel back."

"You're going out dressed like that?"

Rett looked down at her blotchy pajamas. "I look like I murdered somebody."

Natalie took her keys out of her hand. "I've only had one and I've been snacking all along."

"I'm perfectly . . . no, you're right, I'm not." She'd had her first rum punch some time ago, but she'd started another and hadn't had anything to eat. "Thanks, Nat."

The noise of the cars faded into the night.

"Do you realize," Bunny said suddenly, "that in our graduating class four of eleven girls are gay? Four?"

Mary crossed her legs at the ankles. "Maybe that's all for the whole reunion."

"There's what, eighty grads here?" Rett thought it wise to sit down, too. She felt very lightheaded all of a sudden.

"Eighty-seven," Bunny said.

"Then eight-point-seven of them are gay. Four just happen to be in our graduating class. That leaves one each for the other classes."

"How do you get to be point-seven gay?" Lisa stepped over the snoring Kate to get a handful of pretzels. Rett gratefully accepted half.

"Denial," Rett said. "That or lack of imagination."

Bunny laughed. "Well, I won't forget this party for a while."

Maybe Bunny was too deep in her rum punch to see that what Cinny was going through wasn't a laughing matter. "It's going to be very difficult for Cinny. As you said, people aren't going to like it because people feel like they own a piece of her."

"You survived," Bunny said.

"I don't have to live here. I'm not the icon of the all-American girl. She's going to need her friends to stand by her. People like Jerry Knudsen can be very cruel."

"Jerry's a moron."

"Doesn't make him less spiteful."

Kate snored and rolled onto her side. Mary sighed. "You know as well as I do that folks 'round here hate change. Most people are live-and-let-live, but they sure hate mess. It's going to be messy for her."

"She going to need her friends," Rett repeated. "People who will look the Jerry Knudsens of the world in the eye and tell them to grow up."

"That'd be kind of fun," Bunny said. "I think she lied for too long, and she should have never married Sam if that's the way she was."

"She was just doing what those prayer-can-cure-you fanatics preach. They never seem to think about the husbands and wives who get hurt when their partner just can't live the lie anymore."

Bunny put her hand over her eyes. "Can we talk about something else? This is starting to sound like politics, and I hate politics."

Rett shrugged. "It's your party. It's been a doozy."

"You can say that again," Lisa said. "Buns, I'm not looking forward to sleeping on the floor, and I think I've had all the fun I can stand for one night. I'm going to head home."

Bunny sighed. "You sober enough?"

"I just had the one earlier. I'll be fine."

"Who the hell drained the punch bowl? Kate and I did? I did, didn't I?" Bunny tipped sideways on the couch. "I think I'm going to pay in the morning."

Rett would have told Bunny she and Angel were

also going to call it a night, but Bunny was asleep. She gathered up the things she and Angel had brought and waited outside for Angel and Natalie.

Natalie likewise decided to call it quits and promised to have lunch with them the following week after all the reunion hubbub was over. Angel was quiet most of the way back to the motel, and Rett was lost in thoughts chiefly concerned with Cinny's future.

"You're not responsible," Angel said suddenly.

"How did you know what I was thinking?"

"I have your number, Rett Jamison."

"She did it for me."

"She did it for herself. She doesn't know that yet. She's achingly sorry for what she's putting Sam through, but other than that, she didn't utter one word of regret. Don't forget, the Cinny Keilors of this world land on their feet."

"I hope so."

Rett curled around Angel's sleeping body and breathed in the warmth. The past week had been a barrage of memory and discovery, most of it good and some really bad. In those few short days Angel had become so solidly a part of Rett's world that all her visions of what the future would bring had Angel in them somewhere. So they would live in different places. There was always e-mail and frequent flyer miles. It would work out because in Rett's mind there was no other option.

11

Rett rang the doorbell at the Martinettas'. Angie opened it a few moments later and whistled.

"You look almost as good as Auntie Angel."

"Why, thank you." Rett wasn't put out by Angie's bias. She followed Angie to the greatroom where the elder Martinettas were sipping after dinner coffee while the two Tonys and their brothers-in-law, already in tuxedos, were clustered around the television watching a Twins game.

Tia had followed her into the room. "Angel will be right out. That dress is yummy."

Rett smoothed the deep green fabric. Sequins spilled across the shoulders and over the bodice, then narrowed to a thin line that swooped across her stomach to the hem. It made her all bosom, but she'd taken to heart the knowledge that no one ever looked at Marilyn Monroe's stomach. "So is yours." The creamy linen suited Tia's velvety olive skin, a trait all of the Martinetta women shared.

"Mr. Martinetta, sir." Rett made her voice break like a nervous adolescent's. "I'm here to take Angel to the dance."

Angel's father laughed. "Have her back by ten."

"You mean ten A.M., right, Papa? You won't see Paul and me before then. Big Tony says there's a dance club in Minneapolis that's open until four and I'm going to make the most of it. Paul takes me out once in a blue moon."

T.J.'s wife entered next, equally glamorous. "I hope that game is just about over."

The gentlemen made assorted reassuring noises, then high-fived at a home run.

When Angel came in Rett was completely tongue-tied. "Professorial" was the very last word she'd use to describe the breathtakingly beautiful creature in a chocolate brown, form-hugging dress. The body that was molded by the halter top made Rett's hands sweat. The earrings they'd chosen together winked in her ears. Angel turned slowly to the appreciative whistles of her family. The dress plummeted in the back to below her waist, snugly outlined Angel's hips and hinder, then flared out to just above her knees. "What do you think?"

Rett found it hard to swallow. "I think —" Her

voice broke all by itself. "I think we're going to need Natalie for security."

Angel grinned and became human again. "You look pretty good yourself."

"I'm not in your league."

"If that's flattery, I'd like some more."

The other women were attempting to pry their husbands from the ballgame when Angel and Rett left.

"Do I really look okay?" Angel glanced at her face in the passenger mirror. "I don't usually go for something so revealing, but it seemed like a good idea at the time. My nieces have very daring fashion sense."

"You look gorgeous. Maybe we could skip the dance and just go back—"

"Not on your life." Angel extended her stocking-clad legs. "I shaved my legs and they deserve some fun."

"It's going to feel very weird to be dressed like this in the old gymnasium."

"It's going to feel very weird just to walk down the school halls. We're such different people."

"Maybe that's the whole point of coming to a reunion. To be assured you really have changed."

Angel laughed when Rett turned into the parking lot that had always been for students. "I think we can safely park in the closer lot. We're grownups now."

Rett sheepishly drove around to the other side of the school to park closer to the gym. "It still seems strange."

"Shut up and kiss me." Angel had to reapply her lipstick when Rett was done. "Christ, already making out in the parking lot."

"And the sun's not even down."

Walking through the old hallways was indeed strange. Rett detoured Angel to their old lockers. Other people were doing the same thing. The foyer of the gymnasium had a table with name badges no one was putting on, and a display with black ribbons for those who had died in the intervening years.

"Mr. Barnwell," Rett said sadly. "I was hoping he would be here. He encouraged me so much — I think I would have given up if it hadn't been for him."

"Hank Bredelove." Angel touched his picture. "I always thought he was gay."

Natalie's arrival in a tuxedo made Rett exclaim, "Girlfriend! You look fabulous!"

Natalie gestured at their dresses. "After all these years of comfort I was not getting into one of those."

"You are going to make some hearts go pitapat."

Angel turned away to say something to Bunny.

Natalie shrugged. "There's only one that matters."

Rett thought she understood. She patted Natalie's arm. "I think you're going to have better luck than I ever had."

"I hope so. If she even shows, after last night."

They went into the gymnasium, which was festooned with crepe paper and lit with a disco ball. The theme was "Stairway to Heaven" — that brought back memories. *Were we ever this young?* Rett wondered. *We must have been, but I sure as hell don't remember the feeling.*

A D.J. was spinning tunes but no one was dancing yet. Everyone seemed suitably vivacious as the numbers grew. People who hadn't come early enough for the picnic were having "remember me" conversations, and Rett drifted away from Angel for a while.

When she met up with Thor Gustafson she gestured at her dress. "See? Lesbian sequins, lesbian green —"

Thor grimaced. "The whole town knows about Cinny leaving her husband. Don't you girls know the meaning of propriety?"

Rett was tempted to answer à la Barbra Streisand, but was rescued by Wayne Igorson. "There you are, Rett. We're ready to start."

They didn't look half bad as an ensemble in the best bibs and tuckers. There were no microphones, but the gymnasium acoustics were decent enough. Wayne's meticulous guitar work quieted the crowd and their harmonies carried throughout the room. Polite applause followed "Scarborough Fair," then more laughter as they clowned their way through "Leader of the Pack," sung by the girls, and "She's So Fine," sung by the boys. Wayne segued into a mellifluous classical piece that healed Rett's ears, which had suffered far too much from the local radio selections. As he was finishing she recognized the opening strains of her song. Wayne was leading into it beautifully, slowing the pace and finding the tempo and key they'd agreed on.

They'd pitched it low because it suited Rett's voice. It also suited how she felt. She sang the opening verse of "Something in the Way She Moves" at half voice, then rose to full voice in the chorus. Her gaze never left Angel and the reflection of spinning lights in Angel's luminous eyes made Rett want to swim in their depths for a lifetime.

The applause was gratifying and they quickly synched for their final number, led by Jeanette's accordion. "Kodachrome" was their anthem, and more than one person in the audience joined in. The D.J. quickly started up the dance music again when they were done, and after she'd exchanged hugs with everyone, Rett went in search of Angel, who had disappeared into the crowd.

T.J. caught her hand. "Dance with me."

"You bet." The Bee Gees were crooning "How Deep Is Your Love?"

"I'm trying to figure out how not to offend you," T.J. said suddenly after a minute of turning Rett around the dance floor.

"How so?"

"Well, I'm empowered by my siblings to threaten your life if you make Angel unhappy."

He was joking, but not entirely. "I consider myself duly warned."

"Good. It needed to be said."

"I don't mind. I like that you care for your sister."

"You're an only child, huh?"

"Yes." She barely stopped herself from adding, "Thank God." She wouldn't wish her mother on anyone else.

"That must be weird. Then again, you never had to share the shower with three girls."

"We all had our crosses to bear," Rett said lightly. "I am curious, though. You're Catholic and yet you approve — heck, you applaud your sister's life. All of it. Me."

T.J. thought for a moment. "Mama always said we should read the Bible and pay attention to our priests, but listen hardest to God, who speaks to your heart. God will understand and forgive anything you do out of love. I know that God will understand that I loved my sister and Him more than words on paper written by pious but mistaken men."

It was so eloquently said that Rett wanted to kiss him. She contented herself with a hug.

T.J. grinned and let Big Tony cut in. "I already warned her," he said.

"Okay," Big Tony said. He twirled Rett away, then said, "We're serious, you know."

"I know."

Angel was tapping on Big Tony's shoulder. "Can I dance with my date now?"

"I'll treat her like porcelain," Rett said to Big Tony.

Angel gave her brother an accusing look. "What did you say to her?"

Still protesting his innocence, Big Tony faded into the crowd. "Nothing at all. Wasn't me."

"They love you," Rett said. She pulled Angel close and rested her chin on Angel's head.

"Thef feffum mam wuff," Angel said.

"What?" Rett leaned away so she could hear better.

"I said, I can't breathe. I mean, I don't mind where my lips ended up, but I couldn't breathe."

Rett laughed and wiped surreptitiously at the lipstick on her bosom.

They danced for a long time. Rett forgot to notice if they'd shocked anybody. She didn't care.

It was near midnight when they clambered up the hill behind the school and sat in the cool night air.

"We're ruining our dresses," Rett said.

"I think they'll survive. I just wanted to be here with you and know that this time it's all turning out differently."

Rett liked Angel's head on her shoulder. She began to hum.

"Sing the words," Angel whispered.

" 'Unforgettable . . . that's what you are . . .' " Rett put her arm around Angel, who gazed up at her with such love that Rett forgot the next line. "Well, that's a first," Rett whispered. She lost herself in Angel's kiss.

Perhaps half the people had left by the time they returned to the dance, but the music had caught up to the times as Santana's sweat-drenched "Smooth" brought out slow and sexy moves from those who remained. She and Angel were going to follow her siblings to the dance club in a while, but in the meantime the music suited Rett perfectly.

The D.J. had obviously decided to go with Latin rhythms for a bit. "Smooth" gave way to Gloria Estefan's "Conga." The blistering pace of Ricky Martin's "Cup of Life" made most people, Rett and Angel included, yield the floor to anyone with the energy to keep up.

One couple was keeping up. Cinny hadn't stayed away after all. She looked wild in a scarlet sheath slit to her hips as she kept pace with the tuxedoed figure that twisted and turned her to the breathless beat of the music.

"Who's that?" Angel was on tiptoe trying to get a better look. "Her husband?"

"Not her soon-to-be-ex," Rett said. "Would you look at that — it's Natalie."

"Oh my God. Even when she comes out that woman doesn't lack for panache, does she?"

Rett glanced around. There were disapproving and puzzled expressions. She wondered if there was anything she could do to change anyone's mind, but they were jostled aside by Bunny and Tom, who circled Natalie and Cinny chanting, "Go, go, go, *ale, ale, ale*" with the music. Lisa and a man Rett didn't recognize quickly followed suit.

Rett saw the heartfelt look Angel directed at T.J., and he and his wife quickly joined the circle as Angel and Rett stepped forward, too. Then the rest of Angel's siblings were joining the cheering section and even Kate was clapping along. Rett hoped that Cinny could see that she had friends who weren't going to desert her now that the news was out.

Natalie was spinning Cinny into a blur of legs and hair. In a move that took Rett back to watching Cinny's cheerleading squad, Natalie lifted Cinny shoulder-high, then tossed her higher still. Cinny punched the air and shouted, "Go!" Rett gasped — Cinny was going to break her neck. The song ended abruptly. Cinny fell onto her back, stopped just short of the floor by Natalie's grip on her wrists. For a moment the only things that moved were Cinny and Natalie's heaving chests, then Natalie snatched Cinny back to her feet to cheers from the circle of onlookers.

Rett noticed Bunny elbowing Tom hard in the ribs and he quickly stepped up to ask Cinny to dance as the D.J. wisely switched to something a little more sedate. Natalie didn't hesitate to ask Bunny, who laughed and accepted.

"Cinny's going to wonder what she was ever afraid of." Rett put her arm around Angel.

Angel tipped her head back. Her eyes were like liquid amber. "Don't we all?"

Rett hadn't been in Angel's L.A. apartment enough to feel as if she was going to miss it. Angel was taping the last box and the movers were just about through.

Ten weeks, she reminded herself. You'll see her again in ten weeks. Since they had both returned home last month they'd hardly been apart. Only Rett's steady stream of engagements, including a weekend in Seattle and several days in San Antonio, had separated them for more than a day. Angel had thrown herself into passing on leadership of her UCLA project to other researchers she said were equally able. Apparently UCLA had tried to bribe her to stay, but she'd been adamant. The Mayo Clinic was expecting her tomorrow morning, bright and early.

"That's it," Angel said to the last mover. Her voice echoed in the empty apartment. She turned to Rett. "I am so tired — fuck my cleaning deposit. Let's get a bite to eat someplace where they'll ply me with a dozen diet Cokes and food that isn't good for me."

They ended up at Islands for burgers and sodas. Angel's plane left in three hours and Rett was trying not to cry. It's only ten weeks. She told herself that she'd lived for forty years without seeing Angel every day. *You're leaving in two days for Sarasota, re-*

member? Henry Connors liked to rehearse in the warm and relatively inexpensive Florida sunshine while the rest of the country braced itself for winter. Rehearsals were scheduled for principals for two weeks and a full orchestra rehearsal for another week after that. Then they all left for Las Vegas, concluding their run on Thanksgiving weekend. She wouldn't have more than one day without a performance and nothing was going to change that. After Las Vegas she had to come home to complete any studio work that had backed up while she was with Henry.

In the distant future was a nearly signed deal to record two numbers on a future David Benoit project. But at present it looked like once she got to Rochester in mid-December to join Angel, she'd be able to stay through Christmas. The week between Christmas and New Year's was booked solid with performances with Henry in New York.

It'll work out, she told herself. You'll see her again in January for at least a week. Maybe two. Just tell Naomi what dates you're not available. You're in a position to turn work away now.

"Don't look like that," Angel said. "You're breaking my heart."

"I'm sorry." Rett pushed away her hardly touched burger. "I'm not succeeding at being cheerful."

"Me neither. I'm going to miss you so much."

"I'll e-mail or call every day. We can chat-room while we watch our favorite shows." They'd gone over it before. They'd be in close but nonphysical contact as often as possible.

They talked in fits and starts as they picked at their food. Then it was time to go. The drive to the airport was full of frustrating traffic delays, but eventually Rett found a spot in short-term parking. They each carried a small bag as they walked to Angel's gate.

What was there to say? Rett kept reminding herself she was a big girl, but she couldn't help the tears that formed as Angel strode down the jetway and out of sight. The tendrils of electricity between them were stretching. The sensation was agonizing.

She couldn't watch anymore. Half-blinded by tears she wandered toward the terminal entrance. When her cell phone chirped she ignored it. A minute later it rang again, which meant it was Naomi. She answered with a sigh.

"How do you know a woman named Camille Masterson?" Naomi sounded both peeved and happy, a combination only Naomi could achieve.

"She was a D.J. at a charity event. Why?" Her sluggish mind couldn't make the connection.

"You need to sit down. I'm serious."

Rett dazedly found a hard plastic chair. "Yeah?"

"The woman Disney hired for the part Trish cost you? To make a long story short, she's stuck on another movie that's overtime and has commitments for something when that finishes. Basically, she can't do the part now. Camille Masterson apparently moved into casting recently and put in a good word when they discussed how to replace her. A very good word."

"You mean I'm going to get a callback?" The fog surrounding Rett lifted a little.

Naomi sounded like she was going to burst with excitement. "More than that — since you're free the first week of December exactly when they need you, you're hired. The contracts are on the way!"

"You're kidding." Rett knew Naomi wasn't making it up, but it was too much to absorb.

"Rett!"

"You're not kidding. Oh, my God." Her stomach felt as if it were high-fiving with her vocal cords. "I . . . I'm at a loss for words."

"I expected a little more enthusiasm." Naomi sounded hurt.

"I'm sorry." Rett stood up and walked back toward the boarding area. Disney wanted her voice. Angel was leaving. She felt as if she were floating in a different dimension. The people hurrying and pushing around her didn't seem real. "I just said good-bye to Angel."

Naomi liked Angel, probably because Angel had no inclination to advise Rett about her career. "Well, you can be a little blue, then. But you have to be in a better mood if I'm going to take you out for a celebratory dinner. You name the place."

Rett was halfway back to Angel's boarding area. Naomi's voice was coming from far away. They would be closing the gate soon. She knew she would feel it when the door shut.

"You still there?"

Rett broke into a run. "Sell the condo."

"What!"

"Sell the condo. Or rent it out. I'm serious."

"You're nuts."

"I don't have to live in L.A."

"You'll miss out on the commercial work and cont —"

"Home is where the heart is, right? She has my heart." She dodged suitcase-laden travelers and barely avoided knocking over a free-ranging toddler. "Just sell the thing. I'm moving. There are such things as airplanes. I can be anywhere in twelve hours."

"We'll talk this over at dinner."

"I need my flight to Sarasota changed. I'll be flying out of Rochester, Minnesota. Home of the Mayo Clinic."

She cleared the last cluster of people. They were closing the door. With the cell phone in one hand she shouted, "Wait! Don't leave without me!" She fumbled her wallet out of her slacks. "I need to get on this flight!"

People were staring. Naomi's voice was gibbering out of the phone. "I have to go now or they won't let me on the plane." She clicked the phone shut and waved her American Express card at the flight attendant.

"Just get on," the woman said. "They'll settle up on board. All that's left is first class, though. It'll cost a fortune —"

Rett was already halfway down the jetway. They were swinging the cabin door shut. "Wait!"

Gasping for breath she careened across the threshold. The door whooshed shut behind her and the first class attendant — who looked as if she was trying really hard not to look annoyed — pointed at the nearest seat.

"I'm meeting someone," Rett gasped. She pointed toward the coach section.

"There's nothing available in coach."

"Then move her up here. I'll pay the difference." Naomi was going to skin her alive. But she'd have to come to Rochester to do it.

"No one is moving anywhere until we're at cruis-

ing altitude. *Please* sit down and fasten your seatbelt."
The attendant's voice took on a menacing quality.

There were only two people in all of first class.
Rett took a seat in the last row, which was empty.
Angel was somewhere behind her. She could feel it.

She kept her gaze fixed on the cabin indicators,
waiting for the tiniest flicker in the fasten-seat-belts
light. When it finally turned off, she bolted to her feet
and through the curtain that separated first class from
coach.

Angel was just a few rows back. She was resting
her head on the cabin wall and gazing out the
window.

Rett paused to take in the sight of her and let it
calm her quivering nerves. She hadn't exactly asked
Angel if she really wanted to live together at this
point. They'd both believed it wasn't possible and
hadn't discussed it. Rett was going to make it possible.
She just hoped she hadn't assumed too much.

Angel suddenly lifted her head and turned her gaze
to where Rett stood.

Rett's stillness was beginning to attract the attention of other passengers. Angel's sudden question,
pitched loud enough to carry to Rett, startled several
more. "What are you doing?"

Rett had to try three times before she found her
voice. "Moving."

"What?"

She doesn't look glad, was all Rett could think. "I
upgraded your ticket. There's plenty of room up here."

"Are you crazy?"

"Naomi thinks so. I'm sure the flight attendant
thinks so. The people I ran over in the terminal

probably think so too. I just couldn't leave. I couldn't do it."

Angel's chin was quivering. "Are you really going to move?"

"Yes. Right now."

"You don't even have a toothbrush."

"I'll buy one," Rett said drily.

A man in a nearby seat snickered, then turned it into a cough when Rett glared at him. Why was Angel worrying about petty details when the real story was that they would be together?

Angel was breathing in short gasps and her eyes shimmered with tears. "Where are you going to live?"

"Where do you think?" Really, Rett thought. Dr. Angelica Martinetta was dense.

"With me?" Angel was climbing out of her seat. The people between her and the aisle belatedly realized they were hampering the course of true love, and Angel stepped over them until she reached the aisle and landed in Rett's arms.

Rett filled her senses with the scent of Angel's hair and the texture of her skin. She held her tight because it would have hurt not to.

"You have to take your seats now." The menacing flight attendant was back. "We need to start the beverage service."

The man who had laughed said, "If you two are only going to need one seat up there, I'll be glad to take the other one."

Rett rolled her eyes. The man helpfully passed Angel's things to them, then Rett led Angel to the back row of first class. Angel moved like a sleepwalker, but her eyes were glowing with all the welcome Rett needed.

The flight attendant appeared out of nowhere with two glasses of Champagne. All menace gone, she set the glasses down and winked conspiratorially. "Congratulations."

Rett's gaydar went *ka-zing*. "Thanks."

Angel's gaze never left Rett's face. "I can't believe you're doing this."

"I don't know why it took me so long to realize how easy it would be. I'm not losing much, and I'm gaining everything."

". . . As we make our last turn to start our final descent, passengers on the right side of the plane can see Lake Superior and those on the left can easily make out the mighty Mississippi, America's most loved waterway . . ."

Rett stirred out of sleep. She'd fallen asleep with her head on Angel's excellent thigh. Gentle fingers were smoothing her hair.

"I love you," Angel whispered.

It wasn't a dream.

Publications from
BELLA BOOKS, INC.
The best in contemporary lesbian fiction

P.O. Box 10543, Tallahassee, FL 32302
Phone: 800-729-4992
www.bellabooks.com

TANGLED AND DARK A Brenda Strange Mystery by Patty G. Henderson. 240 pp. When investigating a local death, Brenda finds two possible killers—one diagnosed with Multiple Personality Disorder. ISBN 1-931513-75-9 $12.95

WHITE LACE AND PROMISES by Peggy J. Herring. 240 pp. Maxine and Betina realize sex may not be the most important thing in their lives. ISBN 1-931513-73-2 $12.95

UNFORGETTABLE by Karin Kallmaker. 288 pp. Can each woman win her true love's heart? ISBN 1-931513-63-5 $12.95

HIGHER GROUND by Saxon Bennett. 280 pp. A delightfully complex reflection of the successful, high society lives of a small group of women. ISBN 1-931513-69-4 $12.95

LAST CALL A Detective Franco Mystery by Baxter Clare. 240 pp. Frank overlooks all else to try to solve a cold case of two murdered children... ISBN 1-931513-70-8 $12.95

ONCE UPON A DYKE: NEW EXPLOITS OF FAIRY-TALE LESBIANS by Karin Kallmaker, Julia Watts, Barbara Johnson & Therese Szymanski. 320 pp. You've never read fairy tales like these before! From Bella After Dark. ISBN 1-931513-71-6 $14.95

FINEST KIND OF LOVE by Diana Tremain Braund. 224 pp. Can Molly and Carolyn stop clashing long enough to see beyond their differences? ISBN 1-931513-68-6 $12.95

DREAM LOVER by Lyn Denison. 188 pp. A soft, sensuous, romantic fantasy. ISBN 1-931513-96-1 $12.95

NEVER SAY NEVER by Linda Hill. 224 pp. A classic love story... where rules aren't the only things broken. ISBN 1-931513-67-8 $12.95

PAINTED MOON by Karin Kallmaker. 214 pp. A snowbound weekend in a cabin brings Jackie and Leah together... or does it tear them apart? ISBN 1-931513-53-8 $12.95

WIZARD OF ISIS by Jean Stewart. 240 pp. Fifth in the exciting Isis series. ISBN 1-931513-71-4 $12.95

WOMAN IN THE MIRROR by Jackie Calhoun. 216 pp. Josey learns to love again, while her niece is learning to love women for the first time. ISBN 1-931513-78-3 $12.95

SUBSTITUTE FOR LOVE by Karin Kallmaker. 200 pp. One look and a deep kiss... Holly is hopelessly in lust. Can there be anything more? ISBN 1-931513-62-7 $12.95